THE VAMPIRE HUNTER'S DAUGHTER
THE COMPLETE COLLECTION

by
Jennifer Malone Wright

The Vampire Hunter's Daughter: The Complete Collection

Copyright 2012 Jennifer Malone Wright
Publishing Imprint-Jennichad Books
ISBN: 978-0-615-65008-1

Visit the website of Jennifer Malone Wright at:

www.JenniferWrightAuthor.com

ACKNOWLEDGMENTS

I would like to thank my good friend Rose for helping with every step during the process of bringing this story into the world. I would also like to thank my editors at Accentuate Author Services for their excellent skills and help.

Visit Accentuate Author Services at www.AccentuateServices.com. Michy and Lynn, you are the bomb!

A big thank you goes to Paragraphic Designs for my wonderful cover art for each story.

Visit Paragraphic Designs at Paragraphicdesigns.blogspot.com

I also want to give a shout out to all my fellow authors I have met and networked with. All for one and one for all!

And thank you to the fans; without you, this series would not exist. You all kept me writing more and more with each installment.

Finally, thank you to my husband, for his continued support and encouragement of my writing. Thank you, Honey. I love you.

THE VAMPIRE HUNTER'S DAUGHTER
PART I

THE BEGINNING

The Vampire
Hunter's Daughter
Part I

JENNIFER MALONE WRIGHT

The Beginning

"Chloe!" the voice called out sharply. At that exact moment, the earth shook violently beneath my feet.

"Chloe, wake up!"

The ground swayed and gravity took hold, forcing me to sidestep back and forth. I threw my hands out for balance and tried to catch my footing, but I ended up falling onto my hands and knees. The quaking world was suddenly bathed in harsh sunlight. It had washed over me quickly, blinding me. I threw my arm up to shield my eyes from the glare.

"Chloe Kallistrate, get your ass up *now!*"

My eyes snapped open. All the lights in my room were on and my mother stood over me. She held my blankets in her arms. I realized she had impatiently whipped them off me. I lay there in only my boy-short underwear and my favorite sleep shirt: a torn and faded but still ultra-comfy Harley Davidson tee-shirt. Sometimes when she said our last name really fast like that, she developed an accent. It was a strange name, pronounced Kal-lih-strah-dee.

The light explained the sunlight in my dream, and Mom must have been shaking me, which would have been the earthquakes. I groaned defiantly and glanced at the clock on my nightstand. The glowing red numbers told me that it was two forty-seven in the morning.

"Mom!" I grabbed my comforter out of her arms and rolled over, taking it with me. "It's the middle of the night."

Only then did the heavy fog of sleep lift and I realized *exactly* that: It was the middle of the night and my mother was in my room desperately trying to get me out of bed. Something was wrong. Terribly wrong.

I threw my blanket off and jumped out of bed, causing my mother to jump back in surprise.

"What is it? What's happening?" I demanded.

"You have to hide!" she whispered.

She was still in her pale blue-satin pajamas with the matching robe, and her eyes were wide with fear. Her dark brown hair, which was the same color as mine, hung loose and flowing down her back.

She grabbed my arm and dragged me to my closet.

"Quick, get in there." She looked around the room. "There is nowhere else to go. Now, *hide!*"

"Mom, stop it! What are you doing?"

Her fingernails dug into my arm. She opened the door and literally threw me inside the closet. She bent down, took my chin in her hand so that our blue eyes would meet.

"I love you," she told me, and then abruptly slammed the door shut, submerging me into total darkness.

Even though my fourteen-year-old mentality wanted to fight back and open the door, I did as I was told and sat on top of all my shoes that littered the floor of my closet.

Thundering footsteps pounded on the stairs outside my room. I could tell my mom was still in the room because I hadn't heard the door open and shut. My bedroom door burst open, and my mother immediately yelled, "Get out of here! Now!"

I could just see her pointing her index finger at the door, like when she would tell me to go clean my room or something.

A man's voice, low and smooth, answered back. "Really, Felicia, you honestly think we are just going to turn around and leave?"

He tsk'd at her like she was merely a child who had gotten caught with her hand in the cookie jar. This man knew her. He called her by name and spoke to her with familiarity. I was desperate to see what was going on.

"Trevor can't have her!" my mother screamed at him.

The sarcasm was clear when the man laughed and said, "Well, *you* should know as well as I do that what Trevor wants Trevor will get." He paused and then casually added, "He also wants you dead."

I covered my mouth and stifled the urge to cry out.

What the hell is going on?

He continued to speak when my mother said nothing in return. "You messed up, Felicia. He would have let you live if you had just left and gone on with your life away from us. Instead, you chose to steal what was his. Trevor wants his child back."

What? My mom stole a child?

That just couldn't be the truth.

My mother finally answered him, but she did so in a voice that was surprisingly fearless and brave. "Eli, you know he would have never been able to raise her. She is as much mine as she is his. I did not steal her; I *saved* her."

Her?

The smooth voice continued as if her words had meant nothing. "Nevertheless, we must carry out our orders. I would tell you I'm sorry, Felicia, but I'm not. I never liked you, and I'm ecstatic I am the one who gets to kill one of the most renowned hunters to walk the Earth."

Fear grasped me like a cold hand around my throat. I would not just hide in my closet and let him try to kill my mother. I threw open the door and flew out of the closet to face her attackers.

"No!"

I think I may have actually scared them a little, because every person in the room jumped. After the initial shock, my mother's eyes widened in disappointment and that man—Eli—his lips curled up into a smile.

I could put a face with the voice. He was about six feet tall with dark brown hair and cutting green eyes. The weird part was that he looked like he was about eighteen years old. The thought briefly passed through my head that I could take him. That thought was immediately crossed off the list when I got a good look behind him. There were about five other guys and one woman standing just outside my door.

I bit my lip and wished I had stayed in the closet.

"There she is!" Eli declared. "James!"

Suddenly, James was behind me and grasping both my arms hard enough to restrain me. Really, it didn't take much, because his hands were like iron vices. My mother lunged forward with her arms extended out toward me.

"No!" she shouted. "You cannot have her!"

The dark-haired man thrust his arm forward and sent her flying across the room with one hit. I struggled against James's grip.

"Let me go! Mom! *Mom*, are you okay?" I repeated over and over again.

I was scared to death, but I wasn't going to let them hurt my mom. I watched my mom slowly get up and brush her long dark hair away from her eyes. When I saw her eyes, I felt a rush of power. My mother looked vicious. I had never before seen such determination in her. She took two slow steps forward while Eli appeared to wait for her, and then she rushed him.

"Mom, no!" I called out.

But she didn't hear me, or she ignored me. She was on him, pounding away with tight clean punches. He simply grabbed her by the back of her pajamas and yanked her off. He threw her to the ground mercilessly, and that's when I saw my mother do something amazing: She was on her back staring up at him, and then she hopped to her feet without using her arms. Lightning fast, her hand struck out and grabbed my desk chair. She smashed it over his head.

He threw his leg forward and sideways, knocking her feet out from under her so that she fell to the floor.

"Now this is more like the Felicia we used to know, the one with fight!"

In an instant she was up and snagged one of the busted chair legs off the floor on her way. With a quick spin for distraction and then a lunge, my mom did something I never would have imagined: She staked the man.

He laughed at her.

I was so freaked out by the whole situation I couldn't say a word. Shock ate through my body, making my fingers and toes tingle like they were asleep. My head throbbed, and it looked like a fog was rolling into my room.

Yes, he had laughed at her, and then he pulled the stake out. "Felicia, you should know enough to know that you have to get under our ribs. This little piece of wood could never penetrate our bones."

He grabbed her by the hair, and she screamed in pain. He twisted her around until her back was against his chest and the stake was poised above her heart.

"Chloe, look at me!" she demanded. "No matter what happens, you always remember that I did everything for *you*. I did what I had to do to give you a good life." She paused and twisted her neck to look up at the scary, dark-haired man with the smooth voice, and she nodded. Then, with a final look back at me, she whispered her last words, "I love you, Chloe."

He shoved the chair leg into her heart and snapped her neck at the same time. Instantly, her body fell lifeless in his arms. Blood seeped out of the wound and bloomed like a flower around the chair leg protruding from her heart, staining the pale blue silk almost black. In the distance, I heard myself scream. James kept his grip on my arms while my legs kicked at his. I even tried to bash the back of my head into his face, but he was too tall for it to be effective. I ended up thumping it into his hard chest.

Eli turned to me with my mother still in his arms.

"Shut up!" he snapped and carelessly threw my mother's body onto the floor.

I did stop screaming, but only because I wanted to tell that bastard off. I felt so scared and helpless, but for some reason, I knew I was going to live through this. My voice cracked from all the screaming, so I'm sure I didn't sound serious at all, but I told him anyway, "If it is the last thing I ever do, I will kill you for what you just did. I swear to god."

He casually wiped my mother's blood from his hands with one of the towels I had left on my desk from when I had showered before bed. "It's not nice to swear, Chloe. Now let's take you to your father."

I swung my leg up and kicked out at him. "I'm not going anywhere with you! And I don't know what the hell you're talking about. My father died before I was born."

Eli sighed. "Of course he did. Let's go, James."

He waved his hand, and those who had stood by doing absolutely nothing while my mother was murdered in front of me made way for him to pass. James dragged me along behind him, and they followed.

Even though I was sure I was going to live—only because Eli said Trevor wanted me—I certainly wasn't expecting a rescue. I was trying to figure out a way to escape when we reached the landing at the bottom of the stairs. The front door burst open, and people filed in.

Eli's goons rushed forward and more fighting began. Everyone was fighting everywhere and smashing up everything in our house. I could do nothing but watch and scream. I couldn't even struggle any more because I was exhausted from trying to get away from James. I couldn't fight any more, so I just let myself hang there in James's grip.

The people who had burst through the door looked like average people, from what I could see, but the weapons they carried were extraordinary. I saw one of the rescuers drive what looked like a steel arrow into the belly of one of the men and upward under his ribs to meet the heart. One of the women rescuers had a whip. With one smooth flick, the tail of the whip found the neck of the woman on Eli's side and wound around it. When the rescuer yanked it back, it sliced the other woman's head off.

"Ahhh," I wailed and turned my head. The rescuers were winning. I felt newfound hope, just when I had wanted to give in. It suddenly occurred to me what exactly we were dealing with here: stakes to the heart, cut off heads, slayers... it all added up. I didn't want to admit it. The fog continued to build in my head, and my arms were fully asleep from James's grip. I couldn't move them at all.

After what seemed like an eternity of blood and battle, Eli and James were the only bad guys left.

The rescuers all stood together before us.

"Give us the girl," one of them said. He stepped forward. He was tall and extremely muscular. His hair was a dark blond, but it was his flashing green eyes that drew my attention. I just couldn't seem to tear my gaze from his eyes.

"Get out of my way," Eli told them in his smooth voice, which always sounded calm. "You know I could take all of you by myself if I wanted to."

"Well," the blond-haired guy spread his hands out, "it looks like that's what you're going to have to do." He cocked his head to the side. "I'm ready."

Eli flew forward. Yes, he literally lifted himself off the ground and flew at the group of rescuers. The fighting was a blur of bodies, blood and the occasional cry of pain. I watched while the blond guy took one of those arrows and stuck it into Eli's eye for distraction, while another rescuer slammed his long shining blade into Eli's heart.

James and I cried out at the same time. Mine was a cry of triumph, while his sounded painful. He threw me to the ground and rushed to Eli's side, catching his body as it fell roughly to the ground.

I watched from my place on the floor. The fight James put up was nothing compared to what Eli had given them. He didn't last long.

I lay there on the floor with my arms and legs dead. My vision blurred and my eyelids felt heavy. The blond guy stuck his face in front of mine.

"Come on, Chloe. We need to get you out of here and take you somewhere safe," he said. He lifted me into his arms and carried me into my new life.

When I woke, all I could think about was water. My mouth felt like sandpaper, and my tongue was so dry I could barely move it. I didn't try to sit up right away. I wanted to take in as much of my surroundings as I could before I let anyone know I was awake.

Yeah, I remembered everything. I didn't think it was all a dream. I knew I was not in my own bed, and the room I was in was not mine. I turned my head slowly to the right and saw, with great joy, a large glass of water sitting on the nightstand beside a couple of pills. I also saw, with not as much joy, an old man sitting in a chair beside the nightstand. He appeared to be snoozing while he waited for me to wake.

Trying to be as quiet as I possibly could, I slowly sat up. My arms protested. When I looked down I could clearly see dark purple bruises in the shape of fingers where James had had his hands clamped down on me.

"Ugh," I muttered and reached out for the water, clamping my teeth together to keep from crying out.

When I finally got that glass of water to my lips and was able to drink, it felt like what I imagined water would taste like in heaven. I guzzled it down so fast that I felt a little sloshy in my stomach by the time I set the glass back on the table. I left the pills alone. Exhausted from the simple act of getting a glass of water and drinking it, I fell back onto the pillows and shut my eyes again. I passed out within minutes.

I woke again later and the whole place was dark, so I assumed it was the middle of the night. The glass of water had been refilled, and the old man was still beside my bed. This time he was awake and had seen me open my eyes.

"Hello," I greeted him. "Could you hand me that glass of water?"

I grimaced and pulled myself into a sitting position.

"Sure." He handed me the water with a steady hand. "It's nice to finally meet you, Chloe."

By this time, I figured I could be okay with weird.

"What do you mean by 'finally'?" I asked him.

He cracked a grin, and his blue eyes lit up a little, even in the dark. "Why, child, I'm your grandfather."

I choked on my water, even spit a little bit out on him, "You're my... grandfather? Uh... I... okay."

He took my water glass and set it on the nightstand. He took my hand and held it, patting the top.

"Chloe, it is time to explain your heritage to you. You are old enough now to understand these things." He smiled at me. "So are you ready to hear it?"

I shrugged. I really didn't have a choice. I really just wanted to lay in bed and be sad that I would never see my mother again. But his explanation was something I hoped would explain all that had happened last night. Maybe it would explain why they had killed my mother. I wanted to find out who I had to kill to avenge her.

"Sure," I said.

"Chloe, much of what I am about to tell you will be hard to believe, but it may also fill in some of the blanks that you have wondered about at particular times in your life. Have patience and listen.

"Those people who killed your mother, I'm sure you noticed something different about them, like their strength and the way they died. If you guessed they aren't normal, you would have guessed correctly."

He paused.

I opened my mouth to speak, but he quickly lifted his hand to silence me.

"Yes, as you probably suspected, they are vampires. And we... we kill them. We are vampire slayers, or hunters, whatever you prefer. For generations, our family's bloodline has borne hunters. It is our job to kill the evil to keep humanity safe."

My mouth dropped open. I wasn't really that surprised about the vampires and stuff. I think it was more the issue of hearing someone else say there were actually vampires.

"Now a story begins," the man who called himself my grandfather announced. "About fifteen years ago a young woman who had been raised right here in this very community with our hunters fell in love with a vampire. She was one of the very best of us."

The old man's lips turned up into a smile at the memory.

"Even as a little girl, she trained constantly and learned with determination. It was her dream to be the best of all of us. For her, it was either be first or be killed.

"This amazing woman was your mother, Felicia. Felicia could take any of the men here in a fight. When it came to vampires, there was something about her that could almost mesmerize them, giving her the perfect opportunity to attack.

"That was until the day she met Trevor. We found ourselves in the midst of a battle one night in the park. She had tried to catch Trevor's gaze and draw him into her grasp, because he appeared to be the leader. For some reason, her gifts did not work on Trevor. However, when Trevor saw her, he decided he wanted her. He kidnapped her.

"Your mother fought him, but he was the only vampire your mother could not kill. He took her, and they disappeared for almost a year.

"Your mother told me the time she spent with Trevor wasn't so bad. I would like to think he was the most horrible man in the universe, but apparently he treated her pretty good. She was the *only* one he treated well."

My so-called grandfather paused to take a sip from his own water glass, which also sat on the nightstand.

I kept quiet because he asked me to and because the story was getting good.

He cleared his throat and continued. "Trevor's intention was to turn your mother. She told Trevor she loved him, and she would never leave him. But she didn't want to be a vampire. During her stay with Trevor, he treated her like a queen, gave her everything her heart desired. Unfortunately, he forgot one tiny detail: Felicia was a vampire hunter. The hatred for vampires ran deep in her veins and could not be forgotten, even by loving one of them.

"When one of Trevor's men tried to rape her, she killed him. Trevor would have killed him himself, had he known what the man had tried to do. Felicia had been embarrassed and had no intention of letting Trevor know what had happened. She told him the man had assaulted her. She announced she was pregnant, with you, and that she had only acted to defend her unborn child.

"Trevor was ecstatic. You have to realize how rare this was. Perhaps... once every couple hundred years is a child conceived with a vampire. But... a vampire child combined with the blood of a vampire hunter... that is completely unheard of.

"Felicia knew deep in her heart she could not stay with Trevor. She wanted her child to be safe, and have a good life, not to live in a world of darkness with a bunch of vampires. And there was the question of your safety. Children are like candy to vampires... the blood is sweet.

"So Felicia fled and came home shortly before you were born. When you were born a healthy little girl, we sent the two of you into hiding. Your father has been searching for you for years. That's why you've moved several times. That's why your mother drenched herself in that god-awful perfume and made you do the same thing, and that's why your mother was murdered right before your eyes. Because *you* are a very, very special child, Chloe Kallistrate."

He bowed his head and placed his fingertips on his temples. "Trevor will stop at nothing until he has you."

I had been laying back on my pillows, listening to this story. It did explain a lot of the weird behavior I had noticed in my mom. Sometimes she would get all crazy and just decide to move. She would start packing all of our stuff and clean the house with bleach from top to bottom before we left. Really, I just thought she was nomadic and had sudden urges to move. And the perfume, she changed her scent once a year and wore a lot of whatever she chose. She took about three showers a day, too. Yeah, now I get it, everywhere we went we left a scent.

I did have one question though. Actually, I had lots of questions, but just one for the time being: "How did you know that we needed help when Trevor's men attacked us?"

His eyes met mine. "Chloe, our blood isn't regular blood. We have the bloodline of vampire hunters. Our blood is almost magical. I just knew. Your mother is my daughter, and I just knew we had to go to her. We were too late to save her. Now we will honor her life by keeping you safe, because that is what she dedicated her life to doing."

I nodded.

"We are going to let you rest here for a while, because you have been through a trauma. It will take time for you to feel normal again. Soon, however, you will have to get up and begin your training."

"Training?"

He nodded. "Yes, I'm sorry, but one of the only ways for you to be safe is for you to learn how to defend yourself. If you had lived here with us since birth you probably could have helped your mother in fighting them. Sadly, she was out of practice and hadn't trained for fifteen years."

I could see he was becoming emotional.

"I would love to train." I caught his eye, and held his teary gaze. "I'm going to get good, better than my mother, even. I'm going to kill Trevor for having my mother murdered."

He nodded again and turned to leave.

"I swear it," I whispered to myself when he left the room.

I lay in bed for a long time without sleeping. I kept thinking of the guy who called himself my grandfather as 'the old man.' I didn't want to call him 'grandpa', but I didn't know what his name was, so that only left 'the old man.'

The room they had put me in was a bedroom. It was obviously a girl's bedroom. There was a dark purple comforter on the bed, and the curtains were the same color. A large dresser pushed up against one wall had an old-fashioned oval mirror in the corner beside it. I saw an open door on another wall that I assumed was an attached bathroom.

The possibility of a bathroom almost painfully reminded me that I hadn't peed at all since I woke. Slowly, I lifted myself into a sitting position. My arms screamed out in pain and refused to support me. Pushing the covers aside, I placed my bare feet on the hardwood floor and immediately wished I had some socks. The floor was freezing.

After a slow shuffle to the door, I discovered it was, indeed, a bathroom. *Thank goodness.*

On the way to the toilet, I had passed the mirror and immediately wished I hadn't looked. My image was hideous. My eyes were all sunken in and dark underneath, my hair was all matted and greasy, and the handprint bruises on my arms were beginning to do that thing where they turned green and yellow. I had several bruises on my legs too. I noticed them after I sat down to pee.

When I came out, I decided to be nosy and look around the rest of the bedroom. Maybe the dresser had some socks in it. I opened one of the drawers and found a ton of socks in various colors. I chose a plain white pair for myself and shut the drawer.

One of the picture frames on top of the dresser caught my eye. I picked it up to get a closer look. There, sitting on a bench beside an older woman and staring at the camera, was a girl about my age. As a matter of fact, she looked so much like me that she could have *been* me.

My mother.

I couldn't help it. I burst into tears and sobbed like a two year old. I rubbed my hand over the picture and let my tears fall. I wanted to see her again so badly. Knowing that was never going to happen was more than I could bear. My legs lost their strength, and I fell onto my knees, still holding the picture.

I hated those who had her killed. I can't say for sure I had ever really hated anyone before. Without a doubt, I was going to avenge her and kill that man they all claimed was my father. He would never have me on his side.

She died saving me. *How am I supposed to live with that kind of guilt?*

I missed her so much already.

The bedroom door opened. I didn't want anyone to see me sobbing on the floor. Crying was weak, and I didn't think any of these vampire hunters would be found crying on the floor of their rooms. I quickly wiped away the tears.

"Are you okay?" asked a male voice from behind me. "What are you doing on the floor?"

I tried to get up and fumbled because I was still holding the picture. I felt warm hands gently circle my waist to help lift me up.

"I dropped this picture off the dresser and slid when I bent to pick it up," I told him. I turned around and found myself staring straight into those emerald eyes that had saved me from Eli and those other goons.

He nodded. "Well, are you all right? You look like you're crying. Did you hurt yourself?"

"No, I'm okay. It's just... these bruises, my... uh, my whole body is kind of bruised."

He turned his lips up into what almost looked like a sneer. "Gotta get toughened up now. You're going to have a lot more bruises than that after you start training."

While I was busy looking surprised and thinking he should have been a little bit more sympathetic, he gave me a little push toward the bed to get me moving.

I climbed back in the bed, and he sat in the chair that the old man had used. I still had the picture of my mother in my hand, so I placed it on the nightstand next to the lamp.

Finally, annoyed with this guy enough to ignore his cuteness, I curtly asked him, "So are you going to tell me who you are?"

He tilted the chair back a little bit and rocked it. "My name is Drew."

"Why are you here, Drew?"

"I live here."

I shook my head in frustration. "No, I mean, why you are here in this room?"

"Luke told me to come in here and talk to you about where you are and what we do."

"Well, start talking then." It was painful, but I defiantly crossed my arms over my chest.

He narrowed his eyes. "You don't have to be rude."

"Huh?" Against my will, my eyes widened. "You were the one who was rude!"

"I did nothing rude."

Ugh. He was right. All he had done was tell me I needed to get tough. I was just being a baby because I felt sorry for myself.

"I'm sorry," I told him. "I'm just having a hard time right now."

Again, he nodded. "Do you think you're up for taking a walk?"

"I just got back in bed." I paused. "I don't have any clothes."

"There should be clothes in the closet. Why don't you find something that fits you? I'll wait outside the door. I want to tell you about us, and it helps to be able to show you what I am talking about."

I nodded and waited until he left the room. Why in the world did he let me get back in the bed in the first place if he was just going to make me get out again? With an enormous sigh and one last glance at my mother's picture, I lifted myself out of bed.

I managed find a top that looked like it was from this decade and a decent pair of jeans in the dresser. There were also plenty of shoes in the bottom of the closet. How weird that Mom had thrown her shoes on the floor of her closet too. I had never known that about her. Maybe she stopped doing it when she became a mom and had to be all responsible and tidy.

After I dressed, I cracked open the door and peeked out.

"You ready?"

Startled, I jerked backward, but then I realized it was Drew. Boy, I was jumpy.

"Yeah, I'm ready."

I stepped out into the hall and looked around. The floors were a dark hardwood like in the bedroom, and the walls were a creamy pinkish color. There were pictures on the walls, everywhere, in those huge frames that hold, like, ten different photos. While we walked down the hallway, I also noticed that all the doors were shut on the top floor.

"Whose house is this?"

"It's your grandfather's, Luke's," he answered.

"Oh." I had kind of figured it was, but thought it best to ask before assuming. Down the stairs we went and onto the main floor. From my spot, at the base of the stairs, I could see part of the kitchen and what looked like a living room.

Drew saw me straining to see the rest of the house. "Would you like to see the house first or take a look around when you get back?"

I shrugged like I didn't care. "I'll just explore after we get back. That's fine."

Drew opened the door and I followed him outside. It was super chilly and broad daylight. I hadn't realized that when we were back in the bedroom. I wondered just how long I had been sleeping and how long I had been here.

"See that?"

We stood at the railing on the covered porch connected to the house. He pointed directly in front of us.

"I see that we aren't in the city anymore."

He nodded. "We aren't in the city, but we aren't out of it either. Our community is sort of like a suburb. It's gated. No one comes in or out, except mostly just the people who live here."

Wow. They were a whole community of just vampire hunters. That was wicked. "How many of you live here?"

"There are about one hundred homes in this community. We aren't the only vampire hunter community. There are many, many more all over the world."

"Wow!" That time I said it out loud. I could see the tops of many houses poking up through the trees. The view was spectacular. In the distance, the lush green mountains rose high into the clouds. I saw the tiniest bit of snow on the top of the mountains, and the trees cascaded down into the valley where they surrounded the houses.

I turned to look at Drew. "It's beautiful here."

He simply nodded. "Let's move on."

We took a path through the woods instead of the gravel driveway leading out to the road.

"This path is a shortcut into the main village," he told me while we walked.

I followed without saying anything. The path was covered with leaves, so the only sound I heard was our footsteps crunching over them. When we left the forest, we were on a street. A few blocks more and we were on what I assumed was the main drag of a small town. We passed a diner, a quickie mart, a drug store, a video store. There was even a flower shop and a bakery.

Nice.

The street came to a split where we could only go left or right. Drew veered us to the left. We passed a cute little church with beautiful stained glass in the windows and continued walking until we came to a large building that looked like a giant shop. Drew held the door open for me, and I quickly passed through it. Once inside, I stood in awe, with my mouth hanging open.

It was a training area… a very big training area.

Drew appeared beside me. "Most everyone who lives in this community has training equipment and space in their own homes, but this one is open for everyone."

There were people using weight machines, cardio equipment and sparring. On closer inspection, I realized there were also children using the training equipment. Drew followed my gaze to one particular little girl who had her hair in a ponytail and was hacking away at a punching bag.

"We start early here. I have been training for this since I could walk." He paused. "And you probably would have too, if your mother hadn't taken you away."

I jerked my head to face him. "What would you know about that?"

He shrugged. "We all know about it. Trevor has been attacking directly at us since your mother ran with you. Obviously, we would have to know about you guys so we would know why we were being attacked."

"I'm going to kill him," I whispered.

"I'll help you." Drew met my eyes with his flashing green ones, and for a moment, I felt a strange connection to him. With a jerk of his head, he tore his eyes from mine and turned away. "Let's go, we have more to see."

Confused by the brief moment we had, I stumbled through the door behind him. After seeing the gym, we went to the shooting 3333ranges. By this time, I wasn't surprised to see that there was a range for guns and another for bows. When we left the ranges, we paid a visit to the library. The library was awesome. It was a huge, two-story stone building with tons of old books inside. I immediately fell in love with the library. While we strolled through the shelves of books, I wondered how often the people in town actually used the library. "Don't most people use the Internet for researching stuff nowadays?"

"You'd be surprised," Drew told me. "When it comes to killing vampires, and other things, most of what we need to know we find in here." He gestured to the shelves. "These books are ancient. They aren't your basic encyclopedia or articles written by a blogger."

I walked among the books and decided the library was probably going to be my favorite place in town. After we left the library, we went back to the old man's house. Well, I guess I could call him Luke, since Drew had told me his name.

Once back in the house, we found Luke in the kitchen making a salad.

"Hey, Luke," Drew greeted him when we entered the room. Drew pulled out a chair and sat.

It dawned on me, when Drew had said he lived, here he really meant that he lived *here*, in the house. I wondered why he live here with my grandfather. He hadn't said anything about us being related.

"Drew, Chloe," Luke nodded to us. He pointed his chopping knife at the pile of lettuce on the table. "One of you wash that lettuce, and the other can get those red bell peppers sliced up."

"Chloe, did Drew show you around town?"

I nodded. "Yes, it's a very quaint little community."

"Well, I hope you are going to like it here. I had some of the crews who weren't busy go after your things. I hope we got everything you would have wanted. I told them to make sure to get any and all photographs or memorabilia for you."

I stopped slicing the peppers and realized what I had failed to before: This place was going to be my home. My mother was gone forever. Her family I had never known were vampire hunters. My father was a vampire.

Life as I had known it would never be the same.

"I'm sure whatever they bring will do," I told him blandly.

I gripped the knife even tighter. Far off in the distance, I could still hear them speaking, but only one thing was clear in my mind: Trevor, my father, was going to die.

From that moment on, I was Chloe Kallistrate, a vampire hunter.

THE VAMPIRE HUNTER'S DAUGHTER
PART II

POWERFUL BLOOD

"Ouch, damn it!"

I hit the floor on my side, my hip and elbow making the most contact with the hard floor of the gym. I rolled onto my back and rubbed my elbow but stayed on the ground.

I was tired.

Drew stood aside and watched me struggle to get up, without offering to help. I should have been irritated, but I'd become accustomed to his refusal to help me with anything during training. He insisted helping me would *not* help me in the long run.

I had been training with the vampire hunters for two months, and I still fell on my butt about thirty times per day. I had sworn to myself I was going to be the best, like my mother was, but that didn't seem to be happening.

Seriously, I woke up at oh dark thirty and ran the trails in the woods for an hour. I ate breakfast and showered. I went to school, and after school, I worked out in the gym with the machines. Finally, I got my butt kicked by Drew or someone else for two hours. Yeah, it was pure hell. I knew I was getting in better shape, but I really sucked at fighting.

One thing I *was* good at was shooting. With both guns and archery, I had a knack for marksmanship. Twice a week, I went to the ranges and practiced shooting. Turned out I was a natural, and I enjoyed it, which was a plus.

"I'm done," I told Drew while I got to my feet and grabbed my water bottle. "I'm so tired I can't even stay on my feet. I need a break."

Drew shook his head. "Chloe, you can't quit just because you're tired. You have to build your endurance."

"I have been working my ass off every day since I got here. I need a break!" I blew several strands of dark brown hair out of my eyes. My hair never stayed in its ponytail.

"I thought you wanted to be like your mother."

"Don't you pull that crap on me!" I knew what he was trying to do. It had worked on me before, and he assumed it was going to work again. He was using my mother to get a charge out of me. The last time he had done it, I showed more fight than I ever had before. My mother had been one of the best vampire hunters there was, until she fell under the spell of my evil vampire father. She had hidden me from him all my life, but he found us, somehow, and had his minions break into our house and murder her.

Drew shrugged. "Fine, I can't make you train. Take today off, but do not try and back out tomorrow because I'll just keep thumping on you even when you want to quit."

"Fine." I grabbed my water bottle and towel and escaped the place I had begun to think of as a torture chamber. All I did was sweat and get beat up in there.

"See you at home," Drew called after me.

I threw a hand up in a pathetic wave without turning around.

Home. When I had first arrived, I'd met my grandfather and was surprised to learn Drew lived in the house with him. I had thought maybe Drew and I were related somehow, but I had learned he only lived with my grandfather, Luke, to help him out, because Luke was getting up there in years.

Luke didn't fight anymore, but he still sat on the board with the hunters. He still made important decisions for the community. Turns out our family, the Kallistrate, were one of the most renowned bloodlines in the history of vampire hunters.

I never knew there was a history of vampire hunters.

Crazy.

Drew was eighteen. He was in his prime for vampire hunting and was constantly out on missions. I thought it might be uncomfortable staying in the same house as Drew because we weren't related—and he was super cute—but it seemed to be going okay. Mostly, I think he treated me like a little sister. I wasn't really sure just how I felt about that either.

I slammed into my room and fell face first onto my bed. The dark purple comforter puffed up around my face, and for one brief moment, I wished it would suffocate me. I didn't hate this place, but I had no choice other than to be here.

I wanted my mother back.

For some reason, I thought becoming a vampire hunter would be easier. Heck, it was in my blood, so wasn't it supposed to just like… come to me or something?

I rolled over on the bed and stared at the ceiling of the room that used to be my mother's and had become mine. Funny how things like that worked: My mother had to die for me to know my family and heritage. I never would have met my grandfather—or any of these people here—if she hadn't died. I never would have known who my father was either, not that I really wanted to know.

I decided I wanted to go to the library and look for books on vampires and vampire hunters… or anything that applied to my new life. I figured that being knowledgeable could be just as powerful as being strong.

But first, I needed a shower.

I took the trails to the library. It was quicker than the roads and more scenic. Fall had hit hard, so the air was cold and tons of leaves had fallen off the trees. They crunched loudly beneath my shoes while I hurried along the trails into town.

When I emerged from the forest, I could see the little town bustling with activity. Sometimes it was hard to believe the entire community of people who lived there were all vampire hunters. I saw an older woman struggling to open her car door and balance a gigantic turkey in her other arm. It dawned on me why the town was so busy. It was almost Thanksgiving. Everyone was out picking up stuff for their holiday gatherings.

Thanksgiving… without my mom.

I wasn't sure that was something I could deal with. I had been so busy with training and school, I hadn't had time to think about the holidays coming up. Halloween had come and gone, along with my birthday, which had been on the first of November. Yup, I had turned fifteen and had my first birthday without my mother.

I hadn't told anyone it was my birthday, but they had known anyway. It had been celebrated quietly with a cake and a couple presents. Luke had given me a new iPod because mine had been left in my old room in the house where my mother had been murdered. Drew had given me a gun. Yeah, a gun. It was a nice little light-weight forty-five that I could easily handle. Along with my pretty gun, I also got a gun cleaning kit and a lesson in cleaning my weapon.

In any case, it was going to be hard going through the holidays without my mom around. All the emotions only made me more adamant in my desire to seek revenge against my father.

The bastard.

When I approached the steps to the library, I shook my head to clear the thoughts so I could focus on the task ahead: researching about vampires and vampire hunters. I entered the library and realized I really had no idea what I was looking for.

The librarian sat behind a long counter covered with neatly stacked papers and little piles of books. She turned away from the computer she was pecking at and smiled at me. "Can I help you find anything?"

I shuffled a bit and moved closer. "I don't know, I'm... uh, looking for stuff about vampire hunters or vampires."

"Oh, you came to the right place then."

She took off her glasses and set them on the counter. She wasn't an old woman, but she wasn't really young either. I would have placed her at a good-looking fifty or so. Her hair was a light brown with a few grey strands scattered through it.

"Come with me."

She led me down a maze of books that rose far above our heads. She stopped when we made it to a section where the books were huge, leather-bound monsters of books.

"Because of where you are, this library has a special section on the subjects you are interested in. You should be able to find anything you're looking for right here." She gestured at all the books around us.

"Thank you," I told her, gazing in awe at all the books. I turned to her and held out my hand. "By the way, I'm Chloe."

Her lips turned up in a smile once again. "Oh, I know who you are, honey. Everyone does. In any case, my name is Linda."

"It's nice to meet you, Linda."

"Same goes for me." She took back her hand. "I'll leave you to your studying now."

I watched her walk away and decided I liked her.

Letting out a really big sigh, I scanned some of the titles on the spines of the books. After about five minutes of looking at the titles, I found one that read *History and Legends of Vampire Slayers*. That one looked like it would have some interesting material. I lifted the gigantic book off the shelf, and then I made my way to one of the tables and began to read. On the very first page was a description:

The spread of vampirism was a relentless disease, so a

warrior angel was created and sent to battle the vampires. This warrior angel, Andronikos, found love with a warrior woman, Sostrate. She was uniquely gifted: a demi-god, born of a human and a god.

The union of the angel and the woman produced four children: two boys, Alkaios and Alexio, and two girls, Thekla, Lysistrata. These offspring became a new kind of warrior, gifted with both the blood of an angel and a god. Out of this unique mix, the vampire slayer was born.

I looked up from the text. I came from the blood of angels, gods and in my own special case, a vampire.

Now that's deep.

But... it was hardly believable considering how clumsy and without talent I was.

The book continued on with how the children of the warrior angel and the demi-god woman mated with other people of power or commoners and their children had children and so on.

"Good book, huh?"

Startled, I jerked backward in my chair and almost toppled over. Drew caught the back of my chair and steadied it. "Sorry, I didn't mean to scare you."

Annoyed at being disturbed, I shut the book and glanced up at him. "Drew, we live in the same house. Is it really necessary to follow me around all the time?"

Drew ignored me and pulled out the chair next to mine so he could sit. Giving in to the fact that he wasn't going to leave me alone, I opened the book to the pages I had been reading. "How come you never told me any of this stuff?"

"You never asked." He shrugged.

I sighed. He could be so aggravating. "And it never occurred to you that I might want to know my ancestors were angels and demi-gods?"

"Nah, it never occurred to me. But if you wanted to know it, you should have asked Luke. He has a whole family tree drawn out that dates all the way back to the very beginning. It's taken several generations to finish it."

"He does? Why didn't you tell me?"

This time it was Drew who sighed loudly.

"Because you didn't ask," he repeated. "Chloe, you aren't just descended from angels and demi-gods. You are in the direct line of the original hunters. You could possibly be a very powerful woman."

I didn't say anything because I didn't know what to say. I was a direct descendent from these powerful and good creatures, but yet my blood was tainted with the evil of my vampire father.

Yay.

$$\times \times \times$$

Breathe in, exhale, hold and ease back the trigger.

I hit the red dot every time. I felt like I could hit it even with my eyes closed. Shooting was calming for me, something that eased pain yet allowed a release of my anger at the same time.

The big earphone things muffled the shots while I fired clip after clip into the targets. When I finally felt I'd had enough, I cleaned up and put my gun back in its case. I was going to have to remember to give Drew a really awesome present for Christmas, since I didn't know when his birthday was, because I really loved my gun. That also reminded me that I basically had no money and should probably look for a job, but I didn't have time for a job.

The information I had found at the library was definitely interesting. One of the first things I wanted to do when I got home was to ask Luke about that family tree thing.

While I was leaving the range, I stepped out onto the sidewalk and looked up at the gray clouds that covered the sky. There had been no sunshine for several days, and it was beginning to wear on me. I needed sunshine! Dang, how could I ever be related to a vampire? They died in the sun, and I could bask in it.

Just when I veered into the woods, the first snowflakes of the year floated down and rested on the bare tree branches.

"Oh, just great." Instead of enjoying the beauty of falling snow, I was concerned about the fact I was going to have to run in that crap every morning. I picked up my pace and jogged the rest of the way home.

When I burst through the door, I found Luke sitting at the kitchen table reading a newspaper.

"Hey, Luke," I greeted him.

His wrinkled cheeks lifted when he smiled. "When are you going to start calling me grandpa?"

I shrugged. "I don't know. It seems weird because I just met you."

I opened the fridge and grabbed an apple out of the fruit bin. Man, I missed junk food. Every person in the community was a health food fanatic, so I had to be, too. They didn't even have regular potato chips in their stores. It was sad.

"Luke, I was wondering if there was some way I could... possibly... uhm, earn some money."

I took a giant bite of my apple.

Luke looked a bit surprised. "Well, I guess I don't think of everything. I'm so sorry. Do you need money right now?"

With my mouth full of apple, I shook my head. After I swallowed, I said, "I just figure, with Christmas coming up, I'm going to need some cash to buy presents for you guys. Also, it would be nice to be able to get some of the things I need instead of asking you."

"Chloe, you have money."

"What do you mean?"

"Your mother left everything to you. There was a life insurance policy worth more than enough to see you through most of your life, as long as you don't waste it. Of course, it's in a trust. It's in your name, and I'm the trustee, but there's a board made up of community leaders. They approve all transactions and watch out for your best interests. We can submit a request to the board to withdraw a small portion into a checking account and get you a debit card."

He folded his paper. "I'm so sorry. I didn't even think about you needing money of your own. I did not intend to isolate you after everything you've been through."

I shrugged again, pretending that using my mother's death money to buy Christmas gifts didn't bother me. Talk about crappy. "It's okay. I'm just glad I won't have to ask you for money for personal items and such."

He gave a mock shudder and then cracked a grin. "Yes, that's probably for the best."

I decided to just come right out and ask him about the family tree. So, I sat down in the chair opposite of him and fiddled with my apple.

"Luke... Drew said something to me today about a family tree." Luke's eyebrows rose in curiosity, but I kept talking before he could say anything. "He said it took generations to finish it, but that you have it and it shows my family back to the beginning."

He folded his paper and set it on the table. "Of course, I have it. Would you like to see it?" He pushed his chair back and stood. "It will certainly help you understand where you come from, Chloe."

I nodded my head slowly, not certain I wanted to know everything but at the same time, curious.

"I'll go get it," he told me, and I watched him leave the room.

When he returned, he cleared off the table and unrolled a gigantic piece of super-thick paper. We both bent over the paper to examine the names. The family tree wasn't an actual picture of a tree, as I had sort of expected it to be. It was really just lines connecting with each other with spaces for names. Toward the bottom was my mom and beside her was Trevor's name, and then stemming from their names was my name. At the top of the tree it said: *Andronikos and Sostrate.*

"Do we know who the warrior woman descended from?" I looked up and caught Luke's eye. "I mean…the god that was her parent?"

Luke looked thoughtful, like maybe he shouldn't say anything. "No one can be certain, but it is said that Artemis was her mother."

"Artemis, goddess of the hunt. That makes sense."

He nodded. "It does."

"Except she was supposed to be a virgin goddess," I pointed out.

"Not all tales are actually the way it happened, Chloe." He pointed at the names of the warriors children. "Do you see here where the children of the warriors have paired with many people, conceiving children."

I nodded and he trailed his finger down the tree a bit farther.

"Well, look here." He pointed to two names who had conceived a child together.

I couldn't believe it.

"Brother and sister?" It came out like a question, but it was more like a surprised statement.

"Yes. It wasn't uncommon in ancient times for brothers and sisters to be together. Most royal lines have done this to keep their blood pure. I'm assuming that's what happened here, with cousins." He paused to assess my reaction, then pointed to another set of names down the line, "And here."

"Eeeewwww! Our family is incestuous. Gross!"

"Indeed, it is gross, but the result is the same. It kept the blood of vampire hunters powerful."

Confused, I shook my head. "Drew said something about that earlier, about power and me possibly being a powerful woman. Now you're talking about power. What are you guys talking about?"

Luke rolled up the large family tree. "Chloe, think about it. Angels, demi-gods and for you, the power of vampire blood: How could you not be a powerful woman?"

"But I'm not even strong or anything. I don't have anything that could be even close to a special power."

"Not yet, you don't. Most hunters acquire their gifts when they're about sixteen. Not sure about vampires though. You might want to do some research on vampire children."

I had already planned on researching vampires, mostly to know their strengths and weaknesses. "So, I'm probably going to end up getting some kind of superpower."

Luke laughed. "Well, I don't know about superpower. Most hunters have something they are just exceedingly good at, so we call them gifts."

I nodded vigorously. "Like how I'm really good at shooting!"

"Exactly, but some hunters do come into a little more than just gifts. A rare few do have what could be a 'superpower,' as you called it."

As interesting as it all was, I wasn't sure having to deal with some abnormal and untrained power was something I really wanted. Really, my whole life had been turned upside down, and I had enough problems as it was.

"Now help me get dinner started."

Luke opened the fridge, as though our conversation had been as normal as the weather. I guess even demi-god, angel, vampire mutants had to eat dinner.

✶✶✶

The next morning I woke and opened the curtains to look outside. Just as I suspected: Snow had covered everything. It was pretty, though. The moon was almost full, and the white winter wonderland glittered in the moonlight. The trees had all lost their leaves, and the snow that had settled on their branches appeared crystallized.

I sighed and found my pink velvety jogging suit. After tying my hair up and putting on a headband that would also cover my ears, I set off into the woods for my run. Running the trails on the snow could probably be listed as my least favorite thing to do, aside from getting my butt kicked.

My run was actually closer to a walk. I did so much slipping and sliding that, by the time I made it back to the house, I was soaking wet and running late for school.

School in the vampire hunter community was no different from regular school, except that it was smaller. So far, I hadn't made any friends, but I hadn't really tried to make friends either. It had become habit. At my old school, I usually just kept to myself. I guess I've always been a loner. At lunch, I would grab my food and sit on the stairs in the hallway with my eyes closed and my iPod blaring into my ears, blocking out reality.

After walking to school in the snow, I ended up with soaked feet. My quest for making friends didn't go any better. I sloshed into the school and wanted to cry. Was I going to have to spend the whole day like this? Why couldn't I have looked for a pair of boots in my mother's stuff? Things worsened when Christina Livingston—who was considered the school bitch-slash-slut—slid in the puddle that had formed at my locker. Just as she was going down, my reflexes kicked in and my hands flew out to catch her. Well, I caught her all right. Right in the nose with the back of my hand.

"You stupid bitch!" she screamed at me in a nasal voice. She lay on the floor in a puddle of melted snow and held her nose, which was dripping blood all over.

"Oh, I'm so sorry!"

I bent to help her up.

"Get away from me. Just get away from me."

She moaned. Suddenly there was a huge circle of kids around us. She reached up with her other hand and moved her black hair out of her eyes. Her little skirt was hiked up so far that we could all see her lacey pink panties, surprisingly, not a thong. She rolled over onto all fours and slowly managed to stand. We all stood there watching her. I wasn't going to try to help her again, but I sure wasn't going to leave either.

"I'm really sorry," I said, trying again.

Her bleeding nose had slowed, but there were blood spatter marks all over her tight white shirt.

"Shut up!" she snarled and then lunged at me.

She slammed me up against the lockers and rammed her fist into my stomach. I felt like I was going to throw up. Distantly, I could hear the commotion of all the other students in the background. Most were hollering "fight, fight," and I could hear a few others yelling to get someone.

As soon as she backed off, I slapped her. The return I got was another hit to the gut and then another with the other fist. Before I could recover, she threw an uppercut to my jaw.

"Ow, shit!" she screamed. "My hand!"

That hit hurt... bad! We hadn't moved to hitting each other in the face during training yet. Drew said we would do that once I was better at blocking.

"My face!" I screamed back at her. It made me mad that she was kicking my ass in front of everyone. It was one thing in training where I was learning, but this was just plain embarrassing. I felt heat rise in me all the way down from my cold wet toes.

She wasn't expecting it right then because she was jumping around holding her hand, and I was bent over in pain. I lashed out as quickly as I could and grabbed two handfuls of her long black hair. I pulled her whole head down and lifted my knee at the same time. My knee connected with her face. A loud cracking noise echoed through the hallway.

She fell, crying and yelling about her nose.

"Screw this," I said. I grabbed my backpack and sloshed my way by the group of students and out the front door.

By the time I made it home, Luke had already heard about the incident and sat in the living room in his rocking chair, waiting for me.

I dropped my backpack on the floor and pulled off my dripping tennis shoes. "So, you heard?"

He nodded sternly and pointed to the chair next to him. "Tell me what happened."

I sighed and plopped down in the recliner. "My shoes were wet, and Christina slipped on the puddle my shoes made. When I tried to catch her, I accidentally hit her in the nose, and then she attacked me."

"That's all?" He raised his eyebrows.

"After she hit me a few times, I decided I wasn't just going to let her beat the snot out of me, and I fought back."

"You do know you broke her nose, right?"

I nodded. I didn't know for sure, but I had figured as much. "I'm sorry, Luke. I just couldn't stand there and let her beat on me for no reason."

"And I would never expect you to. You defended yourself and nothing more."

The relief I felt at not being in trouble was immense. I had been so afraid Luke would be totally irate over the whole thing.

"This is the problem with raising so many hunter children all in one place. You are all trained well and could actually kill someone without even trying very hard. When the typical teenage fights break out, it's never a good thing. This could have been far worse."

I shrugged. "I've seen worse fights in my old school. Once, I even saw a kid get stabbed."

Luke closed his eyes and shook his head like the thought saddened him. "Chloe, I know you were only defending yourself, but you must try to stay away from situations like this one."

There was nothing else to say about it. He could be damned sure I would try and avoid stuff like this. I wasn't sure what I could really do to avoid it. I already kept to myself most of the time. "okay. Can I go to my room now?"

"Yes. We have to be at the school in the morning. You are going to be suspended for a week because you were involved in the fight. There is a zero tolerance rule, so no matter if it was your fault or not, you and Christina will both be suspended."

"Wonderful," I said, my voice dripping with sarcasm. I headed out of the room. I paused a moment and then turned back to Luke. "Can I go to the library?"

He nodded his agreement and clicked on the television.

✗ ✗ ✗

When I told Drew about Christina, his eyes narrowed. I wondered what was up with that.

"You know her?" I asked.

"Yeah, she was my girlfriend for a year."

I choked on my carrot juice.

"Your girlfriend?" I blurted when my throat cleared. "Isn't she my age?"

"Chloe, I'm only three years older than you, for one, and I just turned eighteen." He sighed. "Christina is a senior this year, so she was only one year behind me in school."

Oh, that made more sense. On the upside though, I was in a fight with a senior, and I didn't lose.

Sweet.

"Well, why the heck would you date her anyway? She's mean and a slut, too."

He laughed. "She's not a slut. She just wants everyone to think she is."

"That's stupid. Why would anyone do that?"

"Christina is one of those girls who just wants attention. She wants attention because it makes her feel loved and wanted. Her family isn't exactly the best family in the world."

When I raised my eyebrows in question he said, "Christina's father had to be banished from the community. One night, he got so drunk he beat Christina's mother so badly she died. Christina was ten years old at the time. She had been hiding under her bed in the other room and heard the whole thing."

"Oh, my gosh!"

"So, when he came after her, she ran for her life. She ran to the nearest neighbor. It took four other hunters to subdue him. Turns out he was a cocaine addict, but no one knew it."

"How come her mother didn't fight back?"

"Her mother wasn't a hunter. Not everyone here has two hunters for parents. You don't."

"Ugh, don't remind me."

As much as I really didn't want to feel sorry for Christina, I couldn't help it. We had both seen our mothers murdered, and in a way, both by our fathers. "That's still no reason for her to go around being mean and slutty."

He turned his eyes away, and I thought for a minute I saw a bit of sadness in them.

"I know," he told me.

I saw in his eyes that he had cared about her. While I should have felt bad for him, or something like that, I felt something else instead. I'm pretty sure it was jealousy.

Two days after that talk with Drew, he obtained permission to take me into the city so I could buy new winter clothes and boots. Oh, how I longed for the busy shops of the mall!

Before we left, Luke gave me a debit card for my new checking account. He told me how much had been deposited and how much would be deposited each month. Luke explained that he was on the account with me because I was a minor. He told me he would teach me about balancing my accounts when I returned from my trip.

I thanked him and tucked the card into my wallet. If it hadn't been so icy on the walkway, I would have run to Drew's truck.

The mall was totally fun. I was astonished to learn that Drew had never had an Orange Julius, so I made him drink one. I also ate two hotdogs and a big thing of chili nachos.

"You're going to get sick," Drew told me from across the table.

"I don't care." To show him just how much I didn't care, I used a big chip to scoop up some chili and shoved it in my mouth. He shook his head in disgust and took a bite of his healthy sub sandwich.

I managed to find two nice pair of snow boots. One pair would work for indoor and outdoor, the other was only for outside. I got a new jacket, several hats, and a bunch of those little gloves that cost a dollar.

Drew seemed to like the Orange Julius because he was slurping it down fast. "Do you want to go see a movie while we're in town?"

"You bet I do!" I was having a hard time containing my excitement. I hadn't had a great day since before my mother died. And to think, getting into a fight at school got me a shopping trip to town.

Not that I would do that again.

It was dark by the time the movie ended. The clouds had parted for the almost full moon that lit up the parking lot with a luminous glow. Snowflakes fell softly on everything. Instead of causing me worry, like when we were at home, the snow felt magical.

Halfway to the truck I felt a prickle on the back of my neck. Drew stopped in his tracks and gazed around at the other people leaving the theatre for their own cars.

"Let's get to the truck," he told me quietly. I sensed a 'don't argue' tone in his voice.

We continued to the truck and climbed inside. I didn't know what was going on, but what I did know was that we both sensed something. That couldn't be good.

"What is it?" I whispered as soon as we were in the truck with the doors shut.

"Vampire," he whispered back.

Oh, crap.

I knew having a good day was too much to ask. I had no idea what to do.

"Should we just go home?" I asked.

"No." He looked away from the crowded parking lot long enough to glance at me, his green eyes flashing. "We have to kill it."

okay, I was scared. The last time I had a run in with vampires, they murdered my mother and tried to kidnap me. It took a whole group of hunters to kill just one of them when they had come to my rescue. "How do we know there's only one?"

"We don't."

Time passed with complete and utter slowness while the parking lot emptied. People chatted with each other and took their sweet time getting in their cars and driving away. Finally, there were only two people left in the parking lot: a couple who were making out against the door of an awesome bronze-colored Chevelle.

"It's them. He is the victim," Drew whispered.

I don't think he was whispering to me; it was more like he was thinking out loud.

The woman had the guy pushed up against the door of the car. When she lifted her leg, he reached around and boosted her up. He then turned around so she was the one with her back against the door. Snow fell onto to them and stuck in their hair and on their clothes, but they were oblivious.

Drew reached behind him and pulled his gun out.

"You were carrying that around all day? In the mall!" I hissed. "We could have been arrested."

"Shut up, Chloe." He didn't take his eyes off the couple, but I saw his hand reach up and turn off the dome light so it wouldn't shine when he opened the door. He rested his hand on the door handle and pulled it up slowly, silently, so the door wasn't completely shut.

"Stay here," he whispered, so quietly I could barely hear him.

I nodded acknowledgement and slid down in the seat a bit while he crept out of the truck and across the parking lot. I watched the couple making out and waited for Drew. After about a minute, clear as day, I saw the woman's eyes lift and look at me.

Fear ripped through my body like a wave. While she looked at me, her eyes suddenly flashed and glowed a blinding red in the darkness and then she smiled. I saw teeth, white as the snow. In an instant her fangs appeared. She threw her head back and laughed, which that guy probably assumed was just a flirtatious giggle. She continued to stare at me while she snuggled back into his neck and bit him.

I knew I would be next if we didn't kill her.

His scream filled the air. I watched, horrified while he tried to push her away. He clawed desperately at her hair and clothes, but soon all he could do was weakly flail his arms. Oh, where was Drew? I didn't want to watch anymore. Finally, the guy's arms dropped down to his side and his stiffened body went slack.

She dropped his body onto the snow-covered parking lot and wiped her mouth with her arm. I realized I needed a weapon and searched the truck for something I could use to defend myself. I glanced up and couldn't believe what I saw: She stole that guy's wallet. Damn it, not one thing in Drew's truck was even remotely close to being considered a weapon. Some vampire hunter he was; he didn't even carry a wooden stake or two around.

Damn, damn, damn.

Frantically, I fumbled and sifted through everything in the truck and found nothing.

And then she was there.

I looked up, and when I saw her, every ounce of fear I had rushed out in a blood-curdling scream. She stood in front of the truck, her red eyes boring into me, her arms folded across her chest. The breeze outside whipped the snow and her long black hair crazily around her pale face. She wore the stereotypical long black trench coat and her scarlet lips matched her glowing red eyes. I back-peddled my feet against the floor of the truck and screamed.

Drew appeared on top of the Chevelle, where she had left the body in the blood-laden snow. She must have seen my gaze shift, because she turned toward him. He had his gun raised and held it steady with both hands in front of him. I had the weirdest thought: He looked like one of the gods we were descended from. His hair whipped around in the wind. His black hoodie was zipped snug against his body. His eyes flashed a green fire comparable to emeralds in sunlight. I could not see her face, but I was sure her confidence turned to fear.

Drew fired.

When the bullet penetrated her body, a glowing white light erupted and exploded. I had stopped screaming when I saw Drew, and I watched with awe while the white light seeped through her and ate away at her body like a spreading disease. It literally dissolved her away, bit by bit, while she screamed in agony. Within minutes, she was reduced to a pile of gray ash that marred the otherwise pure white snow.

I breathed a gigantic sigh of relief, and Drew hopped down from the Chevelle. He climbed in the truck with me, and we raced home as fast as the icy roads would allow. Neither of us said anything until we pulled into the driveway and turned off the ignition.

I was in shock. The first time I had any experience with vampires, I had literally not been able to do *anything*. One of them had been holding me so tightly. With this vampire, I had been able to fight. I had been able to do something about it, and I didn't do anything.

It was an eye opener. I knew I needed to train harder and be more open to learning how to fight.

I finally found my voice through the fear. "What about that guy's body? We can't just leave it out there."

"He wasn't dead." Drew squinted through the snow flurries obstructing his vision while he drove. "She didn't kill him. He will wake up in about half an hour and wonder what the hell happened. The bite marks will still be there, but will only look like a couple of mosquito bites. Even if he remembers what happened to him, we don't have the ability to make him forget."

I was just glad the guy wasn't dead. "What was that light?"

"UV bullets," he replied. "Once you get past the ranges, you will use them."

"Oh." I said. I looked out the window first and then raised an eyebrow. "Why didn't you use them the first time we met, when my mom was killed?"

"Sometimes, it's just as easy to fight." He paused and our eyes met. "When you do this your whole life, being able to actually kill something that is supposed to be evil and immortal is something you take pride in. Most of us love the fight too. But this was a newborn vampire. The ones who murdered your mother were very, very old and these UV bullets would have been like a poke in the eye to them."

"It's okay. I was just wondering. What about her eyes? The

guys who killed my mother didn't have red eyes."

"She was recently changed and for a few years after the change their eyes turn red right before they feed and for a while after, like...uhm, the best way to explain it is like a human's reaction when they are turned on sexually."

"Oh." See, I needed to learn this stuff. "They should teach us this in school."

Drew looked tired. He brushed his hair back with his hand. "They do. When you're a junior, you'll start those studies. Let's go in."

He grabbed a couple of my bags and exited the truck. Once we were inside, he set down the bags. The house was quiet. Luke was obviously asleep.

"Chloe, will you be okay?" Drew asked quietly.

"Yeah, I'll be fine. Are you going to get up and run with me in the morning?"

He nodded. "Uh huh, but I need to go to bed. Good night, Chloe."

He affectionately brushed my bangs back and tucked them behind my ear. I wasn't used to affection of any kind from him. I backed away.

I choked out a hasty, " 'Night, Drew,"

I grabbed the bags and fled to the stairs as fast as I could. Once in my room, I shut my bedroom door, dropping my bags on the floor. Without warning, I burst into tears. I could not believe I was crying. Completely ridiculous. I really needed to toughen up. Wiping at my wet face and snotty nose, I fell onto my bed and buried myself beneath the comfort of my blankets.

While the tears continued to fall, the only thing I could think of to get tougher was to train harder. My mother must have been a completely different person than the one I knew. I couldn't imagine what she must have gone through during those years she spent trying to protect me. I had to make it up to her.

My mother had dedicated her life to protecting me from vampires. The least I could do was honor her memory by protecting *myself* from them. If I didn't, the last fifteen years of her life would have been a waste.

I reached over and took her picture off the nightstand. Gently, I ran my fingertips over the glass. "I promise to do better, Mom."

I pulled the picture against my chest and hugged it.

"Please help me, Mom. If you're up there, watching me fail, then please help me. Help me find the strength to be stronger and better." More tears poured out of the corners of my eyes and slid down my cheeks. "I need you, Mom."

There was no sign, no really cool ghost of my mom that came down and gave me this super lecture on how great I could be. There was only silence.

Silence and tears.

THE VAMPIRE HUNTER'S DAUGHTER
PART III

BECOMING

BECOMING

I thought Christmas at Luke's would be quiet since it would be only him, Drew and me. It turned out that every Christmas, Luke threw a big ol' shindig for anyone who wanted to come.

Vampire-hunter Christmas really isn't much different from Christmas anywhere else, except that vampire hunters love to give each other weapons. Drew had given me a gun for my fifteenth birthday, and it wasn't until the big party that I understood why he gave me a gun. I can't even begin to count how many of the gifts exchanged were weapons. There was one that was really, really cool though. Charlie, who worked at the video store, gave his brother Joe an awesome gadget he could fit inside his pocket. When a little button on the side was pushed, it turned into a full-sized bow. It was pretty wicked.

Because Drew had given me the gun for my birthday, which I totally adored, I'd decided I needed to give him something really great, too. It took forever, but I finally found some throwing stars. They were real silver and I had them engraved with different sayings like: 'Vampires Suck', 'Stick it', 'Bite Me', 'Suck on This' and 'Got Stake'. Everyone who was there when he opened the stars passed them around laughing at the quirky little sayings.

"Thank you, Chloe." He leaned over and gave me a side hug.

I shrugged like it was nothing. "No prob."

The entire day was full of activities I didn't want to do. Everyone was singing carols by the piano and playing charades in the living room, so I found a comfy spot on the window seat by the Christmas tree.

Even with all the people around, I still felt lonely. The lights on the tree blinked their colored pattern over and over again: red, blue, green, yellow, white, red, blue, green, yellow, white, lighting up the whole tree with their beautiful glow.

"What's the matter?" Drew asked. He sat beside me.

"I want to see my mom," I told him without looking away from the tree.

"You know that isn't possible, Chloe."

"No, I mean, I want to go to her grave. I haven't seen her since the night she died. I don't even know where she is buried."

"I can take you."

I looked up at him. His eyes were soft and sympathetic, not his usual intensity. "Do you know where she is?"

Drew nodded and brushed some of his blond hair away from his eyes. "She's here, in the cemetery."

"You guys even have your own cemetery?"

"Do you want to go tomorrow?"

"No, I want to go now."

Drew raised his eyebrows. "Tonight? It's dark outside."

I looked over at him and rolled my eyes. "I don't care if it's dark. I want my mom."

He jumped to his feet and held out his hand. "Come on."

So we bundled up in our winter gear and headed out the door. I expected Luke to spot us and ask where we were going so late, but no one seemed to notice us when we slipped out the door.

The night was partly cloudy, allowing the moon to shine down onto the blanket of snow, giving the world an almost greenish glow.

As we rode through town in Drew's rumbling old truck, I stared out the window. Twinkling Christmas lights and yard ornaments lit up the streets, and this year, the decorating committee had really gone all out. It reminded me of watching old movies, the whole town covered in holiday cheer. Lamp posts held wreaths and gigantic red bows. Every establishment had painted windows and colorful lights. Everywhere I looked, there was something shiny.

My mom used to climb up on the roof by herself every year and staple the lights onto the perimeter. She also had me lug out an entire nativity scene that was to be placed on the lawn in front of the winter wilted rose bushes.

The cemetery was on the farthest end of the small town. When we arrived, Drew parked the truck in front of the large wrought iron gates. I hopped out of the truck and looked around. The cemetery had florescent street lights scattered among the gravestones. Great big maple trees provided a cover for most of the plots, so minimal snow had accumulated on them.

Even though I said I wasn't nervous, I suddenly felt chills, and not from the cold.

Drew came around from the driver's side. He must have sensed my sudden case of nerves because he reached out and took my gloved hand in his. "Ready?"

I nodded. As soon as we passed through the gates, I felt something. The only way I could explain it would be that it felt like a rush of power.

"Over here." Drew directed me toward a bunch of plots near the gigantic roots of a tree.

There had not been a funeral for my mom. She had left it in her last will and testament that she didn't want one. Knowing my mother, she probably thought it would be easier for me.

It wasn't.

I saw the gravestone then. It was a simple but large rectangle with a curved top.

Felicia Annabeth Kallistrate
Loving mother and loyal hunter
Gone but never forgotten.

"Mom." I released Drew's hand and fell to my knees, brushing away the little bits of snow that had managed to get through the branches of the tree. There were tons of flowers all over her grave, still colorful and vibrant but frozen from the snow and cold.

"Mom, its Christmas today." I organized some of the flowers over the dirt while I spoke to her. "My first Christmas without you."

Tears that I had assumed had been all cried out surfaced from the corners of my eyes and slid down my cheeks. Not really knowing what to say to someone I love who would never answer back, I just sat there and cried and cried some more.

Drew didn't say anything, but I knew he was back there watching me. Normally, I wouldn't want him to see me blubbering all over the place, but for once, I didn't care. I just wanted to be near her. It wasn't because I had a whole speech prepared or wanted to sit and ramble about my days. I needed our souls to touch, like they used to.

And so, for a whole half an hour, I sat on her grave and sobbed.

Drew let me be until snowflakes began to drift down from the sky. "Come on, Chloe. We have to go now."

With tears still staining my cheeks, I gave my mother's grave one last caress and then stood. "All right, I'm ready."

Drew took my hand again and led me between the plots as best as we could manage. The air outside had chilled even more than when we arrived. It was cold. Really cold. When we approached the gates, warmth suddenly filled my stomach and spread through my body.

"Oh, my... what the heck?" I clutched my stomach as the tingling spread all the way into my fingertips.

"Are you okay?" Drew asked. "What's wrong?"

"I don't know." I shook my head. Tears threatened to surface again. "I don't know."

"It's your senses, Chloe, telling you something is off."

Drew and I both spun around and Drew whipped his gun out from underneath his jacket.

"Who are you?" Drew yelled.

There, sitting atop one of the gravestones, bathed in the green glow of florescent lights, was a woman. Even though it was freezing, she barely wore anything, and what she did have on looked like leather wrapped around her body and a halter top with crude lacing holding it together. Snowflakes drifted down and passed through her tanned skin, dissolving into nowhere.

"How do you know me?" I shouted. "Who are you?"

My stomach was still flooded with warmth, and it made me feel like I had to pee. I wished I had brought *my* gun.

She clicked her tongue and tossed a wave of dark brown hair over her shoulder. "You do not need your weapons, my children. I do not come to harm."

She slid off the gravestone, and I watched her bare feet sink into the snow. They left no footprints.

"Who are you?" Drew demanded again.

She moved forward slowly. "I am your mother, many times over."

This chick scared me. Was she a ghost? I moved backward a few steps as she approached, using Drew as a shield, since he had the gun.

She smiled, her dark eyes intently focusing on Drew. "Andrew, lower your weapon. You cannot harm me."

As if under a spell, Drew lowered his arms and his gun came to rest by his side. "What do you want?"

"I am here to help, Chloe." She nodded at me and smiled. "You need the help of your ancestors. Your mother cannot help you, so I have come to give you guidance."

The warmth in my stomach turned into fire in my heart. I can't explain it, but I felt the connection with this apparition. I moved out from behind Drew.

"Who are you?" I whispered.

She lifted her chin arrogantly. "I am Sostrate, the daughter of Artemis, and as I have told you already, your mother, many times over."

"Why are you here?"

"I have come to give you the guidance your mother cannot give you. It is my duty."

"Are you a ghost?"

She only shook her head and gave me a crooked grin. "I am a demi-goddess. I gained immortality from my mother. I do not come as an apparition, because I cannot die."

"Holy shit." Drew actually dropped his gun in the snow.

I moved forward, not afraid anymore. I knew she was who she said she was. As we approached each other, I stretched out my hand, wanting to touch her. She also extended her hand and as my gloved fingers connected with the solid fingertips of hers, I gasped. "You're real."

She nodded. "Of course."

"Sostrate," I pulled my hand from hers, "How can you help me?"

"Chloe, it is time that you think with a clear head. Revenge has taken over your heart and your soul, taken over so much of you that you cannot possibly win this battle. It takes more than thinking with your brain. You must fight with *love*," she pressed her fist against her heart "not only hatred."

"I don't understand," I told her.

"Wars are not won because of *hatred* for the enemy; they are won because of love for what is being defended."

"Told you," Drew whispered from behind me.

"Shut up!" I hissed back at him.

"Chloe, I am going to give you something tonight, and I want you to remember to use it with love. The vampire is a monstrous creature, and you are created from them as well as angels and gods, so it is easy for you to hate."

"I don't think I can ever feel differently about this. He killed my mother."

She lifted a bow out of thin air from behind her.

"You take this, Chloe," she extended the bow out to me, "and every time you release an arrow, imagine how much you loved your mother, not how much you hate her murderer."

She handed me a hard leather quiver full of arrows that she also plucked from thin air. The quiver had ornate carvings of little swirls and shapes along its borders. I examined the bow, which also bore carvings of swirls and shapes. It was very light; I imagined that would make it easy to carry.

"But, Sostrate, we are hunters… how can we not use hate as a weapon? Shouldn't it drive us harder?"

Sostrate began to back away from us. With a final smile and nod she whispered, "We *love* to hunt."

And then, she was gone.

"Oh. My. God." I breathed.

"What the hell?" Drew whispered.

I had never seen Drew freeze like that before. He was in awe. A mythological demi-goddess had just appeared before us, and I held in my hands gifts from the gods, quite literally. The tingling feeling began to spread again. The more I tried to ignore it, the worse it got. I clutched my fingers around the bow even tighter and slung the quiver on to my shoulder.

"Let's go home, Drew."

Drew nodded and continued to stare at the spot where Sostrate had appeared.

"C'mon, Drew! It's freezing out here." I trudged through the snow and out the gates. As soon as I passed through the gates, the tingling went away.

⤳ ⤳ ⤳

I woke the next morning certain our visit from Sostrate had been a dream. My gaze drifted over to the chair where I had propped the bow and quiver. Sure enough, they were still there, looking as normal as if I had bought them at a sporting goods store instead of from our demi-goddess ancestor.

I sighed and rolled over. It was still Christmas vacation. I didn't have to go to school, but I still had to train every day. I lay there for so long I knew Drew was downstairs pacing the living room, waiting for me. I threw back the covers and let the cold air touch my bare legs for a minute before I forced myself to get up and throw on a pair of black yoga pants with a tank top and hoodie. I pulled my hair into a crude ponytail, put on a windbreaker over the hoodie and headed downstairs.

As I had suspected, Drew was pacing the living room while the news blared in the background. "Turn that down or you're going to wake up Luke. It's still early."

Drew rolled his eyes at me and clicked off the TV. "There were six robberies within a four-block radius last night. All the people in the homes died, their throats slit," he announced and then continued his pacing.

"Does that mean you're going on mission?" I called from the kitchen where I had gone for a bottle of water.

"Yeah, but probably not until tonight." He shook his head. "I can't believe how bad this is getting, so close together."

I wandered back into the living room "How do you know it's vampires doing it?"

Drew grabbed his own water bottle and shoved it into his back pack. "Lots of vampires cut the throats of their victims to make it look like a murder. A murder by a human. You ready?"

I nodded, and we took off.

Running through the snow sucks big time. On my list of things I hate most about training, running in the snow was probably in the top three. Apparently it was of the utmost importance to learn to run in the elements, because I might have to chase a vampire through the snow or something.

While we ran, Drew veered off into the trails. The snow was actually not as deep in the forest, so we crunched over the icy layer on top of the soil. We were deep in the forest when I began to really detest the slippery ground.

It had become my habit to push through it when I felt this way. I dug in and ran faster. I breathed in deep with my nose and exhaled long with my mouth, forcing the fatigue out of my body. I could feel my heart thumping in my chest, pounding rapidly as the blood pulsed throughout my body.

I dipped my head down and sped up again, passing Drew who jumped a little bit when I did. I smiled with triumph when I passed him, because the whole time I had been running and training with Drew, I had never, ever passed him.

I kept thinking about the ice melting beneath my feet and the soles of my shoes touching the earth beneath it. My feet felt like they were on fire.

"Chloe…"

I heard my name, but I didn't stop because I didn't want to give him the chance to pass me again. I had the lead.

"Chloe!" He called again. *"Stop!"*

I skidded to a halt when his shout carried that tone I had come to know as warning. I turned to face him. "What? What is it?"

He only pointed. I looked down at my feet and there were small flames flickering around my shoes.

"What the—" I jumped back and shook one of my feet. "Ah, what is this?" I turned quickly and stuck my foot into one of the snow banks on the side of the trail. Nothing happened; the flames only melted a gigantic hole where I had plunged it into the bank.

"Stop it!" I screamed, shaking my foot again. The flames immediately went out on both shoes.

"Oh, my god. What was that?" I panted and looked up at Drew, but he wasn't looking at me. He was staring down the trail that we had just run.

I followed his gaze and saw why he was staring down the trail like an idiot. The path was clear. Where I had run, the snow was gone and the earth beneath had been exposed.

"Drew, how…wha…?"

"You melted the snow, Chloe."

"No! My shoes were on fire!" I hollered at him. "My. Shoes. Were. On. Fire!" I punctuated every word to make sure he heard me.

He turned to look at me and awe was clearly written across his face. "I think you have the gift of fire."

"Whatever. I'm not even sixteen yet."

"It doesn't matter. How else can you explain what just happened? What were you thinking about?"

I was still panting, not because I was tired, but because I was scared. My freaking feet had caught fire. "That the ice would melt. That I hated running in the snow."

He nodded knowingly. "See, it's your gift."

"I don't know. I think it's some kind of freak accident."

"Can you do it again?"

"I don't think so." More like I didn't want to try again.

"Come on, try again." He glanced all around us, looking for something. Finally, his eyes settled on a tree. "If you don't want to set your shoes on fire again, do that tree."

"Drew, I am not setting fire to a tree."

"Come on." He was practically begging. I couldn't stand seeing him look like that. He was usually so confident and had this whole 'whatever, I'm just gonna stand here and look awesome' attitude going on.

"Fine."

I thought he might jump up and down, he looked so excited. I adjusted my stance so that I was staring at the tree, squinted my eyes, and thought about it catching fire. Nothing happened.

"I don't know how I'm supposed to do this. It's not working." I told him.

He stared thoughtfully at the tree. "I think you just need to practice. Think about how you were feeling at the time."

"Drew, I'm done with this. I just want to go home."

"Chloe."

"I can't do it. Why don't you understand that?" I stomped my foot and flung my hand toward the tree. "I can't make the stupid tree catch fire."

With a ripping sound, several branches of the tree burst forth sparks and erupted into large flickering flames. Both Drew and I stood with our mouths open. My arm was still extended while we watched the flames crawl along the branches until they reached the tips. I lowered my hand and looked at Drew, who must have felt quite proud of himself, because his open mouth was replaced by a gargantuan sized grin.

"Knock it off," I told him.

"Chloe... Do you know what this means?"

"Yeah, it means I'm more of a freak than I already was."

I didn't want fire. I didn't want a gift I couldn't control. In the course of twenty minutes, I had set my shoes on fire and made a tree go up in flames without even trying.

"I'm going home." I swiveled and marched off down the trail.

Drew chased after me. "This isn't bad, Chloe! You can learn how to control this. You're going to have to."

"I don't *have* to do anything."

"Why are you fighting this? This could be the one thing that helps you get what you want most! If you want to kill Trevor, fire is an ultimate weapon, especially if he doesn't see it coming."

I stopped in my tracks. He was right, absolutely, perfectly right. I could blow Trevor right off the face of the planet if I wanted to.

As if reading my thoughts, Drew said "But you have to learn how to use it first."

I nodded. "Yes, I do."

Once we got home, I stormed up the stairs and into my room. I wanted to get a shower and change so I could go to the library. I wanted to do as much research as I could, and when I had school, I didn't have much time to go the library. Between training, school and hygiene, I didn't have much time for anything.

Drew said we would work on honing my new firepower after he got back from the mission. That left me all day to ponder the visit from Sostrate, not to mention setting stuff on fire. Instead of worrying about that stuff, I headed out to the library.

Of all the places in the community, the place I loved most, besides Luke's house, was the library. It was so quiet there, and the air inside was always perfect. It smelled like history. I entered the two-story stone building and greeted the librarian. "Hi, Linda."

She sat behind the counter and organized a cart full of books into piles. "Oh, hello, Chloe. What are you looking for today?"

She pushed back her chair and smoothed back her hair while she stood. Her glasses sat somewhat crooked on her nose. She looked sort of flustered.

I shifted my book bag to the other shoulder. "I want to look up vampire children today. I thought I'd just start with the computer."

She waved her hand, dismissing the idea. "No, you never know where that information is coming from. Yeah, it can be helpful, but the books are better."

I should have expected nothing less from Linda. "Okay. Well, point me in the right direction."

She smiled and beckoned me to follow her. "Down this way."

We went to the old section where I'd found all the books on vampire hunter history, but several rows over.

"Do you know what the child of a vampire and a mortal is called, Chloe?"

I shook my head. "No."

"A child created by a vampire and a human is called a dhampir." We stopped at a shelf with big, thick books.

"Chloe, you may have a harder time looking up vampires than you did vampire hunters."

I raised my eyebrows in question, but remained silent.

She continued with, "There are many different kinds of vampires. The vampire legends range from the most common, the European vampires, to the rarest vampires, like the bat vampires from Africa and South America."

She lifted a book and hefted it over to me. "I know that you are looking for stuff about being a dhampir, so we can start there." She grabbed another book off the shelf and plunked it on top of the one I was already holding. "But when you start researching vampire breeds and histories, you will have a lot of work ahead of you."

She pulled another leather bound monster book off the shelf and held it in her arms.

"This should do it for now," Linda said.

We hauled the books over to the tables and deposited them onto the wooden surface.

"All right, then." Linda pushed her glasses farther up onto the bridge of her nose. "I'll let you get to it then. Come find me if you need any help."

"Thank you, Linda," I told her. I pulled a chair out to sit while she wandered back through the stacks of books that led back to her desk.

I took the first book off the stack and examined the cover. It was titled *Vampires throughout History*. The cover was leather and so old it was stiff and cracked in spots. The pages showed signs of age too, yellowing and stiff to the touch. There was no table of contents, so it looked like I was going to have to scan the entire book for what I was wanting. I flipped the pages carefully, so as not to tear any of them.

After an hour of scanning and about half way through the book, I found something referring to vampire children.

~~~

Although extremely rare, the natural-born offspring of vampires exist throughout the world. These rare beings are called the dhampir. Dhampir are usually the product of a vampire and mortal. The most common of these unions is a male vampire impregnating a mortal woman. Vampires, both male and female, are seductive in nature and some mortals came willingly to these unions. However, the majority of dhampir born were produced through an act of rape.

Solitary by nature, it is uncommon for a vampire to settle with any one mate for long. The children of vampires, the dhampir, more often than not exhibit all the characteristics of their vampire parent. The strength, speed and agility are the usual hereditary traits that the children develop. They are not always born with these traits but develop them as they grow into adulthood.

The dhampir are day walkers. Some of these children are

sensitive to the sunlight but will not perish in the direct rays. Most have no sensitivity at all. Drinking the fresh blood of mortals is also not usually required of the dhampir; however, some have a liking for it. Very few actually need it to survive.

Most dhampir are rejected by the vampire species because of their mortality and weaknesses. Mortals often reject the dhampir, as well, due to their vampirism, so they frequently remain outcast.

Dhampir are known for becoming vampire killers. Their closeness to the vampires and their vampire characteristics make them powerful vampire hunters. The unique ability to track and kill vampires is specific to only the dhampir and the mythological race of vampire hunters.

Historically, dhampir became vampire hunters as a trade. Towns and villages became plagued by vampires who were terrorizing their homes and killing their people. The dhampir accepted contracts in exchange for monetary payment and used their likeness to their vampire counterparts to exterminate the vampires.

~~~

Holy crap, that was a lot to process. The more I read the passages, the more I understood that my being a hunter was more than my heritage; it was my history and my future. Everything about my bloodlines had hunters involved.

I slammed the book shut, not happy about the realization or any of the information the book had given me. Opening another book and scanning, I found a lot of the same information, only there was some new stuff about the legends of the dhampir originating in the Balkans. Apparently, in these histories of vampires, dhampirs were considered real, whereas a race of vampire hunters was considered mythological. To me, that sounded weird.

I spent the entire day reading through the books and taking notes. My hand began to hurt from all the writing I did. It was almost dinnertime when I realized how long I had been gone. So I packed my stuff, returned the books to their places and headed out.

"See you later, Linda, and thanks for your help."

"Anytime, Chloe." She waved as I passed the desk.

I couldn't wait for Drew to get home so I could tell him all of this. I had to tell Luke, too. I'd rather tell them both at the same time than have to repeat all the information.

The sidewalks were so icy that I couldn't walk on them. I stepped down onto the road and walked in the accumulated snow. It was slushy and brown from the passing cars. I was concentrating so hard on my footing, that I didn't hear the footsteps behind me.

"Chloe, wait up!"

My head snapped up, and I spun around. Well I *tried* to spin around, but, my foot stuck in the snow and the rest of my body tried to turn. Just as I saw Gavin Turner rushing toward me, I fell butt first into the slushy, dirty snow.

His hand was stretched out in front of me. "I'm so sorry! I didn't mean for you to fall."

I grasped his hand, and he yanked me up out of the snow with ease. I could not believe this was happening. Gavin was one of the more popular guys at school, and I didn't see him that often because he was a senior. I did see him enough to gawk at him and his dark-haired, green-eyed hotness from afar. Falling in front of him was complete agony.

I brushed at my soaked jeans. "Oh, no."

"Are you okay?" he asked me, taking my bag from me so I could use both hands to uselessly brush at my clothes.

"Yeah, I'm all right. I guess I was just off in space, and you scared me a little. I didn't hear you coming up behind me."

He smiled. "Yeah, I do have a tendency to walk lightly. It's a hunter trait."

"Well, I don't have it." I told him. There was an awkward silence. We both stood there, facing each other without saying anything. Finally I asked, "Were you calling me for a reason?"

"Oh, yeah," He handed me back my bag. "I was just wondering if you wanted to… uh, if you would like to come to the New Year's Bash with me?"

Stupid took over my personality altogether. "Like a date?"

"Yeah, like a date." He grinned.

The New Year's Bash was a big deal in town. Drew had told me everyone in town always attended, and the dress was formal. And a formal occasion meant having to find a formal dress. "I'd love to go with you!" exploded past my lips. I wanted to sink into the ground. Why couldn't I have said something cool like, 'Sure' with a dainty hair flip, and then called out 'Pick me up at seven.' No, I just wasn't that good. I was a clumsy kid whose crush had just asked her out.

"Okay, how 'bout I pick you up at seven, then?"

I giggled. How ironic. "Seven sounds great. If you don't mind, I really need to get home and change before I get sick from being in these wet clothes."

"Oh, I'm really sorry about that."

I had already started to walk away. I just wanted to get away from him before I said anything else I'd regret.

"I'll see you soon." I called out and started to fast-walk through the slush.

⟩⟨ ⟩⟨ ⟩⟨

"Hey, Luke," I called when I opened the door.

I heard his raspy voice holler from the kitchen, "In here."

I pulled off my boots and peeled off my socks and then went into the kitchen where I found him preparing steaks, seasoned rice and a big green salad. Everyone in the community was a health food addict, but I was *so* glad they still ate meat. I didn't know what I would have done if I'd had to go vegetarian.

"Let me go change my clothes real quick, and I'll come and help you with dinner."

Wondering why I would want to change my clothes, he glanced over at me. "What happened?"

"I fell, walking home from the library."

His gray hair bobbed and he nodded. It wasn't unlike me to do something like fall down while I was walking home. I ran upstairs and quickly threw on a different pair of jeans and a sweatshirt that said 'Whatever' on the front. I hurried down to help Luke. When I arrived, he was just putting on the steaks.

"Will you get the plates and silverware out and set the table, please?"

"Sure," I nodded. "Hey, Luke?"

"Humm?"

I pulled plates out of the cupboard. "Could you not cook my steak too much? It tastes funny to me when it's well done."

"Rare it is," he told me as he flipped the meat.

Just then, the front door opened and closed. Drew.

I ran to the kitchen door and peeked out. It was him. "Hey, I thought you were going on a mission tonight?"

"We will. We leave in about four hours." He threw his bags on the ground by the door. "What's for dinner?"

"Luke is making steaks," I told him and went back to setting the table. Drew had followed me into the kitchen.

"Drew," Luke looked over his shoulder, "I'm glad you're here.

Is the mission planning going well?"

"Yeah." Drew pulled out the chair at his spot, and I set silverware and a napkin in front of him.

"You should wash your hands," I told him, eyeballing his fingernails. Dirt was caked underneath them and had been ground right into his fingertips. He rolled his eyes and got up, but only headed to the sink after I put my hands on my hips and glared at him.

After all three of us were seated and the food was on the table, Luke cut into his meat.

"How are you two doing today? I haven't seen either of you all day."

Both Drew and I glanced at each other. We knew we had to tell him everything, including the appearance of Sostrate. I didn't want him to think we were crazy. I'm pretty sure Drew was thinking the same thing, but we had to tell him.

"Well, it's actually been pretty eventful since last night." I grabbed the salad dressing and doused my salad with it. "We went to the cemetery last night, to see my mom."

Luke swallowed a piece of his steak. "I was wondering when you were going to want to do that. I'm glad you went. Drew did take you, right?"

"Yeah, and I'm glad he did."

"Why is that?"

Again I looked at Drew and gave him a pleading look to explain it to Luke. He knew Luke better than I did, anyway. I was so afraid he was going to think I was nuts.

Thank god, he acknowledged the plea and cleared his throat. "We saw Sostrate, in the cemetery last night."

Luke immediately paused his chewing, raised his eyebrows, and then proceeded to finish chewing. "So the warrior woman showed herself to you?"

We both nodded.

"And she spoke to you?"

"Yes, and she gave me a present." I cut into my meat and forked a big piece of it.

"Chloe! That's gross!" Drew pointed at my steak.

I looked down. "What?"

I didn't see anything wrong with it.

"It's bleeding all over."

"Well, I like it this way. Okay? Leave me alone about it." I shoved the steak into my mouth and chewed.

"Gross," Drew mumbled.

"So anyway," I swallowed, "she came and told me I needed to work on not being so mad and full of vengeance. Then she gave me a bow and a quiver full of arrows. I thought maybe it was a dream, but when I woke up this morning, the bow and quiver were still there."

Luke was shocked. I can honestly say it was the first time I had seen him surprised by *anything* since we'd met.

"It's no big deal. I mean, this happens to people, right?"

"Not that I know of," Luke told me. "You are the first I have ever known to have an encounter with any apparition."

"Oh, no." I waved my fork. "She made it perfectly clear that she was *not* an apparition. She said that she is a demi-goddess and that she gained immortality from her mother."

"Good lord." Luke leaned against the back of his chair. "You have to tell me everything. Can I see the bow?"

I started to tell him he could but before I could speak, loud wailing sirens filled our ears. My hands flew to my ears.

"What is that?" I yelled.

Drew had already jumped to his feet and Luke was on his feet and running. Yeah, he was running.

"We're being attacked!" Drew hollered at me over the sirens.

"What? Attacked?"

"Go get your bow and your gun!" Drew pointed at the stairs. When I didn't move, he pushed me. "Run!"

I took off up the stairs. I saw Luke yanking open a set of double doors, a closet. Inside the closet, there was an arsenal of weapons. Drew and Luke began loading themselves up while I ran up the stairs.

I ran as fast as I could, grabbed my bow and the quiver. I took my gun out of its case and dropped the empty clip and slammed a full one into it. After grabbing the extra clips, I bolted down the stairs.

"Drew! Give me some of those UV bullets for my gun!" I yelled at him.

Without even looking hard, he plucked three full clips off the shelf and handed them to me. He must have had them ready for me, because I was the only one in the house who had a forty-five, and they fit my gun.

The three of us went out to the porch. The sirens were still wailing and the smell of smoke was wafting through the air. I couldn't see any flames, but that tingly feeling started to come back. My gun was stowed in the back of my jeans, and I had an arrow nocked and ready to fire. These bastards were not going to take away the only safe place I knew.

"I wonder how they got past the wall?" I thought out loud. The community was gated, surrounded by a gigantic stone wall, and had security checkpoints around the perimeter. It looked like a jail from the outside. Inside, it just looked like any other town.

"Shhh." Drew put his finger to his mouth.

Luke stood at the ready. I don't think I ever admired him as much as I did at that moment. He stood on the stairs, a gun in each hand and a full bandolier tossed over his shoulders. The moonlight reflected off of his grey hair, causing a beautiful silver glow around him.

Suddenly, the sirens stopped. Drew turned one direction and listened, then the other direction. "They got to the alarm."

I was freaking out. But, thank god I still had my senses. Thinking, *Sostrate, I need you to help me with this.* I chose the bow and arrow above the gun because of what Drew had told me about guns not working as well on the older vampires, and also because the bow and arrows were given to me by a demi-goddess; maybe they had their own superpower.

If vampires had made it to the alarms, that meant they had gotten to the hunters manning the security building. That was definitely not a good sign for us.

A prickle on the back of my neck made my spine straighten. I glanced at Drew and Luke. They felt it, too; I could tell. Both of them stood back to back on the stairs so they could fully cover the circumference around them.

I took a moment during this scary and traumatic time to feel stupid. I didn't know what to do, so I remained by the front door, with my bow and arrow at the ready.

We sat there waiting, in silence, for what seemed an eternity. It was unbearable, knowing we were going to be attacked but not knowing how or when. Plus, I was scared crapless.

In the distance, we heard the smallest crackle, probably a fallen twig in the woods being stepped on. I spun toward the noise.

Suddenly, there was a flash and a vampire appeared. He grabbed Luke. Luke didn't utter a word but did drop his gun when his hand flexed open in surprise. The vampire towered over Luke, his burnt auburn hair and pale skin completely visible in the dark. He held Luke in a headlock, like he was going to snap his neck.

"Stop!" I shouted, surprising everyone, including myself. I aimed my arrow at the vampire. Luke's head was covering the vampire's heart, but I knew I could hit his shoulder. I never missed.

"Let him go, or you die," I said, my voice as cold as I could make it.

I felt my blood rush through my veins, the power, flowing through me.

The vampire laughed, and my anger boiled. No more of my family were going to die. Sostrate had told me to think of how much I loved my mother when I fired, but all I felt was a hot hatred when I released my arrow.

"Burn in hell!" I screamed as the arrow flew.

With the same ripping noise as the tree, the tip of the arrow caught fire and plunged into the vampire's shoulder. He released Luke and screamed a high-pitched noise that could only be associated with death. I nocked another arrow and thought of how much safer the world would be with one less vampire. The arrow sailed into his heart, and he fell to his knees. When he crumpled, he began to burn away until all that was left was a mess of blackness on the snow.

I had killed my first vampire and I felt triumphant. But, there were more, I was sure.

Luke looked at me like I had just farted in church.

"Chloe?" he whispered. I shrugged and put my finger to my lips. More were coming.

We heard them approaching. They weren't even trying to be quiet now. I shook off the nerves that threatened to come back.

You are a vampire hunter, Chloe. Don't let them win.

I turned in the direction of the noise. Drew and Luke fired before the vampires emerged from the woods. They missed a lot, but between all of us, we managed to take them all down. Still more came.

I'd bent down to catch my breath when three really ugly chick vampires and one really hot-looking guy jumped smoothly down off the roof, barely making a sound when they landed right in front of us. Quickly, I moved in closer to Drew and Luke.

"Don't turn your back on them," Drew whispered to me.

The vampires circled around us in the darkness, stalking us, even though we knew they were there. The three of us moved to where our backs were touching. I still had my bow raised and trained on one of the ugly girl vampires.

It all happened so fast. I don't remember much, but they rushed us with their vampire speed. None of us had time to react. With flashes and blurs they were upon us.

Once again, I was locked in the embrace of a vampire. Flashes of my mother's murder and James's iron grip on my arms came back to me full force. I heard myself scream. I heard Drew call my name, but I couldn't do anything. I felt frozen in time, watching my mother die again.

"Chloe!" Drew's voice called me. "Chloe!"

Where is he?

Everything was mashed together. Time had merged the past and the present together.

"Snap out of it!" Someone hissed into my ear. It wasn't Drew, and it wasn't Luke. Whoever it was, it did snap me out of it. My eyes focused, and I saw that Drew and Luke were being held in the arms of the vampire guy and one of the girls.

"Easy with her!" the guy called out to the one holding me. "Trevor wants her alive."

She cackled in my ear. "He said alive, but he didn't say unharmed. This little hunter has caused us a lot of grief." She gave me a hard shake.

"I didn't do anything to you!" I screamed at her.

"Yeah, except that your *Daddy* is constantly sending us on suicide missions to find you."

I didn't dignify that with a response. My bow had dropped when I'd been grabbed, but I still had my gun. Doing anything with that would have been a little hard, considering my backside was pressed up against her. Drew and Luke couldn't move. One thing I had learned from training was not to get close enough to let a vampire get a hold, because they could snap a human neck in less than a second. I was scared for Drew and Luke.

I struggled in the grip of the ugly vampire chick. "Let me go, please. Let me go!"

"Oh, how cute. She's begging."

"Leave her alone!" Luke hollered.

"Shut up, old man," the one who held him menaced. For emphasis, he twisted Luke's arm, and I heard his bones cracking. Luke screamed like I had never heard a man scream.

"Let's just get rid of these two and get out of here," the chick who held Drew told the one who had me. Drew fought against her, screaming obscenities and twisting in her grip while he tried to release his arms.

The ugly vamp's eyes suddenly flickered and lit up bright red as her blood lust took over.

"No!" I screamed and suddenly felt a hot fire awaken throughout my entire body. "Don't touch him!"

I yanked away from the vamp with every ounce of strength I could muster and felt my right forearm snap. I screamed long and hard. The pain was excruciating, and when I screamed my whole body erupted. Literally, I became engulfed in flames. I lunged forward and threw myself at the vampire who held Drew. My screams were joined by those of the burning vampire who had held me. I didn't dare look. The fire wasn't hurting me at all. I veered around Drew and into the vamp who held him. Because she held Drew, she didn't have time to do anything to defend herself when I slammed into her and locked her in a fiery embrace, my broken arm sort of hanging limply around her.

She let go of Drew. I think he had been waiting for it because he immediately grabbed his gun, then spun and shot. Two precise shots lodged into the skull of the vampire who was squeezing Luke tightly around his chest. Luke fell to the ground, his foot twisting at an odd angle when he went down.

I ran at the one who'd been shot, screaming like one of those bloody warriors from Braveheart. I hit him with such force it toppled him to the ground. Even though he was already eroding from the UV bullets, I wanted to make sure. I stood and kicked the body over and over again until Drew grabbed me away.

"Chloe, stop!"

"Where's the other one?" I hissed. "Where is she?"

The flames still flickered and licked around my whole body.

"She ran." Drew panted, then glanced over at Luke, who appeared to be unconscious, lying on the cold snow, and ran to him.

"No!" I concentrated as hard as I could, trying to get the flames to go away. I waved my good arm around and stomped my feet.

Nothing happened. I squeezed my eyes shut and thought of only nice, cool, calming… the ocean. The waves rolled in and crashed on the shore. I felt the water dousing my feet as the surf rolled up the sand.

I opened my eyes. It had worked. The fire was gone. Not that it had been that long, but for the first time, I really, really appreciated having the gift of fire.

My arm still hurt like hell. I cradled it gently and tried to set aside the pain and thoughts of fire for the time being and ran to Luke.

He lay on the ground, with Drew on his knees hovering above him. I fell to my knees beside Drew.

"Is he okay?" I asked while silently begging god, the goddesses of our family, the angels, and anyone who would listen to help him.

"I don't know," Drew replied, and then lifted him off the ground and into his arms. Gently, he carried him into the house while I followed behind. While I watched Drew place Luke on the couch, I realized that if my arm hurt like hell now, it was going to get a whole lot worse when the adrenaline wore off.

"Drew, he needs to go to the hospital." I looked down at Luke. "I think I need to go, too."

Drew yanked a cell phone from his pocket and hit a speed dial number. "Damn it!" he said after a minute. "No answer."

"Who are you trying to call?" I winced as pain shot up my arm. I could feel tears welling up and threatening to spill over. I really didn't want to start bawling in front of Drew.

"I'm trying to call the medics. We have our own little version of a hospital, like an urgent care center, I suppose. They are either really busy with other injuries or the vamps got them."

"Let's just go to the real hospital then." I *really* wanted to go. I knew my arm was messed up.

He sighed. "We're going to have to." He glanced at my face and then down at my arm. "Go out to the garage and start Luke's car."

I did as he said, but first I collected my bow and some of my arrows. I placed the arrows into the quiver and then hurried out to the garage, just in time, too, because the tears finally broke their dam and began their suicide mission down my cheeks.

After starting the car, I waited for Drew to come out with Luke. When I saw them, I opened the back door so he could gently slide

Luke onto the seat. Luke cried out and coughed roughly a few times during the move. I ran around to the passenger side and hopped in. I was ready to go. I'd never had a broken bone before, but I knew that the longer I waited, the worse it was going to feel. I still felt kind of pumped up and was entirely sure that when that completely wore off, I was going to be in even more pain. I guess I could be grateful there were no bones or anything sticking out through the skin.

Drew slid into the driver's seat and pushed the button that lifted the garage doors, backed out slowly and then hit the gas. We flew down the deserted road and into town. The street lights cast an eerie glow onto the empty streets. As I stared out the windows, I thought about where everyone was. I guess I had an image of people running all over in the streets, bloody and screaming, like in some zombie horror movie.

When we arrived at the gates, Drew slowed and came to a stop at the guard shack.

"Oh, great," he murmured.

"What?"

"There isn't anyone in there. When the sirens go off, the controls for the gate in the guard shack shut down. I'm going to have to go up to the control room and turn them back on."

"Really?" I moaned.

Without a word, Drew slammed the car into reverse and turned a wide circle until we were headed back the way we had just come. It seemed like forever to go the short distance to the control room. When we finally arrived, Drew parked the car and asked if I had my gun.

"Of course, I have my gun," I told him, but in my head, I was wondering how the hell I was going to shoot with my left hand since I obviously wasn't going to use my right one.

He nodded, and then he slammed the door and ran through the dark parking lot. I watched through the windshield and saw him punching numbers into what must have been a coded lock. He slipped inside and didn't come out for close to fifteen minutes—fifteen long, painful minutes.

While he was in there, I looked back over the seat to make sure Luke was still breathing, but it was rough and gurgly. When I managed to lean over the seat and feel his face, he felt cold. I got out of the car and opened the trunk. Sure enough, there were two army green blankets folded and tucked into the corner. I grabbed one and placed it gently over Luke's body, trying to be cautious of his arms as I tucked in the sides.

With my arm throbbing and feeling like it was still on fire, I got back into the front seat to wait for Drew. When he finally came back, his face was flushed, and his eyes were blazing.

"What's wrong?" I asked.

He slammed the door and fired up the car. "Nothing," he growled, and then peeled out of the parking lot in reverse.

"Well, it looks like something is wrong."

"Leave me alone, Chloe."

"Fine." Normally I would have crossed my arms because I was so annoyed, but my arm hurt too bad to move it.

Finally, we arrived at the hospital. Drew sped into the ER drop off and jumped out of the car. He ran through the double glass doors and was in there for about two seconds before people dressed in paper coats and gloves came rushing out with him. They gathered Luke onto a gurney and wheeled him through the doors. I watched him go, and said a little prayer that he would be okay. I didn't love him, but he was the closest to anything in my life that I *could* love.

A nurse or doctor or something had stayed behind. "Miss, you need to be seen as well. Come with me."

I looked at Drew. I desperately wanted him to come with me, but he only nodded and got into the driver's seat.

"I'll come in and find you," he told me, and then he slowly drove away.

The first thing they did was a bunch of X-rays. It turned out my forearm was broken, but not as badly as it felt. They set it and gave me a cast that only went up to my elbow. Obviously, I didn't have to stay in the hospital for anything, but we stayed all night in the waiting room because Luke was in surgery. One of the nurses had explained to us that Luke was unconscious from shock, mostly. He had to have surgery on four broken bones, and one of his ribs had punctured a lung. He was going to be in the operating room while they did all the surgeries and made sure there wasn't anything wrong with his brain.

We sat in the pink and white waiting room reading magazines for hours. We drank nasty coffee and ate nasty vending machine sandwiches, and we waited.

At about four in the morning, a young, preppy looking doctor came out and told us that Luke had come through his surgeries well, and that the MRI showed no damage to his brain, but we were going to have wait until he woke up to find out if everything was functioning normally.

"Can we see him? Is he awake?" I asked.

"Of course, but only for a few minutes. He needs rest right now. Your grandfather will probably be asleep anyway; we've given him quite a bit of pain medication."

"Thank you," I told him.

Neither of us said a word while the doctor took his leave. I lifted my eyes and met Drew's green-eyed gaze. We stayed that way for a while, not moving or speaking, just locked in each other's stare. Finally, I became uncomfortable enough to break eye contact. I looked away. "We should go see him now."

Drew nodded and mumbled, "Yeah," under his breath.

We both stood and found our way to Luke's room.

I don't think I had fully prepared myself for what we saw. Luke lay on the hospital bed with a full-length cast on his right arm, a boot cast on his right leg and another one like mine on his left arm. There were tubes coming out from between his ribs that were hooked to a machine, and an oxygen cannula in his nose.

I heard Drew suck in his breath and looked over at him. He looked more angry than sad or worried. I decided to ignore him for the moment and went to the chair beside Luke's bed.

"Luke, can you hear me?"

He didn't move. He looked so frail and old laying there.

"Drew, what are we going to do? He is probably going to be in here for a while."

"We go home, and we see what damage has been done to our people. Then we plan the mission to take our revenge."

I bowed my head. I felt responsible for all that had happened. If it wasn't for me, the community wouldn't have been attacked in the first place. I was sure some of the hunters had died during the attack.

"This is turning into a war, isn't it?" I whispered.

Drew turned toward the window and replied, "Yes… it is."

We went home after sitting with Luke until midmorning. Drew and I both needed sleep and showers. After I showered, I crawled into bed and slept so hard I was certain it would be the next day when I woke. I only managed to sleep for six hours.

Drew was in the kitchen, eating a bowl of cereal and reading the newspaper.

"Hi." I grabbed a bowl and sat across from him.

"Did you go out there yet?" I nodded in the general direction of town.

"Yes. The stats are that we only lost three hunters… not bad, really… considering the attack, but I think they were more or less after you. We lost Eric, from the guard shack, and the two guys in the control room. One of them was my uncle."

Oh, god. He must hate me.

"I'm so sorry." I felt tears sliding down my cheeks. "Are you mad at me?"

Abruptly, he slid his chair out and grabbed his bowl, and then he threw it in the sink so hard it shattered into a zillion pieces. I flinched and sank back into my chair.

"Damn it, Chloe! It's not always about you. Why in the hell would I be mad at you?"

"I don't know." I knew I was whining, but I didn't care. I just didn't want him to be mad at me. "I'm sorry."

I sniffled back a bunch of snot that was threatening to come out of my nose.

He placed his hands on the counter in front of the sink and bowed his head.

I just sat there bawling while he stayed like that. Most likely he was trying to calm himself.

After about five minutes, I couldn't do it anymore. "I'm sorry." I whispered, and then got up to leave. I got as far as the door when he grabbed me by the wrist on my good arm and spun me around. It surprised me so much that I gasped and reflexively yanked my arm back.

"Chloe."

"What? I'm trying to get out of here, Drew."

"Don't go. I don't think any of this is your fault, but I have to grieve, too." He took a step away from me. "Don't you get it? I'm sad, Chloe. My uncle just died and so did our friends."

I didn't know what to say. It seemed like everything I said to him made him yell, so I did the only thing I knew how to do: I moved in and wrapped my arms around him.

It must have surprised him, because I wasn't normally a touchy feely person, but eventually he responded and placed his own arms around my waist. We hugged, staying like that for a long time. His grip tightened around me and I heard him sniffle a couple times. He needed release. I did know enough about guys to know that they don't normally show emotion very well, so I wanted to help him.

When the embrace was over, he released me and turned away. I felt a vibe from him that seemed to say 'If you tell anyone about this, I'll have to kill you.'

I figured the best thing to do would be to leave him alone now. "If you need me, I'll be in my room."

I saw the back of his head moving in a nod.

On the way to my room, I heard my cell phone chirping its stupid ringtone I hadn't bothered to change yet. I ran the rest of the way and threw open my door, then did a sort of flying leap toward my bed where my phone was laying.

"Hello!"

"Chloe?" I hadn't bothered to look at the Caller ID and didn't recognize the voice.

"Yeah, this is me. Who is this?"

"It's Gavin."

"Oh, hi."

"Do you have minute to talk?"

I nodded, even though he couldn't see me. "Yeah, sure. What's up?"

"Well, the main reason I called was to see if you were all right, after all that happened."

"I'm okay. I have a broken arm, but Luke is in pretty bad condition. Drew is all right, too."

I heard him sigh through the earpiece. "Good, I'm glad you weren't hurt too badly. I'm sorry about Luke."

I explained to him all about Luke's injuries and told him how worried I was. After that, we lapsed into silence for a minute. When he spoke, his voice was unsure. "So… this may not be the right time to bring this up, but the New Year's Bash is still on."

"They are still going to put that on, even with all that happened?" I was utterly shocked that they would still go through with such an event after the attack.

"Yeah, its tradition…and I think there will be a lot of discussion about retaliation there too."

Great, just great. I was still going to have to find a dress. "Oh, well I guess we are still on then?"

"Absolutely, that was the other reason I was calling."

"Well... thanks for making sure. I guess I'll see you when you pick me up." I didn't know why, but I suddenly wanted to get off the phone really bad.

"I'll be there," he told me and then we said goodbye and clicked off.

Damn it. Now I had to see if Drew would drive me to the mall after we went to visit Luke later. The last thing I wanted to do was bother him about going to get a dumb dress. I had no other choice; I didn't have anything to wear.

✗ ✗ ✗

"You need to do *what?*" he hollered at me.

"I need a dress, Drew."

"People have died, Luke is in the hospital and all you can think about is what you're going to wear to a party!"

I crossed my arms. "That isn't all I think about."

Drew didn't say anything after that; he just turned away and grumbled under his breath.

"So are you going to take me, or what?"

"You know, I will," he snapped. "I just don't have to like it. Let's go. We can visit Luke and then go to the mall afterward."

Silently, I gathered my things. I sure was getting tired of his mood swings. It was understandable that he was emotional, but it felt like he was taking it out on me.

We stopped to see Luke, who didn't wake up the entire time we were there. We didn't really try to wake him up either. I figured it was probably easier for him to sleep as much as he could.

Afterward at the mall, I searched the stores while Drew went to the food court to get himself an Orange Julius. I think I made him an addict for those things after the last excursion to the mall.

Most of the shops didn't have formal dresses. It took me over two hours, but I finally found a very pretty gown in royal blue. When I tried it on, I was as happy with it as I was when I saw it on the rack. The whole thing fit snug against my body. The top showed off some cleavage, but not enough to make me feel inappropriate, and it had tiny little spaghetti straps. My dark hair contrasted the shimmering blue perfectly. The only thing I needed was a pair of shoes to go with the dress. The dress was long, all the way to my ankles, and had a slit that went up to just above my knee. I hoped people didn't think the dress was too old for me, because it was the only one I liked.

I took it off and put my clothes back on, and then I paid for my dress. Man, it sucked having spent all that money and leaving with one tiny little bag. I wandered over toward the food court to see if Drew was still there.

I scanned the tables, looking for Drew's blond head and pretty green eyes. I didn't see him anywhere. Deciding that he probably just went to the bathroom or something, I got myself an Orange Julius and found an empty table. Slurping the orange liquid noisily through a straw, I continued to look around the food court for Drew.

No Drew.

But I saw someone else.

He sat at a table across the room with his black jean clad legs crossed and a drink in front of him. He had a pale face, pale hands and dark brown eyes that any woman might have fallen for.

It was Trevor... my father. I just knew it was. Something inside me knew that person, just as I had known Sostrate was a part of my blood.

I sat as still as I could, even though I felt the flush of heat rush through my body. I was scared to death, but decided that the best thing to do would be to play it cool. He wouldn't dare hurt me in a room full of people with camera phones.

I sipped my Orange Julius slowly, without taking my eyes off of him. In turn, he stared back at me while he stirred his coffee or whatever it was he had in front of him. He kept his legs crossed and our eyes locked.

I didn't know how long I could stand sitting there staring at him. It was obvious he was threatening me, but I didn't know exactly what kind of message he was trying to send. I wanted to send him a message, too, but didn't know how to even go about that.

I was going to kill him... and he should know it.

Finally, I set my empty Orange Julius on the table and broke eye contact. I turned my head only for a second and he was gone.

Shit!

I waited for Drew for another twenty minutes. After rambling on like a crazy person about what had happened and freaking out on him all over again, he rushed me out the doors with one hand around my waist and another on his gun.

I had brought my gun, too, this time.

"I should have shot him," I told Drew, once we were in the truck and speeding down the dark icy streets.

"Yeah, right, you were going to shoot him, in the mall, in front of all those people."

I clenched my fists, getting angrier by the second. I had let him get away. "I don't care. He needs to die."

"There was nothing you could do, Chloe. He was messing with you."

I wanted to scream, I was so frustrated and angry. "Where were *you*?" I demanded of him.

"I was in the knife shop."

"Figures," I mumbled under my breath.

"What?"

"Don't worry about it," I snapped.

Despite the attack a couple nights before, I felt safer once we had driven through the gates and they were securely locked on the other side of us. We pulled into the driveway and I jumped out of the truck, slamming the rusty old door behind me. I had no idea why I was treating Drew so badly, but I had to take it out on someone. I guess it was how he had felt earlier when he had yelled at me.

"'Night," I called out rudely. I let myself inside the house. I didn't even look back to make sure he came inside. I went straight up to my room.

Once I had stripped off all my clothes and put on my comfy pajamas, I crawled under the covers and hugged my extra pillow to my chest. I wasn't tired at all. I tossed and turned, I tried counting backwards, I tried turning on my iPod, but nothing was going to bring the sleep I needed so much.

My mind kept going back to those piercing eyes, those dangerous eyes...

While his dark eyes haunted me, a realization hit me like a sucker punch to the gut. It was a realization so simple I should have thought of it before. He wanted me.

People were dying because of me.

So, maybe... maybe I should simply go to him willingly. I could protect my other family, by going to the one I hated and making him believe I wanted to be with him.

And then I could kill him.

Well, I could try...

THE VAMPIRE HUNTER'S DAUGHTER
PART IV

DIVIDED

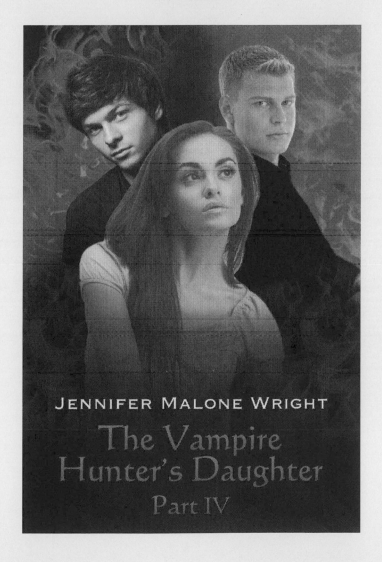

JENNIFER MALONE WRIGHT

The Vampire
Hunter's Daughter
Part IV

The cast on my right arm was more than annoying. It was bulky and sweaty and stinky and itchy underneath. I could not wait to get it removed.

I stared at myself in the mirror and wondered why the heck I had agreed to go to the New Year's bash. My grandfather Luke was still in the hospital. It felt wrong to go to the event without him. Also, Drew was not happy about it at all.

It wasn't all bad, though. Going with Gavin—one of the hottest guys at school— to the dance wasn't exactly a terrible thing. It just felt like the timing was wrong. Besides, I had other plans to get on with. Aside from all that, it really wasn't so bad.

I thought about these things while dressing and doing my hair.

And my dress!

It was certainly nice to wear something pretty instead of jeans or workout clothes. The silky royal blue fabric hung loosely against my skin and went perfectly with my dark hair. My cast stood out stark white in contrast with the blue.

Groaning, I gave my hair one last bobby pin, placing it in with my good hand with the other hundred bobby pins that held up the top half of my hair. I had it piled in a bun type thing with loops and curls, which hadn't been easy to do with the freakin' cast on my arm. The bottom half of my hair lay in ringlets against my back. Finally, after putting on a pair of silver hoop earrings, I turned away from the mirror and grabbed my coat.

I had a wrap, but that certainly wasn't going to keep me warm. I planned on wearing my coat, no matter how out of fashion it might be.

Knowing Gavin would arrive soon, I tried to hurry.

Drew was down there, and I didn't want Gavin to have to deal with him. Drew had been super cranky the last few days. I figured it was because of the attack, losing his uncle and Luke being in the hospital. That was certainly enough to make anyone cranky.

When I finally managed to make it down the stairs in the

dangerous too-high heels I had bought to go with my dress, I found Drew in the kitchen, tying his bowtie and eating an apple. Boy, he looked good in his tux. Weird how some guys looked uncomfortable dressed up and others could pull off a suit with no problem. Drew was the no-problem kind.

"Hey," I said.

His eyes flicked up my way and then back to his tie. I didn't know why he had been practically giving me the silent treatment lately, at least since the town had been attacked. There I was, all dressed up, and he couldn't even tell me I looked nice, not even an approving glance.

Well, see if I compliment him on his tux, then.

"You never told me who you're taking tonight," I tried. I leaned against the counter next to him.

"I'm taking Christina," he said around his apple.

Ugh, what is wrong with him?

I should have known he'd take her. I didn't care how bad her childhood had been, she was still a mean slut as far as I was concerned. After she had started that fight with me at school and got us both suspended, I would have thought Drew would have been on my side. At the very least, he shouldn't have been taking her to a fancy dance.

"Why do you like her?" I couldn't help myself; I had to ask.

"Chloe, we had this discussion already. I dated her. We're still friends. I like her, okay?"

"Fine." I waved my hand and turned to get a glass out of the drainer.

I must have mumbled something under my breath, because Drew practically shouted, "What did you just say?"

"Nothing... I don't know."

"You said something." His green eyes were glowing and he took a defensive stance with his body.

"Jeez, Drew, I don't know. It's not a big deal."

"Well, you don't see me all up in your business about you going with Gavin. He's not exactly an angel himself."

I narrowed my eyes and put down my glass. "What do you mean by that?"

He shrugged and walked out of the room.

I followed him. "Drew, you can't just say that kind of stuff and then walk away."

Still, he said nothing. Sometimes his iciness bugged the crap out of me. I followed him into the living room. He must have felt cornered because he turned around and went back into the kitchen.

"Drew, stop! What the hell do you have against Gavin?"

"Forget it!"

Inside, I wanted to stomp my foot and throw a fit like a two year old. It was infuriating, his acting like he knew something and not telling me. I could feel my body starting to heat up and knew what was happening. Since the attack, I had become more in tune with my fire power; I could sense it coming, unlike before, when I didn't have a freakin' clue. I was, however, still having trouble controlling when it would come and wasn't certain how to make it stop.

I closed my eyes and blocked everything out, trying to think of anything that would calm me down. My mother's face materialized behind my eyelids. She used to sing all the time, no matter where we were: at home, in the car, shopping for groceries. Her voice was a constant in my life, ever since I could remember. Sometimes, even after I was older, she would come into my room and sing to me like she had when I was little.

Now, her voice was my constant... a way for me to put out the fire—both literally and figuratively—that burned inside of me. The one thing I had discovered about this stupid fire power was, once it was burning, I had to put it out with my thoughts. It wouldn't just eventually go out on its own.

"Chloe, are you all right?"

I could barely hear him. He sounded far away. I ignored him and just kept my breathing regular and my mother's voice prominent in my head until I felt the heat pass and my body temperature return to normal.

"Chloe?"

I opened my eyes and glared at him. His eyes had lost their ice and were filled with concern.

"You were fighting the fire again, weren't you?"

"None, of your business," I snapped.

They said *women* had mood swings. Well, I guess whoever 'they' were had never met Drew. The doorbell rang and I spun to answer the door before Drew could get there. I fully expected to see Gavin, in his supreme hotness, when I opened the door. Instead, I flung open the door and found Christina on the other side.

"Oh." Surprised that it wasn't Gavin, I stepped back a few steps. "It's you."

She wore the most hideous dress I'd ever seen. Well, maybe not the *most* hideous dress I'd ever seen, but probably a close second. It was dark green, skin tight and strapless. Her dark hair was in a beehive-looking up-do. She completed her look with hooker boots.

"Chloe." She nodded at me and stepped into the house.

"Christina." I nodded back at her and yelled, "Drew, Christina is here!"

When Drew came into the room, Christina let out a girly squeal and jumped into his arms. She planted a kiss right on his lips. I felt like barfing a little.

"I missed you," she whispered to him, but it was loud enough for me to hear. That was intentional, I was sure.

Ugh... Gavin could not arrive fast enough for me. I wanted out of there. I don't know why Drew didn't pick her up at her house. Why did she have to come to our house?

Drew must have wanted out of there as badly as I did, because he rushed Christina out the door, asking her if she had a coat.

"See you there!" She giggled over her shoulder to me while Drew herded her out. I simply stood there and watched them go. Drew gave me one last look that pretty much told me to behave myself, and then he was gone. Why did he have to act so strange all the time? One minute, he would act like my brother; the next minute, he would act like my father. Sometimes, in those rare moments, he acted like my friend. That was the Drew I preferred. I had no idea what I had done or what was going on that he would have so much animosity toward me lately. It had to be a repercussion of the attack.

Since then, the board members had been in the process of planning a full-scale attack on the vampires. It was fast becoming a full-out war. I knew I was the cause. The vampires would have never attacked if I weren't here. They wouldn't have hurt Luke, and they wouldn't have killed the three hunters, including Drew's uncle. I didn't want anyone else to get hurt. That was the reason I had made plans to leave soon after the New Year's bash. There were just a few things I needed to get done before I could go. I knew I wasn't ready, but it was going to have to be good enough.

The doorbell rang again, and I surfaced from the fog in which I had drifted. I opened the door for Gavin, who looked super-hot in his tux. He held a big bouquet of yellow roses.

"Hey," he greeted me.

"Hi." I smiled shyly. We stood and looked at each other for a moment.

"Well, can I come in?" he asked.

Embarrassed, I backed away from the door and motioned him in.

"Of course. I'm sorry."

"Don't worry about it."

He smiled and his pretty green eyes brightened.

"You look amazing!" he told me, extending the flowers. "These are for you."

Hesitantly, I took them. He didn't know it, but it was the first time anyone had given me flowers.

"I hope you like yellow."

"I love yellow," I whispered, stepping sideways toward the kitchen. "Let's go put these in some water."

He followed me into the kitchen and watched me while I stood on a chair to get a big vase down from on top of the refrigerator. I think mostly he was looking at my legs and butt, which made me feel totally uncomfortable. My dress was tight, and the slit opened up to just above my knee, so I don't think he had much choice other than to look at me.

After balancing unevenly on the chair and getting down without killing myself, I trimmed the roses and stuck them in the vase, filled it halfway with water, and then placed it in the center of the kitchen table. The whole time, he chatted with me about stuff going on with friends of his I barely knew and really didn't care to know.

"Are you ready?" I asked, practically cutting him off.

"Oh, sure. Let's go."

I grabbed my coat off the back of the couch and pulled the bulky thing on over my dainty little dress. Well, at least my top half was going to be warm.

When we arrived at the gym, where they were throwing the New Year's bash, Gavin took my arm and escorted me inside. The moment we were through the doors, I stopped to stare. I couldn't believe what they had done to the place. Normally, it was full of exercise equipment, mats and weapons. For this event, they had moved all that stuff and decorated the entire gym with shiny ribbons hanging from the ceiling, glittery things everywhere, and there was even a band set up on a large portable stage. They blasted out rock music from the eighties.

The place was packed with people. I had no idea how everyone fit, but they did. The center of the gym was where all the people who were dancing had congregated. The perimeter was lined with tables of goodies and people who stood around talking.

I looked up at Gavin and he smiled down at me.

"Come on." He tugged me forward until I bumped into him, and then he wrapped his arm around my waist and guided me to the refreshment tables. Along with all the goodies supplied on the tables were novelty top hats covered in silver and gold glitter. Gavin picked one and somehow managed to get it on my head, even with my hair done up. It was a bit tilted but stayed on. He grabbed another one and put it on his own head.

"There. That's better," he said.

I giggled, and he took me around the waist again and led me onto the dance floor. It felt good to have someone like me enough to bring me flowers and treat me nice. I liked it.

After two dances, I needed something to drink. I stood on my tiptoes and hollered in Gavin's ear that I was going to get a drink and then visit the bathroom.

"Do you want anything?" I shouted.

"I'll come with you," he shouted back. He gripped my hand, and we began to wedge our way through the crowd of dancers. We popped out of the crowd next to a refreshment table, and I practically lunged for the punch bowl. It was so freakin' hot in there from all the bodies. It had begun to smell a bit like body odor.

Gross.

After I guzzled down a plastic cup of punch, I went in for more.

"Here." Gavin shoved a water bottle into my hand. "This might help more than the punch."

"Thanks!" I uncapped the bottle and drank about half of it.

The next song up was a slow one, so Gavin led me out to the dance floor and wrapped his arms around my waist. That awkwardness I'd felt before came back immediately. This was the first time I was ever pressed up against a guy... ever. Honestly, I didn't really know what to do. Gavin took my arms, running his fingers gently from my shoulders to my hands—except for when he skipped over my cast—and then he placed my arms over his shoulders. Finally, he took me around the waist again and pulled me closer.

While we swayed to the slow beat of the music, we turned around and around. I looked up into his eyes and hoped it was affection I saw glimmering there. It was only then I realized his green eyes reminded me of Drew's.

Strange.

On one of our spins around, I glimpsed Drew and Christina. Christina's skanky body was draped all over Drew, and it looked like she was nuzzling on his neck. I looked away as fast as I could. For the life of me, I just could not figure out why I hated the fact he was with her. I just couldn't put my finger on what kind of a feeling it was. It mostly felt like jealousy, but I didn't like Drew that way…or maybe I did.

Was it just Christina though, or would I have felt the same way if it was a different girl hanging all over him? Really, I felt like he deserved better than someone like Christina.

I couldn't take it any more.

"Let's get out of here," I whispered into Gavin's ear.

"Why?" he asked, pulling me back a little bit so he could look at my face. "Did something happen?"

I shook my head and pulled him through the crowd of slow-dancing vampire hunters. After what seemed like forever, we finally made it to the door. We grabbed our coats from the portable closets they had by the door for the many jackets.

Once Gavin pushed open the heavy doors to the gym and we were met with a blast of icy wind, I felt better. I didn't exactly like the cold, but it felt good to be out of the throngs of hot, sweaty people.

"What happened?" Gavin asked me on the way to the car.

I shrugged. "Nothing. I don't know. I just needed to get out of there. It was beginning to feel claustrophobic with all those people all mashed together."

He opened the driver's door and turned on the car while I slid into the passenger seat. We sat there while the car idled and warmed up. As much as I wanted to, I couldn't get that image of Christina kissing on Drew's neck out of my head.

Gavin shrugged. I was pretty sure he knew what was going on but was polite enough not to say anything about it. We sat in the car for what seemed like forever until he broke the silence. "Well, what should we do?"

"Let's just go to my house. No one is there right now."

"All right, then." He shifted car into gear and we left.

My house was dark when we arrived. Briefly, I wondered when I had started thinking about it as my house. I had always considered it Luke's house. I flipped on the light switches as we walked in, and I shrugged out of my coat. I wanted to change my dress, but I settled for just shedding my shoes.

"Are you hungry?" I asked him, trying to keep annoyance out of my voice. "I can go find us some snacks."

"You got any popcorn? We could watch a movie or something."

"Let's go find out."

In the kitchen, we rummaged around until we found a box of light popcorn.

"Well, it's better than nothing." I held up the microwave popcorn bags.

"Popcorn is popcorn." He smiled as I ripped off the plastic wrappers and threw one in the microwave.

"Can I ask you a question?" I asked as opened the fridge.

"Sure. What's up?"

"I was just wondering why you would ask me to go to the New Year's bash with you. I don't hang out with your crowd." I handed him a bottle of water. "I barely know you."

He took the water and grinned. "Isn't that the point, to get to know each other?"

I nodded, not buying that as an answer.

He sighed and leaned back in his chair. "I asked you to come with me because I think you're pretty, and I *do* want to get to know you."

"Why would you want to know me?" I just didn't get it.

"You barely talk to anyone at school. You sit alone with your iPod in your ears so you don't socialize, but you aren't a geek. I just want to see what is behind this wall you've built around yourself."

The microwave beeped and I pulled out the cooked bag and set it on the counter so I could grab a big glass bowl from the top cupboard.

"How do you know I'm not a geek? You just said you don't know me."

"I know some things about you," he told me as he rose from his chair. "I know that you lost your mother, that you witnessed her death."

I sucked in my breath. *Why would he bring that up?*

He moved toward me. "I know that you moved here and have had a hard time adjusting. I know that you aren't very social."

I held the bowl of popcorn in my hands and could feel my fingertips tingle.

"Everyone knows about my mom, and that other stuff is plain observation."

Still, he moved closer. I backed up against the counter as he moved forward. He took the popcorn bowl from my hands and put it on the counter. He took my hands and wrapped them around his waist, pushing his body flush with mine as his own arms circled my shoulders.

"Let me know more, Chloe."

I felt my breath catch, and then flutter out. I wondered if he was going to kiss me.

His eyes were there, staring down into mine. It should have felt uncomfortable to have someone staring so deep into my soul, but I didn't feel uncomfortable. I felt... wanted. It was quite a change from how Drew had been treating me lately.

When his head lowered toward mine, I closed my eyes. His lips touched mine, soft and questioning. I kissed him harder. I pushed myself against him and parted my lips so our tongues could meet.

It was wonderful.

One of his hands worked into my hair, holding the back of my head, while the other one tightened around my waist. My toes and fingers began to feel warm. My heart was pumping harder than usual...

Oh, no...

I pulled back quickly, placing a hand on his chest to keep him away. The last thing I wanted was to catch fire and burn him.

"Chloe, don't. It's okay." He reached out to bring me closer again.

"No. You have to stop," I told him. I was freaked out, so my voice was stern and my hand was still on his chest.

The next thing I knew, Drew tore through the kitchen door and grabbed Gavin by the back of his jacket.

"Get off of her!" He yanked him away from me, turned him around, and then swung at him.

"Drew!" I screamed "Get off of him! He didn't do anything!"

Drew hit him again and again. I tried to stop Drew by grabbing his shirt and pulling on it. I didn't want to get into the line of fire.

"Stop it!" I screamed.

Finally, Gavin came to his senses enough to hit Drew back. He pulled back and cracked his knuckles against Drew's cheekbone. The white of Drew's tux shirt spattered with blood when Gavin's fist connected with his nose.

"Guys! Please, stop this!" I was crazy mad at Drew, but my fear for Gavin was worse than my anger. I knew what Drew could do. I guess, in that moment, I forgot that Gavin was also a vampire hunter.

"Damn it!" I slammed my fist onto the kitchen table and watched in horror as my beautiful yellow roses tipped over, spilling out of the vase. At exactly that moment, I heard a loud ripping noise, and we were blessed with a fire in the kitchen.

Neither of the guys had seen it happen. I looked over, and they were still wrestling, bashing each other into the kitchen counter and grunting.

"Fire!" I screamed at the top of my lungs and ran for an extinguisher. In the last week, a whole bunch of fire extinguishers had magically appeared in the house. I think Drew was worried about stuff like this happening.

Quickly, I pulled the pin from the nozzle trigger and sprayed the table down. I wanted to cry while I watched the foam float over the remaining stems and tiny bits of charred petals. The clear glass vase had split in two, probably from the heat.

They finally stopped when they heard the whoosh of the foam and the hiss of the disappearing flames. I glared at them, with their bloody faces and messed up hair. Both were crouched over, holding their stomachs and staring at the charred table and broken vase covered with fire extinguisher foam. They looked at me in my pretty blue dress holding the damned extinguisher.

"What happened?" Gavin asked.

I lost it then. I grabbed up the brittle, foamy stems off the table with my free hand and threw them in Drew's face.

"How dare you!" I hissed.

I hefted the extinguisher and sprayed them both until nothing was left. Then I tossed it on the ground with a loud clang.

I looked at Drew and pointed. "You get to clean this crap up!"

I stalked out of the kitchen and up to my room.

The next morning, I woke and realized I was still in my dress. I totally was not going to work out or do any training. I didn't want to, and there was no way Drew was going to make me. I was so ticked at him I didn't care if I ever saw him again. I got up and hurried across the freezing hardwood floor and into the bathroom.

I slid out of my dress, grabbed my robe off the hook, put it on and started some bath water. While the water ran, I tried to pick out all the bobby pins. It was a bobby pin nightmare up there, a tangled mess of the little pins and hair. When I finally got them all out, I ran a brush through the mess and, for a moment the air sparkled. After a couple of blinks and a shake of my head, I realized that glitter was falling from my hair and floating around in the air. I smiled while I watched the pretty sparkles float slowly down onto the sink, remembering how Gavin had smiled and laughed when we tried to get the little top hat to stay on top of my up do.

He was probably regretting all that by now.

With a loud dramatic sigh, I finally tied my hair up on top of my head in a big bun and stepped into the hot water. I hadn't had a bath in ages. It felt so nice just lay in the hot water with my eyes closed, soaking and not really worrying about anything except keeping my arm on the side of the tub so as to not get the cast wet.

Then I heard the door open.

"Chloe?"

"Drew!" I screeched. "Get the hell out of here," I ordered.

I fumbled around to get the towel off the chair next to the tub. I flung it over my top half and hoped he couldn't see down in the water from where he stood.

He didn't budge, but he stayed by the door and turned away slightly. "I'm not leaving. I need to apologize for last night. I was totally out of line."

"Yes, you were, and I don't forgive you… not yet."

"I just didn't like seeing him force himself on you."

I sighed. "He wasn't forcing himself on me. I don't want to talk about it."

The last thing I was going to do was tell Drew I didn't want my body to heat up so much while I kissed a guy—kissing my first guy—I almost caught fire.

"Well, I just wanted you to know, I'm sorry."

"The problem here, Drew, is I don't know what you are to me. You're definitely not my father. You're not even my brother, so you don't get to tell me who I can kiss and who I can't."

"Chloe, it looked like he was trying to force you. What was I supposed to do, just stand there and let it happen? I don't think so."

"So instead of just saying something and letting us know you were there, you thought beating the crap out of him would be a better way to exhibit how you feel about me?"

"I was only protecting you. I would have done it for anyone." When he said this, he didn't say it softly. The ice lingered in his voice.

I knew I was making a bigger deal out of it than it was.

"Fine. Just get out of here."

He turned to go and then stopped. Without turning around, he said in a softer voice, "Just because I'm not your brother or your father doesn't mean I don't care about you."

I didn't answer.

"We need to go see Luke today," he told me in a tougher voice. "I'd like to do that as soon as possible."

I stayed in the tub as long as I could, just to spite him. I even ran more hot water into the tub when the water got too cold. By the time I got out, my fingers and toes were all pruned. I picked out a pair of jeans and a dark purple sweater to wear to the hospital. I hoped Luke got to come home soon. I hated seeing him all weak and vulnerable in his bed at the hospital. We went to visit him every day though, and so did a lot of the other hunters in the community. It would be really nice when we didn't have to go to the hospital every single day though.

Downstairs, Drew was sitting at the charred kitchen table. It had been wiped clean of the extinguisher foam. One of Drew's guns was in pieces and spread out all over the table. His cleaning kit was open, and it looked like he had finished cleaning and was putting it back together. My destroyed roses and the vase were nowhere in sight.

"You ready?" he asked as soon as I entered.

"Yup."

"You need to bring your gun."

"I know." I patted the purse I carried when my outfit would make it obvious that I was packing or when I just didn't feel like having a loaded gun stuck into the waistband of my pants.

He nodded and finished cleaning his gun while I grabbed a granola bar and a glass of water. I wandered into the living room with the intention of turning on the news and was surprised to hear my cell phone ringing. No one really called me since my mom died.

Caller ID said it was Gavin. I didn't know if I wanted to answer. I was entirely tempted just to let the voice mail get it. I hoped he wasn't mad at me for what Drew had done. Then again, I had sprayed him with the extinguisher and had run upstairs without saying goodbye or seeing if he was hurt, so he might be mad at me too. Wanting to talk to him overpowered the embarrassment.

"Hello?"

"Hey, Chloe."

"Hey."

"Are you doing okay this morning?"

I think I may have snorted a little. "I think the question is how are *you* doing this morning? *I'm* fine."

"I'm fine too. I just wanted to call and apologize for everything last night. I really wasn't trying to force myself on you." He paused. "I hope you realize that."

"Duh. I know that. Drew just walked in at the wrong time and freaked out."

She could almost see him nodding.

"I just wanted to make sure that you absolutely know I would never try anything like that with you."

"I know," I told him. I really did know that even though I barely knew him, and Drew had said something about him not being an angel… or something like that.

"Let me make it up to you. Let's go do something."

I sat on the couch, relieved. He wasn't mad. "Well, I'm going to the hospital right now, but I'll be home later. Do you want to go to the ranges with me?"

"That sounds awesome. Archery or guns?"

"Both. How 'bout I call you when I get back?"

"Sounds good. Talk to you later."

We both said goodbye and clicked off. Words could not express how happy I was that he wasn't mad at me about the night before.

"You ready?"

I snapped out of my little bubble and looked up. Drew was in the doorway watching me with icy narrow eyes. I was sure he had heard the whole phone call. I hopped up off the couch.

"Yeah, I'm ready." I grabbed my coat off the hook and headed for the door.

At the hospital, Luke's nurse spoke with us for a few minutes before we went into his room. She explained that he was doing well, but that he still needed to stay a few more weeks in the hospital. Apparently, because of his age, it was more of a risk to send him home with the portable chest tube. Plus, there were mobility issues with the casts.

Drew and I both told her that we understood and then opened the door to Luke's room. My goodness, every time I entered that room I felt a million different emotions. I felt sad, because Luke was so messed up and had three casts on. I felt anger at the vampires who did this. I felt guilty because it wouldn't have happened if they hadn't been after me.

I was going to fix it so none of them were hurt again. The only problem was that I wasn't ready. I was barely trained to be a vampire hunter, not to mention the unreliability of my fire power. I didn't want to go in unprepared, but I felt a sense of urgency to protect the only family I had left, and protecting my family was more important than protecting myself.

Where the heck was Sostrate now?

"Hi Luke!" I chirped, going directly to his bedside.

"Chloe!" He turned his head to look at me. Drew went to the counter, without saying a word, and began to organize the flowers, stuffed animals and treats that people had been sending and bringing him. One of the bears just had to have been made at one of those places where you build your own. It had on a camouflage shirt and hat, plus little black combat boots. A tiny little bandolier sat over its shoulder. I don't know where they got it, but someone had stuck a tiny toy cross bow in the bear's hands. The card read, 'It's always vampire hunting season.'

It was hilarious.

"How are you doing today?" I asked him, taking one of his hands into mine.

"Same; nothing has changed. I know I'm healing pretty fast, but not nearly fast enough. All I can do is watch the damn television. It's boring."

I nodded. "I totally understand that. I don't know what I would do if I had to lay here and do nothing all day. Do you need us to bring anything from home?"

He tiredly shook his head. "No, no. I'm fine here. At least most of the nurses are pretty."

"Luke!"

"Well, they are. I'm hurt, not dead. If I have to have someone giving me a sponge bath, I'm just glad she's pretty."

I laughed. "I guess that makes sense."

"Hi, Drew," Luke called out.

"Hey, Luke," Drew responded and came over to the bed. "How's it going?"

"I already just told Chloe, and I know you heard it. Why don't you go down to the cafeteria and get me a banana and a couple of those little cartons of milk. Would you do that, please?"

Drew nodded. "Sure thing."

He left without question. He always did what Luke told him to do.

"Chloe, come here, child." I could tell he was trying to pull me closer so he could whisper.

I leaned my head in and whispered, "What's up?"

"I know what you are thinking about doing, please... please don't go."

How on earth would he know that? But then again, he knew to come to the rescue when my mom was murdered.

"I have to, Luke," I whispered in his ear and looked him in the eye. "I don't want anyone else I care about to be hurt. You are the only family I have left."

"We are hunters, Chloe. This is what we do, and as long as a couple of them go down with us, we are glad to sacrifice ourselves. It is who we are."

"But still—"

"I'm not done," he cut me off. "I will not make you stay with us. I know you will do whatever you want anyway, but at least stay until you're ready."

I was already shaking my head. "Luke..."

"No, you need to be trained more. At least think about it. Also, I know I just finished telling you that we are hunters, and that this is what we do, but child, I don't want to lose you so soon after losing my own daughter. Remember that too."

Oh great... he went and pulled a guilt trip on me.

I leaned in and kissed him on the cheek. "I'll think about it."

"Just don't leave without telling me. I don't care what you do about everyone else, but don't you dare leave without telling me."

"I promise."

I pulled away and sat in the chair next to him. We watched Wheel of Fortune on the little television and didn't speak. Drew returned with the banana and milk. He also had two cartons of orange juice with him.

"Here." He held one out to me.

"Thanks."

Luke's eyes followed from one of us to the other and then an eyebrow rose. "Did you two have a fight?"

Neither of us answered. It seemed like we had been fighting ever since the attack. I had to wonder why that was. It seemed like something like that would only make us closer, you know, help us learn to work together.

"I see," Luke said. "Well, get over it because the two of you still have to train. Chloe still needs help improving her skills and working with her fire power."

This time we both answered. "Yes, sir," Drew said at the same time I said, "Okay."

We sat there for another half an hour in silence, Drew on one side of Luke and me on the other, watching Jeopardy because it was on after Wheel. After Jeopardy, we left. I always hated leaving Luke there in the hospital alone, because he was injured; he had no way to protect himself.

⤙⤙⤙

When we were back at home, I changed my sweater and put on a long-sleeved thermal shirt with skulls on it. I put on my holster that Drew had given me. It was nice to not have to wear my gun in the back of my pants where I might shoot my butt off. Next, I grabbed the bow Sostrate had given me and the beautiful leather quiver. I inspected my arrows to make sure they were all there and carried it over my shoulder. I really needed to practice with the bow, because I hadn't used it at all with my cast on.

I dialed Gavin's number on the way out the front door. I didn't even tell Drew I was leaving. He probably knew where I was going anyway since he had eavesdropped on my phone call earlier in the day.

"Hey, Chloe," Gavin answered from the phone.

"I'm on my way over to the ranges now."

"Awesome. I'll meet you there. Let's start with archery."

"Sounds like a plan," I told him and clicked off the line.

Outside, I blinked against the brightness after being inside so long. It seemed strange for it to be so bright, because the day was gray and threatened to snow. I shrugged the quiver up onto my shoulders and hurried down the driveway.

The walk to the ranges was cold and wet. I was really hoping spring would come soon. I had never in my whole life spent so much time outside in winter. I avoided the trails because I wasn't sure how much snow was on them, so I stayed on the roads. When I arrived in town, I went into the coffee shop to get a latte to warm me up. Funny how in town one could just walk into any business establishment with a bow slung over the shoulder and a gun strapped on.

Jaime, the owner of the Java Bean, was working the counter. The only time I ever saw her was when I came in to get coffee. She was a really nice lady, in her early twenties, I guessed. I liked her because she was one of those perpetually perky people, and she looked like it, too. She always had her blond hair in some trendy style, and she had bright blue eyes that didn't look cold at all. They were warm and inviting.

A few other people occupied the Java Bean, all sitting around drinking coffee and reading newspapers. I had realized recently that most hunters really liked reading the newspaper and watching the news.

"Hey, Chloe." She glanced up from the iced coffee she was mixing.

"Hi, Jaime. How's it going today?"

She grinned. "Busy as always, and you?"

"I'm heading out to the ranges for practice." I shifted my bow a little bit.

"Well, that sounds fun, although it's not exactly beautiful out there." She nodded toward the windows. Snowflakes had begun to float down and stick on the sidewalk.

"I'll live," I told her.

"So what'll ya have today?"

"Can I get a large double-shot latte with hazelnut. Hot." I thought of Gavin. "Better make that two."

"Coming right up." Jaime grabbed a cup off the stack and started to make the lattes.

I turned away from the counter and my quiver knocked the large vase acting as a tip jar off the counter. Reflexively I tried to catch it but missed. It hit the ground with a loud crash and burst.

Millions of shards bounced up, almost suspended in mid-air, and then rained back down. Something went wonky with my vision, because it looked so sharp and clear, similar to how the glitter had played tricks on my eyes earlier that morning. I blinked to clear my eyes, but I realized I could see every single individual shard glimmer under the lights.

What the heck...?

It took a moment to realize people were staring at me.

"Oh, my gosh... I'm so sorry, Jaime!"

She went for the broom and waved it off. "Don't worry about it. Nothing we can't clean up."

I took my quiver off and sat it on a chair and bent to help pick up the larger shards.

"Chloe, don't touch it. You might cut yourself."

Go figure, the minute she said that, I managed to slice my left index finger open.

"Ouch!" I stuck my finger in my mouth and sucked on it. "Damn it," I mumbled around my finger. Suddenly, as the blood touched my tongue, I didn't want to remove my finger from my mouth. It tasted sweet, but metallic at the same time.

"Watch out," Jaime ordered me as she swept the glass.

I jumped up as her voice brought me back to reality, reluctantly pulled my finger out of my mouth, and then went around the corner to grab the trash can.

"Maybe today isn't the best day to go out shooting," I joked, holding the can out for her to dump the glass into.

She chuckled a bit and finished with the rest of the glass.

"I'll get you a bandage," she told me as she brought out a little medical kit from underneath the counter.

"Oh, I'll be okay." I told her, not wanting her to go through any more trouble for me. Plus, I had mostly sucked it dry, still able to taste a faint metallic hint on my tongue and it wasn't bleeding any longer.

"I'm still giving you one. You are not leaving here with a bleeding finger, Chloe."

After I finally accepted the bandage and had it applied snugly on my finger, she set the lattes on the counter in front of me. I paid, giving her a ten and telling her to keep the change. I wished I had more cash on me to help pay for the broken jar. I grabbed my bow and quiver, slinging them over my shoulder so I had both hands free for the coffee.

"See you later, and I'm really sorry about your jar." I nodded to her because my hands were full with the lattes and headed out. The snow came down harder than before, and I had to duck my head to keep it off my face.

My vision really was acting weird. Normally, when my eyes messed with me, everything would get blurry or fuzzy, but my vision was sharper. The snowflakes dropped onto the shoveled sidewalks, some sticking and some melting. I could see each one like I was looking at it through a magnifying glass. Each was so pretty and clear when it hit the sidewalk and then dissolved into beautiful droplets, before finally melting away to join the puddles.

I blinked several times, trying to get everything back to normal and continued on to the ranges.

The ranges had indoor and outdoor areas for both guns and archery. I figured, because of the snow, Gavin would wait for me at the indoor ranges. Sure enough, he sat at one of the metal picnic-type benches, adjusting the sights on his bow.

"Hi!" I called out after I struggled to get through the metal double doors with my bow and quiver on and the lattes in both hands.

"Hey there." He jumped up and jogged over to help me.

"I got you a coffee. It's probably cold by now, though. I didn't think of that when I bought them."

He took one of the lattes from me and took a big swig. "Nah, it's still a little bit warm. At least I won't burn myself."

I giggled.

"True. Sorry it took me so long. I knocked over the tip jar at the Java Bean and cut myself."

I held up my finger and wiggled it around.

"Oh, man. Does it hurt?"

I set my stuff on the table. "Nah, not really."

I took the bandage off so I could inspect the damage now that it wasn't bleeding. "What the…"

There was no cut on my finger.

Gavin looked worried. "What? What is it?"

"It's gone." Shocked, I stared down at my finger. "I know I didn't imagine it. Look at the bandage."

I held it out and, sure enough, the bandage had a dark brown blood stain on the white pad.

"It healed already."

I could still see a faint white line where the cut had been, like a new scar.

"This is freaking me out," I told him.

"Sometimes hunters have quick healing. It just depends on the hunter."

"Oh, well, that makes sense." Unless that hunter is also half vampire. Then maybe it's her vampire half coming through. Maybe that was what was going on with my eyes, too. "Well, in any case, it's better now. Should we get started?"

He ran his fingers over his dark hair and grinned. "Let's do it."

We got to work and stood side by side to fire at the targets. I was a better shot than Gavin. I don't think he really liked that much, even though he pretended to. I was better than him even with my cast on, which surprised me.

"Damn, Chloe. Your aim is impeccable."

"Yeah, I'm gifted," I told him.

He thought I was joking, but I was serious. Marksmanship was one of my gifts. After we shot for about half an hour, we both needed to rest our arms. We sat at the table and sipped on our cold coffee.

"Gavin, are both your parents hunters?" I asked him. I wanted to get to know him better because I suddenly realized that, aside from being the hot popular guy, I didn't know anything about him.

"Yeah, they are both hunters. I was born right here in this community and have been here my whole life."

"Do you have gifts? I heard that some of the hunters eventually develop, like, powers or special abilities around our age."

His eyes narrowed and he stared at me through the slits. "Why do you ask?"

I shrugged. "I'm just wondering, I'm getting to the age where I would inherit gifts and was wondering what kind of gifts other hunters developed."

"Well?" I raised my eyebrows in question.

"I am one of the few of us hunters who is elementally gifted."

"Elements, like air, earth, water and fire?"

He nodded. "Exactly like that, except that I can only control water."

Wow. Water.

"You said control. Can you create water?"

"No, I can only control what already exists."

"Are there people who can create elements... like, um... fire?"

He shrugged. "I suppose there are. I don't think we have any hunters left who are fire elementals. Any who did have it probably passed away long ago. Some of the elders might know better, though."

I was extremely curious. From what I'd read at the library and from being observant and watching the community, I'd learned that most of the hunters who had elemental powers could only control them, not create them. I was a fire starter who could create fire from nothing. I hadn't heard anything about other hunters being able to do something like that.

Then I thought about how odd it was that Gavin and I were basically opposites: fire and water.

"Will you show me something you can do with water?"

He grinned. "Maybe... when we leave." He looked down at his cup, which was empty. "It must be hard, coming into our world and knowing nothing about it."

"Yeah, but I'm learning. I do a lot of research at the library, and Drew helps me a lot."

At the mention of Drew's name, Gavin narrowed his eyes and set his jaw. I just ignored it, figuring it was because of the fight.

"Let's go over to the other side and work with guns for a little bit," I suggested.

"All right." He stood from the table and gathered his things. I did the same and threw my cup in the garbage.

After we spent another half an hour at the shooting range, my arm was aching beneath the cast.

"I think I need to quit," I told him.

"Getting sore?"

"Yeah, but I think it's good that I practiced with the cast on. I was worried about how it would affect my shooting."

"Seems it hasn't," he said.

I thought I detected a bit of jealousy in his tone.

He quickly changed the subject. "Hey, that's a nice bow and quiver."

"Thanks," I told him, totally not wanting to go into where I'd gotten it and hoping he wouldn't ask.

"Where did you get them?"

Crap. Figures.

"My, uh…Luke gave them to me. They were my grandmother's."

Well, they kind of were, so it was only a little lie.

He reached out and touched the carvings on the quiver, running his fingers over them. "They fit you."

I blushed. I don't know why. "Thank you."

He lowered his hand. "Let's go."

We headed back toward Main Street, both of us saying nothing. We were almost there when Gavin veered off toward the trails.

"Where are we going?"

"Come on. You said you wanted a demonstration of the water element."

"Oh, cool." I followed him through the trails until we reached a clearing where a tiny stream ran into a rather quaint little pond. Oddly enough, the pond wasn't frozen. Perhaps it wasn't cold enough.

"This is pretty," I told him.

He just nodded and said nothing while he set down his bow and backpack on a large old tree stump. I watched while he turned toward the pond and narrowed his eyes.

"Look at the water, Chloe, not at me."

"Oh." I changed direction quickly.

The stream poured out of the woods and into the pond with gently running ripples of water. I almost didn't notice when the water in the center of the pond began to swirl. The swirling gradually picked up speed and grew larger until it looked like a whirlpool. But whirlpools go downward into the water. This whirlpool began to rise up out of the water. It rose up maybe six feet and then the water spilled over from the top like a fountain. I glanced at Gavin. He stood stock still, silent, his eyes focused on the water.

Slowly, the swirling fountain of water receded back into the pond. I stood there, enthralled by the magic Gavin could do with his power.

"You're amazing," I whispered to him.

"No," he shook his head, "*I'm* not amazing. I can just do amazing things."

"Well… I think you're amazing."

He turned his head and caught my eyes. "I think you're amazing, and you haven't done anything like that."

Oh, little did he know. For some reason, his comment made me want to show him what I could do, but I didn't even know if I *could* do it on command. So far it had only happened when I was angry.

He stared at me so deeply I felt naked.

"Gavin, what I just saw was magical. You make magic."

He took my hand. "Chloe, I don't know what it is, but I feel drawn to you. Not in the way you might think, but I feel like you're my best friend. Almost…it's almost like I've known you my whole life."

I sucked in my breath. "How could you feel like that? You just told me last night you barely know me, and you want to get to know me."

"No, no, it's a different feeling than that. I can't explain it."

Suddenly, I made a decision and took a chance that was extremely out of character for me. I reached out and took his other hand. "Well, you can be my best friend if you want. I don't have any friends, so it wouldn't be that hard to score that coveted spot."

He burst out laughing and squeezed my hands. I laughed too. We both laughed so hard tears eventually sprouted in the corners of our eyes. I didn't know about him, but I really needed a good laugh like that.

⚔ ⚔ ⚔

Back at home, I skipped dinner and went straight to my room. For hours, I lay on my bed, staring at the faint white scar on my finger. It had to be part of the vampire change; I just knew it. These changes only made me wonder what else was going to happen. There were bound to be more changes ahead.

I rolled over on my bed and looked at my cell phone. I clicked open the contact picture of Gavin and stared at it, wondering how fire and water could survive each other. He didn't seem cool and icy. That was more Drew's thing. Up until that point, Drew had been my only friend, but he took care of me so he was also like a big brother.

My phone rang in my hand and I jumped, because the dang thing hardly ever rang. Caller ID said restricted. That was weird.

"Hello?"

"Chloe," a clear and soft male voice came through the earpiece.

"Yeah, who is this?"

"This is your father."

I let that sink in for minute. I wanted to scream and yell and tell him he could stick it. I think I knew, as soon as I heard his voice that it was time for me to go on with my plan.

"What do you want?" I asked him.

"I'm here with your grandfather, Chloe."

Luke. He was at the hospital. "Don't hurt him."

"Why should I spare him, Chloe? Would he have spared me if the tables were turned? Even if it had meant he could have gotten your mother back all those years ago?"

I took a deep breath and tried to stay calm. "If you even touch him, I will not go with you. If he remains unharmed, I will come to you."

"Ah, that is just what I was hoping to hear. Where shall we meet?"

"I'm coming to the hospital. I want to see Luke and make sure he is alive when we leave. I need to make sure you keep your end of the bargain."

"You have my word. Your grandfather will live through this night if you show up."

I clenched my teeth and then forced myself to relax.

"You had my mother killed. What on earth makes you think that I would ever trust you? I'll be there in two hours."

I clicked my phone shut and threw it across the room.

After exactly one minute of steaming, I jumped up and grabbed my big duffel bag out of the closet and ran around the room grabbing clothes, my iPod, my toiletries, anything I didn't want to leave behind. I collected my phone from where it had landed by the bathroom door and dialed the cab company. I had some cash stowed in a shoebox on the top shelf of my closet. There was no way I was going to ask Drew to drive me. I don't think he would have taken me. He would have just tried to go and kill Trevor all on his own. I knew better than to tell anyone.

After I finished calling the cab, I called the gates to let them know I had a cab coming and I would be up there to meet it. I pulled up Gavin's contact picture, giving myself a minute to embed the picture of his face into my mind before I erased it from my phone. I pulled up Drew's picture and did the same thing. I didn't want Trevor to know what anyone I cared about looked like.

I looked over at my bow and quiver resting on my desk chair and sighed with sadness. I couldn't take them with me because I couldn't go into the hospital with them.

Sadly, I sat and wrote a note to Drew.

Hey Drew,
I can't really explain why I had to leave, but I think you know. I don't want anyone else I care about to get hurt, so I'm leaving. There is so much more to this I should tell you, but I can't right now. Please don't come after me. I am hoping I will see you again soon. I'm leaving my bow and quiver Sostrate gave me. Would you please put them away for me because I will be back for them some day. Take care of yourself, and please make sure to go see Luke as soon as you get this. I think he may even need one of the hunters to guard him. Please, keep him protected.
Love always,
Chloe.

After I folded the note and wrote Drew's name on it, I wrote one to Gavin, too.

Gavin,
I can't explain why I had to leave, especially right after we got to know each other. But I'm hoping that you will figure it out somehow and forgive me for leaving us hanging. I'm going to try my hardest to come back some day. I'm not sure when it will be, but I'm going to try. I hope that when I get back, we will still be friends.
Thank you for showing me that magical side of yourself. I will never forget it.
Love,
Chloe.

I folded Gavin's note and then put on my coat. I threw my gun into my bag, zipped it up and slung it over my shoulder. It was time to go.

Before I left, I put Drew's note on the kitchen table where he would see it. Then, after contemplating, I set Gavin's right beside it. I hoped Drew would set aside his animosity and give Gavin the note.

I didn't look around the house with long, lingering looks; I just turned and left.

I ran most of the way to the gates, my heavy gym bag thumping against my hip the whole way. I did my best to stick to the side roads, rather than the main road, just in case someone saw me running. I certainly wasn't dressed for a daily run just for exercise.

The cab was just pulling up outside, so I ran directly through the gates as they opened for me, flung open the door of the cab and hopped into the back seat.

"Can you take me to St. Joseph's Hospital, please?"

The man in the front seat turned and looked me over, giving me a knowing look, like he knew I was running away from something. "You got it, kid."

✗ ✗ ✗

The ride to the hospital was long and grueling. All I could do was panic and hope Trevor kept his hands off of Luke. When we pulled up in front of the main entrance, I looked through the giant glass doors and took a deep breath.

Be brave, Chloe, I repeated silently.

"You gonna get out?" the driver asked me.

"Oh, yeah… Here. Thank you." I handed him a wad of cash and told him to keep the change. Gathering my bag and my strength, I opened the door and got out.

I stood on the sidewalk, staring inside and trying not to be afraid. But I was. I was terrified about what was going to happen. Mostly I was apprehensive because I really had no clue what to expect. I needed to suck it up. I straightened my spine, adjusted my bag over my shoulder, and marched inside.

I entered the elevator and pushed the button for the sixth floor. No one else was in the elevator with me. It was silent, like I had been suddenly blocked off from the world. It was one of those moments in which I wished I *was* blocked off from the world.

When the elevator doors opened into the hallway of the sixth floor, I stepped out and felt the familiar prickles of warning on the back of my neck. Man, I really hoped that would go away after spending more time around vampires. Just that thought caused more panic. I felt pretty certain Trevor wouldn't hurt me, but how was I supposed to know all his little vampire minions wouldn't?

I turned the corner where it opened up into the waiting room beside the nurses' station. It only took a quick scan for me to spot Trevor. He was sitting in one of the pastel blue chairs, legs crossed, reading an old issue of Reader's Digest. His hair was gelled back away from his forehead, and he wore the same leather jacket he'd had on the last time I had seen him.

Suddenly, as if he felt my presence, he lowered his magazine and our eyes met.

"Chloe," he called out. "There you are."

I stood where I was, trying to find my voice. That monster had sent the order to kill my mother, and he was part of me. How in the hell could I be half of any kind of being who would do such a thing?

He put the magazine aside and strode over to me. Still I said nothing. When he grasped my casted hand in his, he said, "It's been too long."

I felt my body begin its process of heating up, the warm tingles in my fingertips. To avoid any fiery accidents, I took several deep breaths in and out.

"I need to see Luke," I whispered, trying to keep the rage out of my voice and yanking my hand back from him.

"Go right ahead." He waved for me to lead the way and moved to follow me.

I turned and glared at him. "Alone."

A momentary glimpse of hesitation flashed across his pale face, but he nodded. "As you wish. I'll wait here."

As much as I hated to turn my back to him, I turned around and continued down the hall. When I reached the door to Luke's room, I found him wide awake and apparently waiting for me.

"Oh, Chloe, I'm so glad you're here."

I ran to his bedside.

"Was he in here?" I whispered, even though I knew he must have been because he probably got my number out of Luke's phone. I grasped his hand as best I could with both our casts.

Luke nodded. "Yes, he was here. I saw him, but I said nothing because I can't defend myself here. I'm so sorry, Chloe."

"No, Luke. Don't be sorry. If you had tried anything, he may have killed you. I left Drew a note to send protection for you, so they should be along soon." I bowed my head. "I have to leave."

"I know." He looked fearful and sad at the same time. I was sure he was flashing on my mother and losing her. Now he was losing me. I felt horrible.

"I'm going to come back." I hugged him and whispered into his ear. "I'm going to come back as soon as he's dead."

"I hope so, child. Just please, please... be careful."

"I will." I pulled away. "I also wanted to say thank you. Thank you for saving me and taking me in."

"There is absolutely no need to thank me for that. You are Felicia's daughter, my granddaughter."

I needed to go, before Drew showed up, but I didn't want to leave.

"I need to go," I told Luke.

He nodded his understanding. "Oh, one more thing."

He beckoned me forward and whispered, "I'm going to keep putting money into your account every month. Be careful. Don't waste it. You may need it when you want to come home. And make sure to keep your card hidden."

I nodded and stood again. Clutching the shoulder strap of my bag, I yanked it up onto my shoulder.

"I really have to get going." My voice was starting to choke and tears were welling up. I did not want to give that monster who called himself my father any satisfaction by letting him see me cry.

"I love you, Chloe," Luke called out.

I stopped short in the doorway. No one had said that to me since before my mother died.

"I love you too… Grandpa," I choked out, and then let the door slam behind me.

I was so upset while I marched back out to the waiting room. I was sad, mad, angry… you name it. Trevor stood when he saw me stalking past him.

"Chloe, wait."

"I'm not waiting for you. You're a vampire. Don't you have like… super speed or something? Just keep up."

"Shhh," he tried to quiet me, appearing by my side in an instant.

"See," I told him. "Super speed."

"Chloe, you cannot go around saying things like that."

I didn't stop to look into his eyes, but I knew he was frustrated with me already. Well, what did he expect? I was a teenager, and I was going to say anything I wanted. I did not intend to make his transition into fatherhood easy, after all.

Once outside, standing underneath the overhang in front of the main doors, I shivered against the cold and stopped.

"Look," I told him, "I don't know what you want from me. I'm coming with you because you want me for some reason. Do not think for a moment that I'm going to enjoy being around you."

His pale face almost glowed in the moonlight. "In time, you will adjust to it, and we will get to know each other. You are my daughter, my blood… and you're important to me."

"You killed my mother!" I spat at him.

A couple walking by snapped their heads in our direction, and Trevor shushed me again. "I did not kill your mother. I wasn't even there."

I shook my head in disgust. "Don't lie! I heard Eli say you issued the order that she needed to die for taking me away from you."

He neither denied it, nor did he acknowledge my accusation. I figured his silence was probably because he knew it was true. He just strode off into the parking lot. He stopped when we got to a brand new black Mustang. He pulled out his keys, and I heard the locks disengage.

"Get in," he told me.

I opened the door, threw my bag into the backseat and slid into the passenger seat. Trevor slid behind the wheel and started the engine.

"Nice ride," I told him.

"You have no idea," he replied as he pulled out onto road that led to the freeway.

So off we drove, into the night and away from my family, away from my best friend, and away from the guy who had been everything to me since my mother's death.

Off we drove into the next chapter of my life.

THE VAMPIRE HUNTER'S DAUGHTER PART V

LIVING WITH VAMPIRES

JENNIFER MALONE WRIGHT

The Vampire Hunter's Daughter
Part V

Living With Vampires

The headlights glared off the dark, wet highway ahead of us. Trevor's Mustang flew across the pavement at breakneck speed. I sat in the passenger seat, scared out of my wits and stared out the window into the blackness, just to avoid looking at him.

It took about an hour to reach Trevor's house. I tried to guess which house was his, but little did I know, it couldn't be seen from the highway. Eventually, we slowed, and I realized the house was hidden down a small paved driveway, beyond a large iron gate, surrounded by trees. Well, it wasn't even really a house... It was a freakin' mansion.

We pulled into a brick driveway that circled a large fountain with stone fairies that danced around falling water. Lights in the bottom of the fountain created a magical glow for the dancing fairies.

"Why is your house so big?" I asked him. I leaned over the seat to grab my duffel bag.

He got out of the car and slammed the door. "A little extravagance never hurts," he replied.

"*Okay.*" I rolled my eyes and didn't bother to keep the sarcasm out of my voice.

"Follow me." He motioned for me to come with him.

I slung my bag over my shoulder and followed him up the brick pathway to the French doors that served as the front entrance.

"Welcome home," he told me and flung the doors open.

I spun around in a slow circle. Never in my life had I actually been inside a home as nice as his. The floors looked like they were white marble with black swirls. A gigantic chandelier hung directly above us, each delicate crystal glimmered and reflected the lights. Because of my new wonky vision, I could tell that every one of those crystals were real. Expensive Persian rugs were thrown over specific spots on the floors. To my left, I could see a large living room area, the couches and chairs were all smooth black leather that looked so comfy and soft.

"Are you hungry?" he asked.

I looked at him like he was an idiot. "Seriously, do you even have anything here I can eat?" In my head I was thinking that he was going to offer me a big glass of blood or something.

The corner of his mouth lifted in a semi grin.

"Vampires do not require the sustenance humans require. We can, however, consume human food if we choose to. I also have human donors who live here. They must eat well in order to feed me well."

I wanted to barf. *Human donors?* "That is disgusting."

"You would rather I bring home an unsuspecting young girl and take her against her will?" He waved his hand in the air a bit. "I have tried that and found it distressing when I have to kill them because they can't keep silent. The donors are here of their own free will, and I pay them more than enough. None of them will have anything to worry about for the rest of their lives. Come now." He beckoned me again to follow him.

I was still disgusted.

"Alice!" he called out. Within seconds, a human girl with blond hair, who couldn't have been much older than me, emerged from one of the rooms beyond where we stood.

"What can I do for you tonight, Mr. Trevor?" At least she wasn't wearing a degrading maid's uniform. She had on a tee-shirt and jeans.

"Alice, my daughter and I would like to have a late supper."

"Yes, sir." Alice rushed off in the direction of what I assumed to be the kitchen.

I was still so taken with the house and continued to look around. There were many pieces of art on the walls and shelves housed authentic-looking statues and vases. The only reason I knew they looked old was because we did a section on art history in school. The majority of the art on the walls were paintings of sunsets, sunrises and ocean scenes. The pinks, purples and oranges of the sunset and sunrise pictures contrasted the black and white decor, giving it warmth and color.

Trevor watched while I examined the house. "Chloe, I hope that you will make yourself at home. This is all as much yours as it is mine."

I nodded trying to keep my expression blank.

"Why don't we take your bags up to your rooms?" He headed up the stairs. The stairs and the second floor were carpeted in white.

Really, more white? For some reason, my one thought when I saw the white carpet everywhere was that it would be terribly hard to keep blood stains off of it.

The walls upstairs were burgundy. Instead of paintings, the walls were accented with artistic photographs.

"Did you take these pictures?" I asked.

He shook his head. "No. Most of these are daylight shots, so I couldn't have taken them." He stopped to examine the pictures, gazing longingly at one in particular of a farmhouse surrounded by lush green fields and large oak trees. "Although, they do remind me of what I am not able to experience."

He turned away, and we continued on until he paused at a set of double doors at the end of the hallway.

"This is your suite." He opened the doors with both hands.

I passed through the doors and then stood in awe. The room we entered was a living area with couches and a television in the center. A desk was pushed up against one wall and there were about six book shelves along another wall, bulging with books. Across from the couches, tucked into the corner of the sitting area, was a small dining table with two cushioned chairs.

The only thing I didn't like about the room was that there were no windows to let the sunlight in.

"This is your sitting room, and if you come this way," he moved through an adjoining door, "this is your bed room."

I followed him into the bedroom. As soon as I saw the queen bed with a pewter frame and sheer curtains, I wanted to crawl in and go to sleep. The bedroom also had a flat screen television mounted on the wall.

"This is amazing," I told him. I continued to explore. I found a gigantic walk-in closet and an adjoining bathroom.

"It is yours," he told me.

His words echoed loudly in my head: '*You're very important to me. You are my blood.*'

I just nodded. I didn't want to be grateful to him. No matter what, I had to remember my mission. He had killed my mother. He was trying to buy me off, or it seemed like he was.

Alice appeared in the doorway of the other room and cleared her throat. "Your supper is ready, Mr. Trevor." She nodded my direction. "Miss Chloe."

I hadn't realized she knew who I was. Trevor hadn't bothered to introduce me.

"We will be down momentarily." Trevor dismissed her with a slight wave of his hand. He didn't thank her, but what else should I have expected? She hurried out of the room. "Shall we eat?."

I wasn't really hungry, but I figured it was best to eat to keep my energy up. I threw my bag onto the bed and followed him down to the dining room.

Later, we sat across from each other at the long dining table while Alice served us thick steaks, potato salad and corn on the cob. I picked at my food and stared down at my plate.

What exactly should I talk about with a father I have never known and whose guts I hate? Maybe he was thinking something similar, because he didn't say anything either, except to ask if I wanted some of the red wine he had uncorked and was pouring into the crystal wine glass beside his plate.

I passed. I didn't want to do anything that would cloud my thinking while I was around him.

I didn't trust him.

I studied him while I messed around with my food. He was dark. Everything about him, except his skin, was dark. His hair, his eyes, his demeanor, all of it was just... black.

"So, how old are you now anyway?"

He tilted his head thoughtfully. "My mortal life was taken when I was twenty eight, the age which I will forever appear. As an immortal, I have lived nearly one thousand years."

I almost spit out my water. "Wow!"

"Yes, it is a very long time to have lived."

Against my vow to loathe him, my interest was piqued. I wanted to know more. "How did you become a vampire?"

He took another sip of his wine. "That is a story barely worth mentioning. It happened so long ago."

"I think it's worth mentioning. You should tell me."

He shook his head. "Perhaps another time."

I shrugged and stabbed a piece of steak. "Whatever. If you would rather sit here and stare at each other, that's fine with me."

"Chloe, you're being insolent."

I shrugged again and chewed my steak then took a big swig of water to wash it down.

He leaned back in his chair, turning to the side so he could cross his legs. "I suppose, if it pleases you, I could tell you how I came to be who I am. Seeing as I am your father, it would not be a terrible thing for you know."

After another rather delicate sip of wine, he spoke. "I was born in the Balkans. My parents bore no other children. For most of my life, I stayed home with my parents and worked the land.

"When I was twenty-two years, they both died from the sickness that had spread rapidly throughout our small community. Nothing could help them."

As much as I wanted to hate Trevor, the look of sadness on his face when he spoke of his parents made my heart wrench a little bit, I knew what it was like to lose the ones you love.

"After their passing, I had no desire to keep our land. An inner anger I had not known before had surfaced. I wanted vengeance for something that could not have been helped. I wanted to kill people who had no part whatsoever in the spreading disease that took my parents. With this anger, I became a soldier and killed for the good our people."

I leaned forward and ate a few bites. This was actually a good story. Much better than I expected.

"Eventually, the nobles of Italy hired foreign armies to fight for them. Their country had much wealth; however, their armies were miniscule. They were known mercenary soldiers, led by Condottieri. We were basically contract killers. Some called them soldiers of fortune.

"Italy found war and blood. I reveled in it and fought my way into one of the highest-paid armies. Years passed and my soul hardened. Death and becoming a vampire are not what made me the way I am. It was life that made me a killer."

He paused for another sip of wine, then continued. "One night, in the calm between battles, I stood on the cliffs and looked down at the black sea. Below, I saw a woman who sat on a lower cliff, letting the spray of the waves rain down upon her white gown. I called out to her, telling her to remove herself or she would be drowned when the tide came in. Still, she sat on the cliff, staring out at the waters."

"She was a vampire!" I guessed.

"If you want to hear my story, be silent."

I shut my mouth, because I did want to hear it.

"Frustrated with the idiot woman, I climbed down the cliffs to retrieve her. I was a hardened soul, but I wasn't going to stand by and watch a woman be taken by the sea for her stupidity.

"When I arrived on the cliffs below, I bellowed at her that very thing ordered her to climb back up the cliffs with me.

"When she turned and looked into my eyes, I saw the most beautiful woman, perhaps aside from your mother, that I'd ever seen. Her face was pale as ivory and hair dark as the rolling sea beneath her.

"She stood and said softly to me, 'Have no fear for my life, sir.' I felt entranced by her beauty, though my harsh words continued to flow freely from my lips. She took a few steps toward me, and I reached out to grab her by the arm and drag her back to the top of the cliffs with me."

He shook his head, remembering his frustration with the woman. "As I clamped my hand around her arm, she had me in her arms quicker than lightning, as I have no memory of how I got there. Her lips caressed my earlobe and whispered again 'Have no fear.'

"I felt the pierce of her fangs when she bit me; they drove deep into my neck. Her lips formed around the wound. The last thing I remember after screaming in fear until I was breathless was that it was the most amazing feeling I had ever encountered.

"Ever since then, we traveled, and then I left her and traveled on my own. I built my power within the supernatural realm as well as the living, and killed to live instead of living to kill."

I fell back in my chair and pushed some hair out of my eyes. I didn't want to feel sorry for him. I regretted asking him to tell me his story. I didn't even know what to say to him.

I set my fork down. "I'm tired. Can I go to bed, now?"

"Of course." He nodded and rose from the table. "Go on up to your room. If you require night clothes, you will find a few things in the armoire."

There was no way in hell I would wear anything he had gotten for me in anticipation of my being here.

"Thank you." I slid my chair out and rose to leave.

"I feel I should warn you, there are guards all over the grounds. They will stop you if you attempt to leave."

Seriously? "So, I'm a prisoner, then?"

His eyes were cold. "Only if you make yourself one."

"I understand," I told him and marched out the door.

What a freakin' jerk.

I should have known he wouldn't let me have freedom. Well, to be fair, it seemed like I would have a little freedom, as long as I was on the grounds.

Once upstairs, I put on my Harley shirt and sweatpants out of my bag and slid into them. I hadn't worn the Harley shirt since the night my mother had been murdered. I wore it this night on purpose, because I needed it to bring back memories of her death. I had to stay focused on my goals. That's the only way this time with Trevor would be bearable.

I pulled back the covers on the bed and slid beneath the cool sheets. Curling up into a ball, I pulled out my cell phone and turned it on. Immediately it buzzed that I had messages and texts. I checked them. There were four texts from Drew, two of them were of him yelling at me and demanding to know what the hell I was doing. Then the last one was him, finally, begging I come back or call him, anything.

There were also several voice messages and texts from Gavin. His were all simply wondering why I had left, asking if I was in trouble, and asking me to call him as soon as I could.

Tears slid down my cheeks and soaked the pillow. I sniffled and sighed, and then I turned off my phone. As much as I wanted to, I couldn't call them.

I just couldn't.

When I woke, I couldn't even tell if it was morning, because there were no windows to let in the light. I rolled over and looked at the clock. It was almost nine in the morning. I never, *ever*, slept that late. Even on vacation days from school or during the summer, I still woke up at the butt crack of dawn to go for my run and train.

I pulled back the covers and sat up on the edge of the bed. I wondered what I was supposed to do all day. I assumed Trevor would be asleep, being a vampire and all. I picked out an outfit to wear and then hurried to the bathroom. After I'd showered and dressed in jeans and a plain black tee-shirt, I wandered into the sitting room and immediately smelled food. A quick glance around the room proved there was, to my surprise, an entire breakfast sitting on the little table in the corner of the room. On closer inspection, I saw an omelet, hash browns, a bowl of fruit, coffee and orange juice. My stomach rumbled, and I realized the long rest overnight had stirred up my appetite.

"I hope you like it."

"Ahhhh!" I jumped back and reached for my gun—that wasn't

there—on instinct. When I realized it was Alice who had spoken, I put my hand on my heart and released a big sigh. "Jeez, Alice. You scared me!"

"I'm so sorry." She held out a little dish with toast on it. "Please, don't tell Mr. Trevor I scared you so badly. I was just getting the toast off the cart over there."

I was still catching my breath from the scare. "Don't worry. I won't tell *Mr. Trevor.* You didn't do anything wrong. I was just surprised; that's all." I pulled out the chair and sat. "Would you sit and have coffee with me?"

She shook her head quickly. "Oh, no. I couldn't."

"Why not?"

"Uhm... I just... I—I don't think I'm supposed to. I'm just the help."

"Well you're not *just* 'the help' to me." I pointed at the chair across from me. "Sit," I ordered.

She smiled shyly and sat.

"Well, now, that's more like it." I handed her the coffee mug and took the orange juice for myself. "Tell me about this place, Alice."

"What would you like to know?"

"I want to know everything. Do you like it here?"

She shrugged. "I don't really know much else any more."

"How long have you been here?" I asked her.

"Since I was thirteen."

I set my orange juice down so hard it sloshed over the sides. "Wow. And how old are you now?"

"I am twenty two. Mr. Trevor found me sleeping in a rest room at a bus station. He asked me if I wanted a better life, asked what I was willing to give up for that better life. Then he brought me home."

For a moment, I wondered if her blood was the only thing she had given up.

"Are you happy here?" I leaned in, speaking softly.

"Like I said, Miss, I don't really know much else any more. I'm not unhappy."

I nodded. Perhaps, it was a better life for her. I, however, refused to accept that bringing a thirteen-year-old kid home to drink her blood, and do whatever else with, was an acceptable thing to do.

"This place is beautiful, but I'm wondering what I'm going to do all day." I looked around the room.

"Mr. Trevor says you can go anywhere in the house or on the grounds, as long as you don't leave."

I nodded. "I kind of figured that."

She slid out her chair and stood. "Miss, Chloe, I really should be going. I have several things to do, and then I nap in the afternoon so I will be awake when Mr. Trevor wakes."

"I'm sorry to have kept you," I told her. Actually, I was a little sad to see her go. I didn't want to be alone in a gigantic house with nothing to do. I glanced at the bookshelves. I guessed I'd find something.

"Goodbye," I called to her while Alice quietly slipped out the door.

After I ate some of the breakfast she'd brought up for me, I decided to take a walk on the property and explore. I needed to know who was out there watching, where the exits were, that sort of thing. I strapped my gun on and then bundled up, even though I didn't know what it looked like outside. I hated not having windows. It made me feel even more like a prisoner.

Outside it was brisk, cold and snowing. The clouds covered the sun and a thick fog had settled in, misting like smoke in the trees. I wondered then if Trevor was the kind of vampire who could actually come out as long as there was no direct sunlight. Maybe he had to actually sleep during the daylight hours. I realized I had no clue.

I couldn't even see the fence. The property was outlined by trees and the fence ran along the inside of the tree line. I walked the perimeter, staying on the snow-laden lawn, where it would look like I was simply out for a stroll.

I didn't see any guards along the way. They must have been hidden, because I was certain there were guards. It also occurred to me that during the day, they had to be human. Oh crap, if I had to escape and a human tried to stop me... I didn't know if I could handle killing a human being.

I could just hear Drew in my head: *They aren't human, Chloe. They are evil... we kill evil.*

I just don't think I could do it.

I tried hard to come up with a plan of action. I'd come to this house with Trevor to kill him. It actually wouldn't be that hard for me to kill him, but the odds of my killing him and then getting away weren't so good, if he really did have guards posted everywhere.

When I wandered into the backyard and saw a deep rectangular in-ground pool underneath a huge covered patio area. The pool had steam rising from it; it was warm and ready for use. Beside the pool was a miniature hot tub version of the pool. A large brick grill was built into the patio and two patio tables accented the area with their bright blue chair cushions.

Thinking about getting in the pool and stretching my muscles made me wonder if Trevor had gym equipment in this house. I couldn't see why he would, because he was a vampire and vampires didn't need to work out. Did they?

Back inside the house, after finding out that there were more bathrooms than I thought anyone would ever want, a theater entertainment room, and a recreation room with a pool table, I did indeed find a large room with gym equipment. There were only a few weight machines, a treadmill and a rowing machine, but beggars couldn't be choosers. I hadn't trained for a few days, and I couldn't afford to let my muscles go like that.

Yeah, like I could ever overpower a vampire.

I needed to keep telling myself I was a vampire hunter. We overpowered vampires all the time, but it did bother me that I was so weak compared to a vampire. The other thing that bothered me was I needed to practice my special ability, my fire power. I couldn't really do that in Trevor's house. I was pretty sure he knew about it anyway, from that one little vamp who had gotten away during the attack. But maybe he didn't know, and if he didn't, then I sure as hell didn't want him to find out.

⚔⚔⚔

When Trevor woke around sundown, Alice informed me that I was expected for supper in the dining room in thirty minutes. Somehow, the properness of this request made me feel I should change my clothes. So, I took off my jeans and put on a pair of slacks with my pink blouse. While I changed, it became clear I was going to need more clothes than I had brought with me. I still didn't want to wear anything he had picked for me, simply on principle.

Once downstairs, we sat across from each other at the dining table. It was much like it had been the night before, only this time he tried to have a conversation with me.

"Have you come into your abilities, yet?" he asked while he cut into the tender pot roast Alice had served us.

I shook my head. "No, I'm not yet sixteen, so I haven't noticed anything different." I didn't want him to know I was developing my gifts on both sides. Not yet. The weaker he thought I was the better off I would be.

"When you begin to sense these abilities are present, make sure to tell me. I cannot help you much with your hunter heritage, but I can help when your vampire half develops."

I took a long swig from my water glass and then stabbed a piece of lettuce in my salad.

"I'll let you know."

I chewed and swallowed the lettuce.

"Hey, is there any literature or anything I can read up on about coming of age for my vampire side? I'd like to know about this stuff."

He waved his hand in a dismissive gesture. "There are likely plenty of books on the subject in the library. I will have some brought up to your room."

"That would be great, thank you." I paused and chewed the last bite of my roast. When I finished, I asked him, "Do you have a computer here, or something I could use for researching on the internet?"

His eyes narrowed and flashed a bit. "I would prefer that you use only the books. Under the circumstances, I would rather you not have access to communicate with the outside world." He took a dainty sip of his wine. "Which reminds me: I'll need your cell phone, please."

He wanted my phone, the very last connection I had to the ones I cared about. I could not believe this.

"If I can keep it, I promise not to make any calls."

He shook his head. "I am sorry, Chloe. I also need you to bring me the gun you brought with you."

This time I couldn't keep the anger from boiling over. I was pissed. I slammed my fork onto my plate and shoved my chair away from the table. I marched to his side of the table, reached into my pocket, grabbed my cell phone and threw on the table in front of him.

"Happy now?" I asked and stalked out of the dining room.

"You'll see this is all for the best," he called after I was already out of the room.

Back in my room, I grabbed my gun and removed the clip, then tossed them both out into the hallway. After slamming my door, which was quite unimpressive and not really what I was going for, I threw myself on my bed and pouted. I curled up with my clothes still on and pulled the covers over me. I let the faces of the people back home lull me to sleep.

⤙⤙⤙

Before I knew it, months had passed. The snow slowly melted and spring settled in. It was nice to finally see the forests around us turn green again. When the snow melted off the grounds, the large expanses of green lawn could be seen along with the new pretty flowers that popped up all over the place.

Trevor had a doctor come to the house and take my cast off in early March. Words simply cannot express how happy I was to have that thing off, to finally have full functionality of my hand.

Every single day I did the same things, and it became a monotonous schedule. The one thing I absolutely refused to do was become a night owl to suit Trevor. I woke at six a.m. Then it was shower, workout, another shower, breakfast, take a walk, read for a few hours, and then lunch. After lunch, I would repeat the same thing until dinner, minus the first shower.

I was getting strong, really strong. I was training double what I had been doing with Drew. I tried to use all the weight machines exactly the way Drew had shown me. I did the same with the other exercises where I didn't use a machine. It was crazy, seeing my body build muscle mass and tone up. One day, I was totally shocked when I looked in the mirror after my post workout shower and saw definition in my abs. I smiled at myself in the mirror because I knew Drew would be proud of me.

When I was out for my walks, I used that time to play around a little bit with my fire power ability. I was probably being watched by guards or cameras the entire time, but I just didn't have anywhere else to practice. I didn't want to do it inside, just to avoid setting the house on fire and it was getting to the point where I really didn't care if anyone saw it anyway.

I was getting better. With a lot of practice, I discovered I could make fire whenever I wanted, not just when I was angry. This process was like pulling energy from all around me and centering it inside of me, then pushing it out again. I think it was the same way it happened when I got angry, it just happened without me thinking about it.

I only saw Trevor at dinner and for a little while after. I didn't really want to see him, so that little bit was more than enough time for me. He didn't really bother much with me, which I found odd. If he thought I was that important, then why didn't he even act like he wanted to get to know me? It seemed like he wanted me only because I was his, like a little kid with his toy…he only wanted it because the other kids wanted to play with it, but when they didn't want to play with it anymore, neither did he.

It seemed the whole eating dinner together thing was an obligatory time to spend together. Trevor was confusing to me. It seemed like he wanted to be my father, but at the same time, he didn't spend much time with me, and I was sort of a prisoner in the house.

It had been months since I left the community. I didn't want to admit it, but I was beginning to wonder why they didn't try to come for me. I told them not to, but a part of me sort of thought they would anyway, especially since Luke knew the truth about why I had left, even if the others didn't.

Alice had become the first girlfriend I'd had for a while, since before my mom's death. The more we got to know each other, the more she trusted I wouldn't talk about her with *Mr. Trevor*. Oh, how I hated it that she called him that. I really liked Alice, and I wished that she would understand life could be better for her outside of this place. She wouldn't hear of it. For her it was as good as it was going to get. She didn't care that Trevor used her for food and sex; she was taken care of and would never want for anything, so she let him.

So sad, I knew I couldn't help someone who didn't want to help herself.

Secretly, I vowed to get her out of this place. I loved Alice, but I had to restrain myself from talking with her about Gavin and Drew. I didn't talk to her at all about any of the hunters. I knew she had grown to trust me more, but that didn't mean I trusted her.

During the time I spent reading, I only read the books Trevor had given me about vampires. I learned about the different types of vampires, half vampires, gifts and abilities, how vampires can die, myths and legends, the list of topics went on forever. I guess when you've been around as long as vampires have there was a lot of information to document.

It was early April by the time I decided that if I was unable to leave, I needed to learn something besides vampire history. So one night at dinner I said to Trevor, "I'm a little worried about not being in school. I'm actually a little discouraged that *you* haven't been more concerned about it. I'm still in high school, and I need to learn things. If I can't leave to go to a regular school, could we at least hire someone to come in and teach me?"

Trevor nodded and shuffled his food around on his plate without actually eating it. Sometimes he did that. I think most of the time he didn't eat real food when he was already full on human blood. "I don't see a problem with having a tutor come in and homeschool you."

I breathed a sigh of relief. It would be really nice to see someone else in this house other than Trevor, Alice, and the occasional guard. "Thank you."

"I will look into it immediately and hire someone with excellent credentials."

"Thank you, I'd appreciate that."

And there ended another of our short conversations. He never asked me anything about myself, like what my favorite color was or what I enjoyed doing. Not that I really cared to tell him that stuff anyway…it just baffled me.

Two days later, a tutor arrived. His name was Oscar Williams, and he was not the kind of man you would think would be a school teacher or a tutor. He was hot! Oscar couldn't have been more than twenty-five years old. His hair was a light blond color, and he styled it in kind of a punk spiked style. He always wore a casual jacket over a button up dress shirt and jean. He also rode a motorcycle. I couldn't help but wonder where Trevor had found the guy and what kind of qualifications he could possibly have that would convince Trevor he was good enough to tutor me?

We immediately began lessons. Having someone else to talk to and something purposeful to do was a huge relief. I studied with vigor, impressing Oscar right from the start. He seemed to like my spongy ability to retain everything I learned. I liked that he was impressed.

Alice had a crush on him, too. I saw her more when Oscar was around than I ever did before. If anything, Oscar's presence gave us something juicy to gossip about, and a reason to primp a little more than we had been. I'd been getting so lazy that some days I'd just walk around in sweat pants. But there was no way that I was going to let Oscar see me in them. Alice normally wore her hair in a ponytail, but on the days Oscar came, she would style it. Trevor noticed Alice's changes, too. I could have sworn he acted peeved about it. For the first time, I wondered if he actually cared about her.

In any case, having Oscar around was really nice, and learning stuff was easy with him. Plus, he was full of surprises. Only a week or so after our first tutoring session together, Oscar showed up in my room carrying a big black guitar case.

"What's that?" I asked him, not bothering to sit up. I had been lounging on the couch reading and munching on a big bag of potato chips. At least Trevor was okay with buying me chips. I couldn't get those back home.

He rolled his eyes. "It's a guitar, Chloe. A musical instrument with five strings—"

"I know *what* it is." I cut him off. "Why do you have it?"

"I thought I might play you a song or two." He set the case down on the table and opened it. Inside was a beautiful acoustic guitar. I noticed the body was an awesome teal blue that made me think of tropical water.

He pulled out one of the straight-backed chairs from my little breakfast table and sat with the guitar on his lap.

"Any requests?" he asked, and he strummed once.

I shrugged and shoved a chip into my mouth.

"Play whatever you want." I shifted on the couch until I was sitting up and pulled my legs up onto the couch with me.

He played a slow ballad, a song I did not recognize, but it was beautiful and moving all the same. Even more amazing was when he sang. Oh, my god, I wanted to melt in to a puddle of goo. Wishing the song would never end, I leaned forward, resting my chin on my hands. What I really wanted to do was close my eyes and lose myself in the music, but I just couldn't take my eyes off of him.

When his fingers strummed the last chord of the song, I felt my heart sink. I wanted more. "Can you play another one?"

"Just one more, and then we have to get on with learning." He adjusted himself in the chair and played again. This time, the tune was faster, but my reaction to it was the same. I'd never felt such a pull to someone before, not even Gavin.

That day, he left his guitar in my room and every day thereafter he would play me a song before we started lessons. Alice came into the room for the song as well, and we would both sit like star-struck kids and watch him play.

If, anything, it made the days enjoyable.

XXX

Months passed far faster than I expected they would. The wet, colorful days of spring turned into summer, and I was able to spend more time outside. I didn't like being in the house all the time. It was too confining without any windows to let the light in.

One day in July, after a practice session with my fire power ability, I quietly slipped inside the house and took my shoes off by the front door so I wouldn't track anything all over the beautiful floors Alice had spent so much time cleaning. I hurried upstairs.

The silence of the house was thick. I had noticed several times recently that I could almost hear the air as it passed by my ears. On my way down the hallway, I heard a slight clanking noise coming from the opposite end of the hall from my room.

Knowing Alice was downstairs asleep and Trevor's rooms were also downstairs, I decided to check it out. I turned around and crept silently over the carpet, listening as closely as I could.

I was actually a little afraid some random vampire might be roaming around, and I had nothing to protect myself.

Wait, I did have something.

I stopped for a moment and closed my eyes. I flexed my hands by opening and closing them, pulling energy from around me, letting it fill me up. I opened my eyes and continued down the hall. Another sound came from the room Trevor had said not to go in because he used it for his office. I was kind of nosey, but I had never had the urge to go in there. The noise sounded more like a squeak that time.

I came to a stop in front of the door and took a deep breath, wondering if it would be better to try to open the door quietly or to fling it open and storm inside. I flexed my hands again and reached for the knob.

"Stop hovering out there and open the door, Chloe."

I jumped back away from the door at the sound of Trevor's voice. I hadn't realized I'd been holding my breath and my heart was beating rapidly in my chest. I let out a long, slow breath before I grasped the handle and opened the door.

The first thing I noticed about his office was the gigantic desk made of a heavy dark wood. It was littered with stacks of books, and papers were scattered across it. It was a little shocking, because Trevor was normally such a neat freak. The laptop sitting amongst the clutter kind of ticked me off, too.

The next thing I noticed was that the room had a window. It

was covered by thick curtains, but they were left open just a crack, just enough to let sunlight stream through, leaving a long strip of light that cut across the carpet.

Trevor sat leaning back in his office chair with his legs stretched out in front of him and crossed at the ankles. He was staring at the stream of light that was only mere inches away from his feet.

"What are you doing?" I asked, approaching him.

He looked depressed. He looked how I felt when I thought about everyone at the community. I missed them something fierce.

His gaze didn't stray from the light. "I am dreaming of the past and wishing for the future." He waved his hand toward the chair on the other side of his desk. "Please, sit with me."

I dragged the chair beside his so we could stare at the strip of sunlight together. Like him, I kicked my feet out in front of me and crossed them. After about three minutes of complete silence, I asked him "Why are you sitting here staring at sunshine on the floor."

He almost cracked a grin. "Do you know what a vampire most desires, Chloe?"

"Blood?"

He shook his head. "No, most vampires detest having to drink blood. We do love it, and we do desire it, when the bloodlust kicks in, but it is most certainly *not* what we desire most."

"Well, I don't know then."

He rocked his chair a little bit. "I have not rested my eyes upon a sunrise for almost a thousand years. I rarely see any sunlight, other than shafts shining onto a floor or wall." He gestured at the floor, "The daylight is my enemy, an enemy I shall never defeat. A vampire most desires what he cannot have, the sunlight. The day."

I bowed my head. "Oh."

"What do you most desire, Chloe."

I thought for a moment before answering. "I've never really thought about it. I don't know... my mother I guess, if we're talking things we want but can never have."

He ignored my sass, like he usually did. He simply nodded.

About two months later, we were having dinner and Trevor made a surprising announcement. "Chloe, tomorrow night, we are going to entertain some friends. I think it's time I introduce you."

I raised my eyebrows. "Why haven't you asked them over

before to introduce me?"

"I've asked them to stay away to give you time to adjust." He pushed his full plate away, looking irritated. "Alice," he called out. She popped her head around the corner. "Would you bring me a glass of the reserve wine?"

"Yes, Mr. Trevor." She disappeared.

"Well, I don't know why you would ask them to stay away just because I'm here. There is no reason to live your life any differently than you did before," I told him. Really, the last thing I wanted to do was meet any of his blood-sucking buddies.

"I was concerned with how you would react in a room full of vampires. Now, you are more acquainted with our ways, so it will not be such a shock, and my friends will be coming around more."

I sensed there was more to it than just my needing to adjust. "Is that the only reason?" I questioned. "Should I be worried about something?

Trevor sighed and pushed his chair out a bit, then crossed his legs.

Curious, I caught his eyes and raised my eyebrows in question.

Finally, he relented and explained. "I simply could not take any chances with you, your mother..."

I felt my spine stiffen. "What about my mother?" I demanded.

He ran a hand through his dark hair, smoothing it down. "Your mother lived with me for about a year. During that time, she was attacked by one of my men. I will not take that chance with you."

I think I snorted a little bit. "Really? Because, when you had all your goons attacking my family all those times, that was me in danger... that was you taking a chance with me."

"That is hardly the case, Chloe. I had ordered that you were to be taken alive."

I felt myself heating up. "Are you crazy? I was still in danger of being killed!"

"Why must you always be so insolent? I simply will not continue to tolerate your attitude. You are here now and must accept things the way they are."

"Fine." I crossed my arms. "What should I wear?"

He looked thoughtful, tilting his head and staring at me as if he were imagining me in a certain dress or something. "There are several dresses in the armoire in your room. You should pick out one of those to wear."

"Can I go shopping tomorrow?" As much as I hated shopping, I wanted the illusion of freedom and going off the property would have allowed me that.

Alice came back with his wine and sat it in front of him. He looked up at her briefly and then dismissed her with a slight nod. Jeez, what an ass. Alice smiled and nodded at me on her way out of the room.

"No, you cannot go shopping. There is no time. Besides, if you were to leave the grounds, I would want to go with you."

"Oscar could go with me," I hopefully suggested.

"Chloe, there are dresses upstairs. You don't need to go buy one. It's only a simple dinner party."

"Fine." I pouted and looked down at my food. I should have known better, but I also didn't like him having so much control. It felt awful not having any say in what I was going to wear.

After dinner I went upstairs and opened the armoire. There were four dresses there. I immediately cut the blue one because it was more of a formal gown, all fluffy and stuff. The next dress was red, and even though I looked good in red, I thought it was too flashy for a dinner party. The green one was a color that reminded me of Christina and her hooker dress, so that left the always dependable little black dress.

While I tried it on, I considered showing up in jeans and my Harley shirt. Strangely, I ended up surprised how nicely the dress fit and how appropriate it was. It had a skirt that stopped just above my knees, the neckline was scooped and the straps were about an inch wide. I ran my hands over my hips, feeling the soft cottony fabric beneath my fingertips. It felt good, so I decided to wear it. After digging around a bit, I found a pair of open-toed heels that matched in the bottom of the armoire.

$$\times\times\times$$

The next night, after the sun went down, Alice rushed around trying to prepare everything for the guests. Hired help prepared food in the kitchen, and I chased Alice around, asking her every two minutes if there was anything I could do to help.

"Stop asking me that and go sit down or something!" she finally snapped at me, pointing at the couch. I was about to do just that when the doorbell rang. Expecting vampire guests, I wandered slowly to the door and pulled it open. It was a complete surprise when I saw Oscar on the other side.

"What are you doing here?"

"I was invited," he told me and stepped inside.

I closed the door behind him. For some reason, I felt like a puddle of goo whenever Oscar was around. I just couldn't place the feeling.

"I didn't know you socialized with vampires," I said, attempting to tease him.

"When I am invited by one of the most prominent vampires in the supernatural community, I certainly do socialize with them." He shrugged out of his coat and hung it on the tall rack in the entryway.

"Well, come on then." I waved him into the house. "No one else is here yet, but they should be soon."

Oscar regarded me with slanted eyes. "You're nervous."

I nodded. "Yes, yeah, I'm very nervous." I paused. "What if one of them wants to eat me or something?"

Oscar laughed "I highly doubt that one of them would try anything like that here, even if they did want to eat you."

"It's not funny, Oscar. I'm actually a little scared."

The back of my neck tingled just as the doorbell rang again. I wondered if that tingling thing was ever going to go away. I glanced at Oscar and raised my eyebrows. Well, there wasn't much else I could do except get it over with. I turned and opened the door.

On the other side, framed by the darkness, stood a man and a woman. We examined each other for a moment. He was tall, with dark hair and bright blue eyes and was dressed in black slacks and a dark blue button up shirt. His arm was protectively wrapped around the waist of his lady friend.

She was a pale goddess. Blond ringlets cascaded her back to her waistline. Her skin was so smooth, like porcelain. I wanted to reach out and touch it. She had big, wide, grey eyes, and she wore a dress almost the same color. The dress was classy: tight-fitting, touched the knees, showed just enough cleavage, elegant sleeves. I liked it.

"Hello, I'm Chloe." I greeted them and opened the door wider. "Come in."

"I am Vincent." He ushered the blond inside. "This is Dahlia."

He held out his hand for me to shake once they were fully inside and I was able to shut the door. I grasped his cool hand and nodded.

"It's a pleasure to finally meet you."

He smiled at me, showing me his perfect white teeth. I couldn't see any fangs.

"I'm happy to meet you as well." I told him. "Have you met Oscar?"

Oscar stepped forward with his hand extended. "I don't believe I've had the pleasure. I'm Oscar Williams, Chloe's tutor."

I glanced at Dahlia and saw her watery, grey eyes scale up and down Oscar's body and briefly flashed with red.

Oh, my gosh!

I hoped she wouldn't try to drink *his* blood while he was here. I thought *I* was going to be the only one I had to worry about.

Before I could worry about it too much, the doorbell rang again. This time the couple in the doorway were women, both dark haired, dark eyed and dressed to impress. I escorted them in, introduced myself and learned their names were Vanessa and Constance.

"Do you know Vincent and Dahlia?" I questioned as we approached the couple, who were speaking with Oscar in the hallway. Vanessa shrugged out of her wrap, and held it out for me to take. I stared at her for a moment before grabbing it from her and hanging it on the coat hook.

What was I, her maid?

Immediately, I took back the mental comment, because of Alice.

"Yes, I'm quite familiar with Vincent and Dahlia." She practically purred Dahlia's name and ran her fingertips down the length of the other woman's arm.

Uh, weird.

I was beginning to think all these vampires were kind of perverted. Maybe that was another reason Trevor had told them to stay away. Before I could wonder about their odd relationships, the doorbell sounded again. Trevor swept into the room in his usual black clothing, only this time instead of jean, he wore black slacks and button up shirt.

"I'm so glad you all could make it." He greeted his guests on his way to the door. Vincent, Dahlia and all the rest of us moved into the living room to mingle while Trevor ordered Alice to answer the door and take coats.

Trevor made formal introductions. Turned out Vincent was his business associate. For some reason, when he told me that, I thought of Eli and how my mother made it sound like *he* was Trevor's main man.

I stuck closely to Oscar's side and spent as much time helping Alice as I could. At dinner, the twelve of us sat at the table. I was bombarded with questions: How did I like it here? What did my mother tell me about my father? Did I have any vampire abilities? The list went on and on. I lied about all of them. Lying seemed to be something I was good at lately. Funny, I could never get one by my mother.

I thought it was just the dumbest thing that vampires were all sitting around a dinner table and they didn't even eat. The whole dinner plate thing was probably just to give them something to play with while they questioned me.

Alice came in and out, serving us the courses and keeping our glasses full. Everyone's goblets were full of some kind of blood wine mixture while mine only had water. Oscar had opted for a beer. I didn't even know we had beer in the house.

Trevor sat at the head of the table while I sat directly to his right. "Chloe, would you like some of the wine?"

Oh, how I desperately did want some of that wine. If it was anything like what my own blood tasted like, then yes, I wanted some. But, I knew what weakened me, and I knew what I was here for. I didn't want to become a vampire. I wanted to kill them.

"No, thank you. I'll just stick to water."

Trevor nodded and then proceeded to question the rather ugly looking male vampire to his left. Vanessa sat on the other side of me and Dahlia straight across the table. Dahlia, seemed like a quiet one. She hadn't said anything since she had arrived. Suddenly, I felt a hand on my leg.

My head snapped over and I glared into Vanessa's dark eyes.

"Take your hands off me," I hissed at her under my breath.

"Oh, honey," she whispered back. "I will place my hands anywhere I damned well please."

"Take them off," I repeated.

In complete defiance of my wishes, she ran her hand up farther onto my thigh. What the heck was wrong with this chick? Well, if she wanted to play with fire, she picked the right person. I looked into her eyes and smiled, then reached underneath the table. I used my fingertips, to gently walk her short dress up until enough skin was exposed. I then rested my hand on the cold bare skin of her thigh.

Everyone around us was chatting, not paying any attention to what was happening between us. Vanessa smiled and ran a fingernail over my skin.

I gave her one more chance. "I *said*, Take your hand off me."

She leaned in like she wanted to tell me a secret.

"Why don't you make me, *Hunter*."

I closed my eyes and pulled in the energy in the air around me, channeling it down to my hand where I wanted to release it.

"Ow, damn it!" Vanessa screamed and jumped up out of her seat, snatching her hand off my thigh.

"Vanessa!" I exclaimed, feigning surprise, like I hadn't just burn her. "What happened? Are you all right?"

I hadn't used fire. I had only warmed my hand, but against her cold vampire skin, it probably felt like she had been scorched. Our eyes locked. She read my silent message loud and clear: Touch me again and it will be worse.

She shook her head. "It's nothing. I'm sorry. I haven't eaten all day and my stomach is paining me today." She caught Trevor's eyes. "You know how it feels when you haven't eaten."

Trevor assessed the situation. I almost certain he knew she had lied.

"Alice!" he called out. His eyes held Vanessa's. When Alice appeared, he asked, "Would you take Vanessa downstairs and assist her? Her stomach is *paining* her."

Alice understood the code he spoke and nodded. "Yes, sir. Come with me, Miss Vanessa."

Oh, my gosh! He meant for Alice to give herself to Vanessa, to give her blood. I didn't even know there was a downstairs from the main floor. I thought we were downstairs. I wanted to get up and go after them, but I knew I couldn't. I knew Trevor would never let me near whatever was going on. I barely touched anything else on my plate for the rest of the meal because I was so nervous.

When the meal was finally over, I felt relief wash over my body, except for needing to pee. The vampires rose and spread through the house, mingling and talking about one of the nightclubs Trevor owned—apparently one Vanessa ran for him—and how they needed to find a way to keep the hairballs out.

I didn't know why there would be a problem with hairballs in a bar. I shrugged it off and hurried down the hall to the bathroom. Before I could turn the knob, I heard voices on the other side.

"Do you think she knows?" I recognized Constance's whispered voice.

I heard a giggle followed by Vanessa saying, "She doesn't have a clue. I hope he drains the little bitch dry. I'm sick of her already. Even though she smells wonderful, she is a pain in the ass. I don't know why Trevor insisted on bringing her here so early."

"He had to. He had to make sure she was here when she turned sixteen. It would have been really taking a chance to wait until closer to her birthday," Constance answered.

What the... What were they talking about? It had to be me.

"Yeah, I guess," Vanessa answered. She sighed audibly. I could just see Vanessa on the other side of the door, glossing her pale lips in the mirror. "I can see that, considering she had all those Hunters around who never left her alone."

Constance lowered her voice even more. "I'll tell you what, if I knew I'd get away with it, I'd snag her up and keep her for myself. The ability to walk in the sunlight would make me the most powerful vampire. Trevor doesn't deserve it. We do all the work for him anyway."

"Shut up, Constance," Vanessa hissed. "Talking like that will just get you killed. What if someone hears you?"

What the heck is going on?

I felt my heartbeat and my body shook violently. It wasn't clear exactly what they had meant, but it was clear I was in trouble. Big trouble.

Constance told Vanessa she needed to shut up, that she would say whatever she wanted. I turned around and crashed right into Alice, who had been standing behind me. I had been so intent on listening to the conversation on the other side of the door, I hadn't heard her approach.

She took a step back to steady herself and looked at me with sadness in her eyes.

"Did you know about this?" I demanded in a whisper.

She took two steps back and lowered her head. I took that as my answer and balled my fists. I lurched forward, grabbed her by the throat and slammed her against the wall. "I should kill you! How could you?"

She only shook her head a bit while tears slipped from the corners of her eyes and ran down her cheeks onto my hand. Fury washed over me and I could feel my hands getting hot. Alice winced in pain and squirmed against the wall.

"What is going on out here?"

Vanessa and Constance came out of the bathroom and saw me standing there holding Alice by her throat. I looked over my shoulder and watched them stop short, stare at me for a moment and then instinct kicked in. Before they could do anything to stop me, I ran.

I ran as fast as I could through the house and out the front door. I heard the women screaming at Trevor, "She knows! She's running!"

They chased me out the door.

Even though I knew in the back of my mind there was no possibility I could outrun them, I kept going. When I hit the lawn, with my mind racing, I decided to take a chance and stopped. I turned around to face them, lifted my arms into the air, palms out toward them, mustered all the energy I could and forced it toward them. From each of my palms, huge bursts of fire flew forward, curling and licking as the air gave it more fuel.

Vanessa and Constance, not expecting me to have such a weapon, ran right into the flames. Their awful, screeching, banshee-like wails penetrated the air all around us. I saw more coming out the front door and bolted.

I picked up my speed as much as I could, running like I'd never run before. I knew the wall was coming soon, and I had no idea what I was going to do except try to jump. I heard more footfalls behind me.

Damned vampire speed.

When I was about three yards away from the walled fence, I willed my weight to be as light as I could. I sprang into the air and almost made it, but not quite high enough.

I caught the edge of the stone fence with my hands and held on. My legs dangled halfway down for anyone to grab and yank me down. My hands hurt like hell, but I managed to swing my legs up and over just when one of the vampires reached the fence and grabbed for me. I literally fell over the other side and down onto a ton of branches and bushes.

"Ouch!" I cried out, feeling a stick jab its way into my leg. I didn't take any time to worry about it. I turned over on my hands and knees, getting ready to stand, when suddenly my head was yanked backward by my hair.

"Gotcha!" a male voice cried out triumphantly. "Got her," he called even louder.

I tried to turn my head, but his grasp was too tight.

"Let me go!" I screamed, willing the energy again. I tried to pull it over my whole body. A sudden ripping noise echoed through the darkness and unlike the times before when I didn't expect it, I *willed* the fire to engulf me, feeling it surround me like a force field.

The guard released my hair and I was free. I began to run again, pulling the fire out with my mind as I flew over twigs, fallen branches and rocks of the forest floor.

Then there was a gunshot.

My mind told me to stop, but my feet kept going. It never occurred to me they might try to shoot me.

"Stop this instant, Chloe!" It was Trevor's voice carrying through the air, but I didn't stop. "I *will* shoot you. I do not have to kill you to stop you. I can shoot you in the leg."

I didn't want to get shot, especially if he wasn't going to kill me. Yeah, that's right; he wanted me alive for some reason.

I stopped.

"Go ahead!" I cried out, turning around to face him. I spread my arms wide open and pulled some flames up for him to see. "Shoot me, and we both go down in flames."

I watched him step forward across the forest floor, his white face so pale against the night. "Do you really think that power you possess could possibly reach farther than a bullet from this weapon?"

I hated him more than ever.

He shook his head. "Now, come with me back to the house and we will talk."

"The last thing in the world I want to do is talk to you. Just let me go."

"I'm sorry, but I need you far too much to let you go anywhere."

Discreetly, I placed my feet and prepared to run again.

"I wouldn't do that." He waggled the gun in his hand. "Let's go."

I had no choice but to follow him. I wasn't going to be able to get away. My superpower wasn't so super after all if a modern weapon could outdo it.

"You would really shoot me, your own daughter?"

I swallowed the fear and stepped toward him.

"If I had to I would, as long as it kept you alive."

I continued past him in the direction of the house. "You're sick, Trevor, like…mental institution sick."

He followed behind me a few steps. "Possibly," he replied.

Once we were back at the fence, we followed it around until we reached a guard who punched a key code into a little pad on the fence. The gate of the fence swung open. With a nudge from Trevor, I stepped through the opening and onto the lawn.

I could see the vampire guests and Oscar standing on the porch, looking in our direction. Things were getting serious and it looked like my chances of killing Trevor had just gone straight down the tubes.

As we approached the porch I watched Vanessa eyeball me and Constance raised her eyebrows, turning her lips up in a smug grin. I grinned back and pointed at her. "Watch out for those two, Trevor, I heard them talking about taking me for themselves and how they do all your work so you don't deserve to have the power."

If anything about that night was satisfying, it would have to be getting them in trouble with Trevor. It was awesome. I watched both of their mouths drop open and their eyes widened with fear. Only then did it occur to me that maybe they didn't know that I'd heard the *whole* conversation they had in the bathroom until I busted them out.

Oscar followed me with his eyes as I walked past him in my torn and dirty dress.

"You knew too?" I whispered, aware all the vampires were watching us.

Oscar didn't lower his eyes in shame or turn away, but he said nothing.

"Trevor planted you here, didn't he?" Without taking his eyes off me, he nodded. Aside from Alice being a traitor too, Oscar being a spy was something I didn't see coming and was far more disappointing than I would have expected. If I got the chance, I'd kick his ass too.

"Go on. Move. Get in the house." I felt the nudge of Trevor's gun in my back. "I'm so sorry, but I'm afraid the evening must come to an end now. I have an issue with my daughter I need to address."

"It was so nice to meet you all," I called out sarcastically and even took a chance of getting shot by waving to them as I stepped into the house. Trevor kept the gun pressed into my back, following right on my heels. "Can you put that thing down? I'm not going to try anything."

"Once we have you safe in your room."

I couldn't help but laugh a little, "Really? Now you want me safe?"

He grabbed me by the arm with one of his strong hands and pulled me up the stairs. When we reached my room, he kicked open the doors and shoved me inside.

I whirled to face him. "What the hell is going on here? What exactly is it that you want me for?"

I crossed my arms over my chest and locked gazes with him.

"Sit down." He waved the gun at the couch.

"I don't want to sit. I want you to tell me what the hell is going on here!" My gaze moved to his hands and zeroed in on his gun. "Is that *my* gun? Seriously, don't you have your own?"

He didn't answer me. He stepped just outside the door, leaving the gun trained on me and moved aside one of the photographs on the wall, exposing some kind of switch. He flipped it and a loud clank echoed through the walls.

"What is that?"

Again, he didn't answer. He let the picture fall back into place, came back into the room just as some kind of metal sheeting emerged from the ceiling, covering the walls and everything on them.

Appalled, I looked up and down, back and forth, watching the metal slowly imprison me.

"You truly thought I didn't know about your little gift? He pulled out a straight-backed chair from the table and sat in it, crossing his legs.

I continued to stand.

How in the hell will I ever get out of this room now?

My mind raced ahead of actual time. I knew I was going to be left alone at some point, and I needed an escape route.

As though he had read my thoughts, he said, "I've fireproofed the entire room, even the furniture and carpet are resistant. Not completely fireproof, but resistant. If you light it up, sprinklers will extract from the ceiling, so using your fire won't do you any good in here."

"How did you even know about it?"

"I've known since my vampires tried to bring you back once

before, the day you broke your arm. Shelia managed to escape you and the other Hunters. She immediately came back here to report why they hadn't returned with you."

I finally went to the couch and plopped down onto it. "Why didn't you say anything?"

"I do not have cause to voice my reasons to anyone. You are no exception."

"At least tell me why I'm here. You owe me that much."

I leaned back on the couch, put my feet up on the coffee table and waited for him to talk.

He uncrossed his legs and then crossed them the other way. "All right. I suppose I should explain it to you now."

He paused, turned his head away for a moment and stared at a far point on the wall. I refused to break the silence and speak first, so I sat and waited for him. Eventually, he sighed and then turned back to face me.

"Do you remember the conversation we had about what a vampire most desires?" he asked.

I nodded, but stayed silent.

"Above all else, a vampire desires the sunlight. To be able to walk about under the deadly rays of daylight would make any creature of the night extremely powerful, simply because of what he can do. Not only powerful, but I could experience something I have not experienced—and have missed—for hundreds, if not thousands, of years."

"About a year before I met your mother, I came across a book that contained a recipe for a vampire to become a day walker." He paused and let that sink in. "This recipe called for the vampire in question to drink the entire blood supply of a dhampir, who is also half Hunter, on the day the dhampir turns sixteen. As you know, both dhampir and Hunter are rare to come by. So, instead of searching the world with minimal chance of finding someone with those traits, I found a woman with whom I could make my own."

I felt my stomach turn over and lurch. I even gagged. "You... you... *bred* me. You used my mother to make me for your sick desires?"

It took every ounce of control I had not to jump over and strangle him. Like that would do any good anyway, being that he was dead already.

"I did love your mother. I didn't think I would, but sometimes things don't always turn out the way you want them to. I never intended to tell her my plans for you. I would have staged an accident to explain your death in order to keep her with me."

My jaw hung open. I was speechless.

"Don't look so shocked, Chloe. I never treated your mother badly. I loved her, and if we could have one child, then we could have others. Everyone would have been happy."

He sighed. I closed my mouth.

"When Felicia found my books and research papers containing all the information about my plan, she ran, escaped with you in her womb."

I watched his facial expression fade until he appeared to be far away and lost in thought.

"She loved you so much without even knowing you... she ran from me to protect you."

I planted my hands on my hips and stomped my foot. "I'm tired of hearing all this crap about how much you loved my mother. You are a lying bastard, and I *hate* you. I should blow us both to bits right now."

He shrugged, calling my bluff and then stood, challenging me, seeming almost hopeful. "Yes, I figured as much," he said, actually sounding disappointed when I did nothing but stand there. "You are going to stay in here. If you try any funny business, like trying to burn the place down, you will be removed from this room and taken elsewhere. And believe me, this room is far better than the alternative."

He backed away from me, toward the door. I was fuming, my hands were hot... they were just begging for me to bring on the fire.

"Go to hell," I told him as he slipped outside the door and shut it.

I heard a lock click inside the door and voices outside.

Great. He probably had one of his goons standing outside the door, just in case I decided to try any "funny business."

As soon as I heard the lock click, I rushed to the door and put my hands on the cold metal. I tried the door, even though I knew it wouldn't open and then felt along the walls for gaps or seams. The only gap was the one where the doorframe was. I ran my fingers over it and then tried to get my fingers inside it but couldn't because they were just a tad too big. *Damn it.*

Panicking, I racked my brain, trying to remember if I had

anything in the room that would fit in that crevice. I spun around, rushed to the desk and rummaged through things on top of it, trashing the place in the process. My hands finally fell onto a wooden ruler. It would have to do.

I gripped it and ran back to the door. It barely fit in the tiny gap. I wanted to pry the metal away from the door and to see how pliable it was. Sadly, the ruler snapped on the first try.

"Piece of crap!" I screamed to the empty room and chucked the broken ruler half at the door.

How could he call me his daughter? Better yet, how could he call himself a father? Sick, daylight-obsessed, murdering vampire!

"Arrgggh!" I yelled and kicked the door several times.

Suddenly, the anger diminished. I'd never felt a change so sudden. One second I was kicking the wall, the next I was on the floor crying, really crying, not just tearing up, but tears drenching my face, snot dripping out of my nose and all the mascara I'd put on for the party smearing around my eyes.

Sitting wasn't good enough. I fell to the side, laying on the floor and curled up as much as I could into the fetal position. I tried meditational breathing to stop the panic. Slow breath in the nose, exhale through the mouth. In...out. My little black dress was dirty and torn, but I had no desire to take it off. And my leg was stinging from where the stick had punctured my skin when I went over the wall.

I have no idea how long I lay there, bawling my eyes out, but eventually I heard the locks release again. I didn't even move. I just stayed where I was, wishing Drew and Gavin and the rest of the Hunter's would hear my mental plea and come for me.

I was in serious trouble.

When the door opened, someone slipped quietly inside.

Whoever was there must have just stood there watching me, because I didn't hear anything after the door sealed again. After a few minutes of complete silence, I heard, "Chloe, are you all right?"

It was Oscar, the traitor.

"Go away, you phony. Just get away from me."

"I just came to get my guitar," he told me. Instead of getting his guitar, he crouched down right in front of my face. I squeezed my eyes shut, trying to block him out.

"I'm sorry," he whispered.

There was no way I was going to let him get to me. He betrayed me.

"I didn't know what Trevor had planned for you, Chloe, but I did know he needed you to become a day walker. I had no idea he meant to kill you."

I opened my eyes. "How could you?"

He grabbed my hands and tried to pull me into a sitting position. I burned him for his efforts.

"Ow! Damn it, Chloe!" He yanked his hands away from me and stood. "Why did you do that?"

"Why do you think? You don't get to touch me." I rolled over and faced the other way.

"Damn it. You have to listen to me."

I could hear the frustration in his voice, but I didn't care. I was going to die here, and he had helped.

"I didn't know the whole story. The reason I was called on to tutor you was to keep you occupied. To keep you from wanting to leave here."

"Whatever, Oscar. You're not *that* hot."

I heard him pace the floor beside me a couple times. "I can make you do whatever I want, Chloe. Just as you are descended from angels and gods, I am descended from the ancient sirens."

Seriously? Would the mythology and supernatural crap never end? I rolled back over and sat up. "You're a *what*?"

"A siren. Mythological women who could lure men with the sound of their beautiful voices." Sarcasm was thick on his voice.

"I know what a siren is, but you're a… a guy."

I am descended from the sirens, so I have traits. Just as you are a Hunter and have certain traits of the gods."

"Ugh! This is completely insane. Why did you agree to this?"

"I don't know if you noticed, but you're father pretty much runs the vampire community. I'm not about to deny him when he asks me to do something."

"You suck." I moaned, planting my face into my hands. "How am I ever going to get out of here?"

"Look at me, Chloe."

"No!"

"Look at me!" His voice didn't become angrier, it softened.

"What?" I barely whispered.

"Give me a hug." He held his arms open.

Even as I went to him, I was thinking, *Why in hell am I hugging this jerk?*

Then, his arms were around me and it felt good. I needed the human contact. There truly was some comfort in his touch.

He pulled my head close to his and whispered into my hair. "There are cameras in here. I will do everything I can to help you. I'll make this up to you, but I will die if I'm caught."

Finally alert, I whispered back, "If you get me out, I promise you protection."

He released me and nodded. He backed away and turned to grab his guitar case. "It's been nice knowing you, Chloe. I'm truly sorry."

With some hope finally rushing through my body, I played up the show a bit. "See you in hell, asshole."

Lifting his fist to the metal on the door he rapped on it a couple times. The locks released and he slipped out. Only seconds later, I heard the locks click back into place.

"Damn it," I whispered and went into my bedroom. I flopped onto the bed and stared at the ceiling, thinking.

Well, it was September, so that meant I was a least going to be safe until November. I still had a few months to figure out a plan. There had to be a way to get out of here. Maybe he was lying about the sprinklers and stuff. I tried looking harder at the ceiling to see if I could find any evidence of hidden sprinklers. It was pretty far up, but nothing I could see indicated there were any up there.

Oh well. I'd just burn myself alive if I tried lighting the place up. I hated being trapped. I jumped up and tore the dress off my body. I wanted to get clean. I really hoped there weren't any cameras in the bathroom, even though I knew chances on that were slim.

I stuck the dress into the trashcan and turned the water on in the shower. I let it run for a few minutes and then stepped underneath. The water was hotter than I expected, but the sting on my skin felt good, because it was washing away dirt and grime, the filth of the evening.

I closed my eyes and tipped my head back, letting the water rush down over my face and shoulders, down my hair and back. I breathed in deeply through my nose and exhaled through my mouth. I wished for the Hunters—for my family—most of all, for my mother.

I opened my eyes and reached for the towel hanging over the door. I wiped the water out of my eyes before they could begin to sting and pulled the towel away.

When I opened my eyes, Sostrate was there, in the shower with me.

"Ah!" I Screamed. "What are you doing here?" I tried to cover myself with my hands. When that wasn't sufficient I yanked the towel off the door and held it over myself.

"Shhh…" Sostrate held her finger to her lips. "This is the only safe place to speak with you."

Her face and body were surrounded with steam, but I could see she wore the same crude leather over the only areas that needed to be covered. Her beautiful dark hair was loose and flowing. The water didn't seem to touch her body at all.

"What are you doing here?" I whispered.

"Do you not need me?"

"Of course I need you! I need to get out of this house. I need to get back home before my own father kills me."

"There isn't much time," she leaned in to whisper to me. "This place is the only place you will not be seen."

"Great," I muttered.

"Chloe, on the other side of this wall is the outside." She touched the wall above the faucet. "You can escape."

I think she forgot that the wall was completely tiled over. "Sostrate, this is a shower wall. Those tiles are grouted in there." Even as I spoke, I realized what she was telling me.

"You can do this." She told me in a whisper, and then she shimmered and faded into the steam.

Quickly, I moved to her side of the shower and inspected the wall. It was the only part of the walls in the whole suite that wasn't covered with steel. The tiles were small, blue squares, sealed in with grout. I'd once seen my mother re-tile the back splash in our kitchen.

She was right. I could do this.

I washed my hair as fast as I could and scrubbed the grime off my body. After I turned the shower off I wrapped myself in the wet towel and sped over to the shelf where the dry towels were. I wanted as little naked time in front of the cameras as possible.

I finally wrapped the dry towel around myself and threw the wet one into the shower. Then, I opened the medicine cabinet behind the mirror and searched around. I needed something for my puncture wound on my thigh. The bottle of peroxide was hidden behind the bandages. I grabbed both and sat on the toilet to pour the peroxide onto the wound. Afterward I covered it with the bandage and hoped it would heal itself like my finger did that time.

Back out in my bedroom, I shrugged into my sweats and began to plan. It looked like I was going to be spending a lot of time in the shower.

✗ ✗ ✗

I smelled breakfast before I even opened my eyes. The scent invaded my dreams, forcing my eyes to open so that I could go and discover what was causing that delicious smell. As soon as I opened my eyes, I rolled onto my back and stretched, and then immediately regretted it because every part of me ached at the slightest move.

Wonderful.

I peeled back the blankets and sat up with my feet hanging over the bed. If it wasn't for hunger, I would have just laid in bed all day, sulking.

After about five minutes of sitting there, I finally got up and shuffled into the bathroom. I peed as quickly as I could. I wasn't sure if there were cameras aimed at me, and the last thing in the world I wanted was people seeing me pee. After that, I opened the medicine cabinet and grabbed the bottle of over the counter pain reliever I'd seen the night before.

I poured two into my hand. After a few seconds of contemplation, I added another one in the hope they would kick in quickly. I closed the lid on the toilet and sat so I could gently pull the bandage off the wound on my thigh. As I suspected, nothing was there. The only evidence of the injury was a thin, white, misshapen scar.

Well, at least that was one less thing to worry about.

After tossing the used bandage into the waste basket, I wandered back into the sitting room and found the breakfast that had smelled so good consisted of hash browns; eggs, over easy; sausage links, and toast.

It surprised me he was feeding me so well, although I knew Alice had most of the say in what was done in the kitchen. I kind of figured I might be made to eat bread and water for the next several months.

Alice was damned lucky I hadn't been awake when she brought the cart up though. I still wanted to finish things with her.

While I ate, I tried to ignore the fact I watched by cameras. I also suspected there were far more vampires in the house now that I wasn't allowed to roam about.

Crap.

When I finished eating, I put my napkin on top of my plate and turned to get up. Intentionally, but making it look like an accident, I brushed all of my silverware and the half full glass of orange juice onto the floor.

"Dang it!" I muttered loudly. "Just great."

I grabbed the napkin off of my plate and got down on my hands and knees. I wasn't really sure where exactly the cameras were, but I had to take a chance.

Using the napkin, I scrubbed away at the juice and discreetly placed my knee over the butter knife. After scrubbing it sufficiently I leaned over just a tad and used the napkin to wrap the silverware, except the butter knife, which I quickly slid into my boot.

I crawled backward and stood. I set the bundle and glass on the table, making some annoyed noises for the show, even though I was actually triumphant.

With the intention of killing some time and making it look like I was just bored, I wandered over to the couch and flopped onto it, stretching out with my feet up. I turned on the TV and flipped through the channels, trying to find something interesting. I stopped at "Blade." I'd forgotten about him. He was supposed to be a vampire hunter too, and like me, was half vampire.

Interesting. At least there was something besides reality shows to watch while I waited. I never could understand how people could watch those. Like real life didn't have enough drama, people wanted to go watch someone else's on TV.

I let my mind go a bit numb and was deep into watching Blade kick ass, when the door locks released.

I looked over and watched a tall male vampire slip inside the door, head straight to the breakfast table without even glancing my way, and cleared the used dishes onto the cart.

"Hey!" I hollered at him.

Obviously, he knew I was there, because he glanced over and nodded at me.

"I just came in to get the cart," he told me.

"Well, have fun being Trevor's little maid," I said to him, turning back to Blade.

He didn't bother responding; he hurried back to the door and rapped on it.

"It's me," he called out to whoever was on the other side. The locks released, and he wheeled the cart through the open door, and then quickly shut it. Again, the locks slid back into place, the sound confirming my imprisonment.

After Blade was over, I got up and messed around with the stuff on my desk for a while, organizing and straightening. When I thought enough time had passed, I grabbed a book off the shelf and went into the bathroom.

I slid open the door on the tub and set my book down on the ledge, started the water and flipped the stopper. I bent and tested the temperature of the water and then looked around for bubble bath, when I found some vanilla scented bubbles, I dumped an ungodly amount underneath the stream of water and watched the bubbles begin to form.

While the tub filled, I put my hair way up on top of my head in a big bun. I backtracked into my bedroom to the closet. With every ounce of my being, I hoped the closet didn't have a camera inside. I opened the door and stepped inside. I bent over to take off my boots. Discreetly, I slid my hand down into my boot, like I was trying get the boot off my foot, and palmed the butter knife. I stood and slid the butter knife beneath the waistband of my pants and underwear. It fitted snugly against my skin. At the same time, I lifted my left hand and sifted through the hanging clothes for a shirt. Feeling certain the knife was safely hidden, I ripped a shirt off a hanger without really looking at it and backed out of the closet.

Back in the bathroom, I checked the tub. Seeing it was full and almost overflowing with vanilla bubbles, I shut off the water and grabbed a fluffy white towel. I hated the fact that there were cameras in the bathroom. I knew I was taking it for granted Oscar's comment about being videotaped was true, but I couldn't take a chance, because it was more likely than not.

First, I took off my shirt and wrapped the towel completely around my body. Only then did I remove my pants. I had to be really careful while I was taking them off. Luckily, it probably looked to whoever was watching like I was just sore from the escape attempt the night before. I wiggled gently out of them, holding the towel closed around my private areas.

It also occurred to me I wasn't supposed to know that there were cameras. Realistically, it wouldn't matter if Oscar had told me or not. Trevor knew I was smart enough to know he'd been watching me outside with cameras, so it wouldn't be strange for me to assume cameras would be installed in my rooms. He managed to lock me inside a metal prison. Why not watch what I'm up to as well?

After getting in the tub, I shut the door and quickly removed the towel and put the knife underneath the water, on the floor of the tub. I hung the towel over the top of the door. Finally, I could strip off my bra and panties. I opened the door a crack and let them fall to the floor.

Whew. The hardest part was over. Only then did I realize my heart was beating wildly in my chest. I released a huge amount of air I'd been unintentionally holding inside and exhaled while I sank into the near-scalding water. The bubbles rose and surrounded me like I was sitting on a cloud. As hot as the water was, it felt amazing on my aching muscles, and I let my eyes closed for just a moment.

Unfortunately, I didn't have time to savor it. It was time to get to work.

I felt around on the bottom of the tub until my fingers closed around the knife. I scooted as close as I could to the wall above the faucet. The tiles were about three and a half, maybe four inch, squares.

Grasping the knife in my hand, I raised it up and scraped at the grout separating each square. I scraped and dug until finally I was able to pry one square off the wall. Chunks of grout and dust particles drifted down, settling on top of the bubbles. It was messy, but it was done. Relieved and tired from the stress, I laid back and opened the door a crack to look at the clock. It had been twenty-five minutes.

Man, I really, really wanted to get more done than that. But, I knew if I was in the bathtub too long that Trevor would start to get suspicious. So, reluctantly, I flipped the plug and let the water drain. I set the knife and the tile on the side of the tub underneath the faucet, then stood and wrapped myself in the towel again.

⤝⤝⤝

It took two weeks before I was able to take enough tiles off the wall that a hole big enough for me to fit through appeared. After the tiles were off, there was a huge pile of them sitting in the tub.

I was actually surprised Trevor hadn't sent anyone in to clean the bathtub yet. Normally Alice did it once a week, but now I hadn't seen her at all. I think Trevor was afraid I was going to kill her. Part of me wanted to, that was for sure.

Maybe he figured since I was in here with nothing else to do, I could clean my own bathroom. I probably should pretty soon, just so the cameras could see that it was being cleaned and no one needed to come in and do it.

As a matter of fact, I hadn't seen Trevor either. The only one I saw was that tall vamp who had come the first morning I'd been locked up. He collected the cart, the dishes and my dirty laundry. He also brought me anything I requested or that was sent up to me. I didn't really care. I didn't want to see any of them anyway.

Except Oscar. He had promised he would help me get out. What a liar. I shouldn't have expected anything from him, really. He was just another of Trevor's goons now, as far as I was concerned.

After I got all the tiles off, I dug at the wall underneath. It was actually harder than doing the tiles and that took another two weeks. I left the thinnest part of the outer wall where the plastic siding covered it. I was going to have to push the pieces of siding out so I could slip underneath them. That would come when it was time. There was one last thing I needed to do before I could escape... I needed to make a rope.

For three days more I plotted when I would make my escape and managed to tie several of my garments from the closet together, forming a crude, makeshift rope. Hopefully it would hold until I was safely on the ground.

When the day of my escape attempt arrived, I woke, just like every day, to the smell of breakfast. I wandered out to the table and found biscuits and gravy waiting for me. How strange. Biscuits and gravy was my favorite breakfast meal of all time, and I just found it a little ironic it was being served on the day I was trying to escape.

I ate it like I was never going to eat again.

After I had practically licked my plate clean, I set my fork down then picked up my coffee and took a big swig. Hoping it looked like an accident, I spilled a whole bunch on the front of my shirt. "Ugh! Man... just figures."

I really, really hoped I sounded annoyed enough that my shirt was stained, because I wasn't annoyed at all. I wasn't even scared; I was excited.

Taking my shirt off on the way, I went to the closet and threw the dirty one in the hamper that I'd stuffed the clothes rope into. I grabbed another shirt off a hanger and put it on.

Phase one... accomplished.

I lay down on the couch with a book and tried to concentrate on reading until Mr. No Name Vamp came to get the cart. He never spoke unless I spoke directly to him, and he had to answer me. I let him come and go in silence; I preferred that anyway. He probably did too, all things considered.

Once he was gone, I went back to my book for a while. After a while, I stood and stretched. I then changed my clothes, making sure to put on my running shoes. After that, I looked around as if I were considering what to do next. Pretending the decision was made randomly, I went to the closet, retrieved my laundry basket and hauled the whole thing into the bathroom. I set it next to the tub and slid the door open. I stood in front of the opening to the shower door and snatched my shirt of the top of the basket and examined the coffee stain for a minute, showing the cameras what I planned to do.

It was time to just go for it. I dumped the entire basket into the tub and hoped whoever was watching—if they were watching—wouldn't question why I just threw a bunch of dirty laundry in the bathtub. One thing I was positive of was that they would never guess there was a Chloe-sized hole in the wall and I was about to slide through it and hang from a homemade clothes rope from the second story of the house.

Nope, they would never guess. I felt victorious already.

As quickly as I could, I got into the shower and shut the door. I tied one end of the clothes rope into a loop, securing the knot by tugging it as tight as possible.

I took a deep breath. "I can do this," I whispered and then hung the loop on the faucet. I was worried about going out feet first, because I didn't want anyone to see me before I could see them, but I had no other choice. I dumped the entire clothes rope through the hole, letting it fall all the way down. I stuck one leg through and followed with the other, sliding myself underneath the siding and wiggling my body out of the hole. Finally, I was hanging all the way down with my hands still gripping the hole and my head still underneath the siding.

The fresh air hit me. I hadn't smelled the outside for so long! It was amazing. I breathed in deeply through my nose and exhaled through my mouth. The daylight was another story. The fall sunshine felt like daggers in my eyes. I hadn't seen actual sunlight in over a month. As for the air, I couldn't get over how wonderful it smelled and tasted. Unfortunately, I didn't have time to hang around breathing air. I needed to get moving. It was time to grab the rope and climb down.

Slowly, I forced my fingers to release their death grip on the edges of the hole and grabbed the rope with one hand, then the other. Finally, I was within feet of my freedom.

My feet flailed for a minute until they found the wall and I was able to start slow walking down, holding tight to the top of the clothes rope. It was a darned good thing I'd kept to working out, even after I got locked in, or else I wouldn't have had the strength to hold on. It was slow going, a lot slower than I would have liked. I had only gone about four feet when the rope suddenly dropped about three inches, causing me to almost lose my grip, I did lose my footing.

I swung back and forth, trying to catch the wall and steady myself. Not much luck. When I finally slowed enough to get my feet up against the wall again, the unthinkable happened, something I didn't think over or anticipate: The faucet came loose, freeing my homemade clothes rope from its safety.

I don't remember falling.

I opened my eyes to see a vision I was sure was a hallucination from the pain in my head and back. Through a fuzzy cloud that was reminiscent of a heat off the sidewalks in the summer, I watched Drew drop over the wall and sprint toward me in a full-out run. He drew his guns while he ran.

I closed my eyes again. The pain was horrendous. Throbbing and scorching in my head and back.

"Chloe!"

I opened my eyes again to see him there, bent down in front of me. His eyes were scaling over my body, and so were his hands.

"What are you doing?" I muttered.

"Checking you for breaks."

I sighed and realized that I could actually feel his hands on me. "You're real."

"Yes, now let's go. You have to get up." He sounded just like Drew, always ordering me around.

"I've escaped," I told him in a whisper.

"Chloe, you haven't escaped yet. We have to get out of here, now!" He reached down, lifted me up and ran back toward the wall. I bounced around painfully in his arms while he ran. I wrapped my arms around him and clung to him.

"I have a six pack now," I told him.

That was when the best sound I'd heard in almost a year rang out through the air: his laughter.

We made it to the wall and he set me down on my feet. "You have to stand. I'm going to climb over, then I'm going to reach down for you. Okay?"

I think I nodded because he began his ascent. I moved over and leaned against the wall where he was climbing and looked toward the house. I saw my clothes rope in a pile on the lawn. The sunlight reflected off the silver faucet, which was sitting on top of the clothes pile like a cherry topping on a hot fudge sundae.

Suddenly, Drew made some kind of gurgling sound and fell over the wall on the other side.

"Drew!" I screamed. Finally, the haze was lifting. Something was wrong. "Drew!"

I heard a strange voice say, "Over there."

There was shuffling and pain pierced my shoulder. I looked down to see what had caused the pain and saw a dart sticking out of my bicep.

"What the…?" I lifted my hand to pull it out but never made it. Everything faded to black within seconds.

⤢⤢⤢

I woke slowly. The first thing I realized was that I was lying on a cold stone floor. I reached out and felt the floor. It was rough and damp. The darkness was thick and the air was musty. It smelled like dirty socks.

"Drew," I whispered.

I heard him shift and crawl toward me. "I'm here."

"What happened?"

"I tried to save you, but you met me half way." He laughed a little. "I was just climbing over the wall when I saw a rope drop out through the siding followed by you climbing down. I thought I'd see if you got to the bottom before I ran over there. Then you fell, and I had to cross out into the open." His voice lost its excitement. "They got us before we could get back over the wall."

I felt myself nodding, remembering, "The dart."

I sat up and felt around for him.

"Yeah, they tranquilized us." He scooted toward me until we were sitting close together. "Any idea how to get out of here?"

I shook my head. "I don't even know *where* we are," I admitted.

I looked around now that my vision was finally clearing the fuzz. I could probably see better than Drew could, with my vampire vision. I saw bars.

"We're in a cell." I heard my voice waver with panic.

He sighed deeply. "Yes. Now let's get to thinking of some kind of plan.

We heard a clang and footsteps echo, coming right toward us. I got up and went to the bars, trying to look out. Trevor stood there. He shook his head and made a slight tsk-ing sound.

"I told you if you tried to escape the alternative would be far worse."

All the panic I had felt vanished in an instant, replaced by waves of anger.

"Go to hell." I told him, emphasizing each word, through clenched teeth. Without thinking, I lifted my hands and blasted him. His speed was faster than the fire, because when the flames withered out, he was far out of reach.

. "You will stay here now," he told me and then flicked his head at Drew. "The hunter will die tonight." With those final words, he turned and left, walking at a normal pace so we were forced to listen to the creepy echo of his footfalls again.

"Oh, my god. We are screwed!" I wrapped my hands around the bars and tried to shake them. "I hate you!" I screamed after Trevor.

I then did the most juvenile thing I think I've ever done: I had a fit, kicking the bars, throwing fire out into the hall on the other side of the bars, screaming curse words, and crying. I'm not sure how long I carried on, but Drew sat back and left me alone.

Maybe he was afraid of me.

Finally, my anger receded. I looked at Drew, who sat on the floor against the wall of the cell. His blond hair appeared almost luminescent against the darkness. He sat with his knees bent up, leaning forward with his head resting on his arms.

I paced the length of the cell, thinking. We needed to get *out*. If we didn't, the rest of the community would come soon enough because Drew was here. It was one thing for me to be here; they thought I had come on my own. They would come after Drew for certain. I spun to face him.

"Why did you come here, Drew?

His head snapped up. "Are you kidding me? *Seriously?* Chloe, I came here for *you!*"

"Well, I didn't need you to come. I would have gotten out of here on my own. Now we're both stuck in here."

"We'll find a way out."

Rage bubbled to the surface of what little composure I had left.

"Damn it!" I stomped my foot and spun to grab the bars again. "Let us out of here, you filthy scumbag!"

"Knock it off, Chloe. He isn't going to let us out. Come sit down so we can try to come up with a plan."

He was right, as always. I wasn't doing any good standing there screaming when no one would hear me anyway. It was only wasting energy. I slid down the wall and sat next to him.

"But, why… why did you come after me. You knew I wanted to come here. And why did you come by yourself?"

Drew sighed but said nothing. I didn't say anything either. Eventually, he reached out and grasped my hand in his.

Surprised, I reflexively tried to yank it out of his grip. But he only tightened his fingers around mine. "Chloe, I'm not sure what exactly I feel, or what it means, but I care about you. I can't really place the feeling just yet, especially because you are young still, but I care about you different than I would care about a sister or something."

I opened my mouth to say something, but couldn't think of anything.

"I… I don't know. What I do know is that I like you more than I should."

I still couldn't say anything, so I just sat there, letting him hold my hand. Could it be possible I felt this way too? It would explain that confusion of not knowing where to place Drew when I thought of friends and family. It would explain the jealousy when he was with Christina.

But then there was Gavin.

"*That* is why I came for you." He gave my hand a squeeze.

I felt a tear escape from the corner of my eye and was suddenly grateful for the darkness that enveloped us. "I… I know I care about you too. But, I…I don't know what it is either."

I finally managed to choke out.

"Why didn't Gavin come?" I couldn't help it, I had to ask.

Drew pulled his hand back. I glanced over at him and saw his eyes had narrowed before he turned his head away from me.

"What...what is it?"

"It's a long story. I could make him look bad and say he didn't want to come, but that isn't totally true."

What? They planned to bust me out, and Gavin didn't want to come.

"Tell me."

Drew sighed and settled back against the mossy wall. "He wanted to come. Since you left, there have been several meetings about coming to get you. It was vetoed three times because you left of your own accord. Even Luke wasn't pushing for a rescue, until just recently."

I opened my mouth to speak, but Drew cut me off before I could get a word out. "Just let me talk for once."

I nodded into the dark.

"Chloe, regardless of why you're here, I know it's not because you want to be. It's because you think it's going to keep all of us safe from your father. I've known this since I got your note, and you're stupid if you think I would just sit back at home and let you sacrifice your life to that bloodsucker. I went to the only other person besides Luke who I figured would feel the same."

I shifted on the floor and shivered. Then, after a second thought, I moved closer to Drew, pressing up against his side. *It's freakin' cold, screw propriety.* I just wanted to keep warm. He ignored me and let me lean up against him.

"Gavin did want to come and get you, but he wanted to do it organized. You know, a planned attack with lots of Hunters backing us. He wanted the same kind of rescue that the board had already vetoed three times. I begged him to come, and he said he would but that we had to plan it better. Dumb ass." He shook his head. "Anyhow, we argued about it... a lot. He insisted we needed more Hunters to come with us, and I just wanted the two of us. It's quieter that way, and we could infiltrate more places before anyone would have noticed we were here. He stood by his idea of convincing the board of a rescue. And, well...here I am."

"Why would you come here by yourself? This is probably the stupidest thing I've ever seen you do."

"Well, even perfection makes mistakes."

I could see pretty well in the dark, so his grin wasn't hidden from me.

"Knock it off!" I slapped at him. "This isn't a time for joking around. We have to get out of here. My birthday is in about a month!"

He shifted to face me better. "What does that mean?"

"Oh, that's right. You don't know."

"Know what?"

"Well, apparently, I was bred to allow my father to become a day walker."

Drew visibly startled. "What the hell?"

"Yeah, the only way a vampire can become a day walker is if he drinks the blood of a human who is half vampire and half vampire hunter. As you well know, those are kinda hard to come by, so my genius father decided he would just use my mother to make his own."

"What the…are you freakin' joking?"

I shook my head. "No, I'm not joking one bit. I didn't even get to the part where he has to drain my entire body of blood on the day of my sixteenth birthday for it to work."

"Oh, god! Chloe! We have to get you out of here."

"Yeah, you think?" I mumbled. "I'm more concerned about getting *you* out of here. He needs me alive, at least for another month, but you are expendable. Like he said, he wants to kill you tonight."

He stood and paced, like I'd done before. "How the hell are we going to get out of here? We need the other Hunters."

I nodded. "Luke will know. He always knows when I'm in trouble." I watched him pace. "Is that Luke's gift? Does he have some kind of psychic ability or something?"

He nodded, but continued his voyage from one end of the cell to the other. "Yeah, mostly it's just like a strong feeling, but with people close to him, he has been known to have visions or dreams."

I pretty much knew this, but it was nice to have confirmation.

"Drew, come sit down."

"I can't sit down; we have to get out."

He went to the bars and tried to look down the dank hallway on the other side.

In an effort to get him to sit down so I could think for a moment, I said, "I need you to tell me why you hate Gavin so much."

"Chloe, I don't want to talk about that now."

The outside of the cell had suddenly become important to him.

He looked from side to side, up and down.

"You will never want to talk about it unless I hassle you. Get over here."

His hands dropped to his side, and he turned to face me. "Fine."

I patted the hard stone floor, offering him his spot back. "Besides, I need you over here to keep me warm."

"Can't you warm yourself up with your fire?"

"Uh, no, it doesn't really work that way."

He slid back down the wall beside me.

"All right, now spill it, mister."

Drew was silent for a moment, trying to gather his thoughts, I suppose. He leaned forward and wrapped his hands around his knees. "Gavin is my brother."

"What!" I knew something was up with them, but I never suspected they were brothers.

"He is my half-brother. My mother is also his mother. Right after I was born, my mother left my father for Gavin's father. She left me too. She had been having an affair with Gavin's father. When I was six months old, she found out she was pregnant again. This time the baby wasn't my father's. My father kicked her out and told her never to come near him or me again."

"She just left you? Her baby?" I was having a really hard time believing a woman could do that.

"Yes, she just left me. I think she knew my dad would have fought for me, physically, if he had to." He closed his eyes. "She probably figured that she had another baby coming, so she would be able to replace me anyway."

"But... you all live in the community, how is it that you never see her?"

"I don't know. She avoids me, I think. I pretty much hate her for screwing around on my dad and leaving us, so I'm okay with not seeing her."

"She never tried to talk to you?"

He shook his head. "Nope."

"And Gavin... how is it his fault that your mom did this to you?"

"It's not. He has tried to be my friend over the years, get to know me or whatever, but I don't want to be his friend, and I especially don't want to try to be brothers."

"That is just stupid, Drew! Why not?"

Suddenly he slammed his fist into the floor and I flinched in surprise, the thud resonated throughout the cell. "Because! He is the reason my mother isn't my mother! He is the reason she left. If he had never been…then my mom would have gotten over that damned affair and would have stayed with us."

"Oh…" My heart ached for him. I couldn't imagine going through that. "I'm so sorry."

He was quiet, head turned away from me.

"Drew?" I placed my hand on his arm and tried to turn him toward me. When he resisted, I only tried harder. Still, he didn't want to turn toward me, so I crawled around until I was in front of him. I knelt and took his face in both my hands and stared into his now watery green eyes. "I know it hurts. I know that you don't want it to hurt, but hating Gavin isn't going to make the hurt go away."

Suddenly, without warning, he grabbed my arms and yanked me forward until I was kneeling between his legs and our chests were touching.

And then… he kissed me.

He kissed me better than Gavin had kissed me, I'll admit that. Drew's kiss felt like he had been waiting a hundred years for our lips to finally meet. I placed my arm on his shoulder, around the back of his neck and kissed him back, not wanting it to end.

All too soon, he pushed me away.

"I'm sorry," he mumbled, almost under his breath.

I shook my head. "Why are you sorry?"

"I just had to do it, just once." He caught my eyes with his.

"I don't understand. Why only once?"

For some reason I felt the tears starting again. Damned tears always showed up when I didn't want them.

"Chloe, I'm not about to be second choice for anyone. I care about you, but you want to be with Gavin. If that's what you want… fine. I just don't want to be a choice you made because he wasn't available to you at the moment."

Now the tears were really rolling.

"Gavin and I are friends, Drew." I sniffed. "Don't ruin this."

"Ruin what? We are stuck in a freakin' dungeon!"

"Ugh! You can be so frustrating." We'd just had our first kiss and he was ruining the moment with every word that came out of his mouth. "Drew…"

He held up his hand in the dark. "Stop, I know what you're

going to say, but I'm simply telling you not to make any decisions right now. I don't want to hear that I shouldn't have done that, I don't want to hear that it was wrong, and I don't even want to hear that it was right! Let's just figure out how to get the hell out of here."

I kept my mouth shut and only nodded. I don't know what kind of decisions he was talking about anyway, him or Gavin, I guess. He was right. After a kiss like that and Gavin not being here, especially after hearing he didn't want to join Drew on the rescue, I was feeling drawn more to Drew than ever before.

I heard a door clang somewhere in the distance and sat straight up. "Did you hear that?"

"No, what is it?"

"I heard a clang. Someone's coming."

"I didn't hear anything." He got to his feet and held his hand out to help me up.

"I can hear it because I've got vampire gifts, too."

He nodded, trying to listen. "I forgot about that," he whispered.

"They're coming," I told him.

"I hear them now. It sounds like more than one."

I moved forward toward the bars that enclosed us into the tiny dank cell. Whoever was coming down the hall way was being extremely careful and quiet.

"Who's there?" I called out.

"Chloe!" Drew chastised me in a loud whisper at the same time as Alice popped into my line of vision. She held her finger to her lips, shushing me.

"What the hell are you doing here?" I demanded. I was so ticked off at her for what she had done..

Drew joined me by the bars.

"Who is she?" he asked.

"It's Alice, and she's no one," I told him.

"Chloe, I'm sorry. I'm so sorry." Alice came up to the bars and stood on the other side, straight across from me. "I came down here to let you out. You have to get out of here."

"Yeah! You think?" I yelled at her.

Drew put his hands on my shoulders. "Calm down."

I shrugged him off. "No, I don't want to calm down! How the hell am I supposed to trust her anyway? How do we know she's not just trying to lead us into a trap or something?"

"Who cares, Chloe? She's letting us out."

Alice nodded and withdrew a set of keys from her pocket, searched for the right one, and then turned the key, releasing us from our prison.

"Which way?" Drew asked.

Alice pointed the same direction she had come. "This way," she told us and sped off in that direction.

I grabbed Drew's hand and bolted after her. We ran through the stone hallways as quietly as we could, knowing that even footsteps echoed loudly.

Suddenly I heard a whimper. "Stop!" I hissed at both of them.

"What?" Drew asked. "What is it?"

"Shh." I held up my hand. "I heard something."

I heard it again. I followed sound. I turned a few corners and found more cells. Finally, at the end of a hallway full of cells, I found the source of the noise.

"Oscar!" I rushed toward the door and realized then why he had never come for me. He hadn't been a traitor. "Why are you in here?"

Oscar tried to stand, wobbled, and then fell to his knees. He crawled to the bars and lifted himself to stand with the help of the bars. "They locked me up as soon as I left your room. I guess they figured I might be a problem." He coughed and gave a little laugh. I looked closer at him. There were bite marks all over his neck and arms.

"They've been feeding on you?" I asked him.

He only nodded and turned his head away.

"Alice, let him out," I told her.

Immediately, she had the key in the lock. I'm sure she had it ready before I even asked.

"Who is this?" Drew asked "Can we trust him?"

"Drew... look at him. Does he look like he is on Trevor's side?"

Drew nodded. "Good point. Let's go."

As Oscar exited the cell, Drew grabbed him around the waist to help him walk.

"Oscar," I looked him in the eye. "I know you're hurting, but we are trying to get out of here, and I need you to be as strong as you can so that we can move quickly."

He nodded and we ran again, not quite as fast as before, but hopefully quickly enough.

We ran until we reached a narrow door. Alice whipped out a key and opened it. "Down here is a tunnel. The tunnel is for Trevor, only. I only know about it because I've seen him use it. It comes out in a parking garage down the street from one of his night clubs. But there are exits along the way that are closer."

Seriously? Wow.

"Alice." I looked her in the eye. "You can't stay here."

She accepted my stare and our eyes locked. "I know. I'm coming with you."

I felt like jumping for joy and decking her at the same time. She finally decided to leave Trevor, but only after she had ruined my trust. I couldn't leave her though. She would die for letting us out. We had to repay her.

"Let's go, then."

I turned and lowered myself on the ladder Drew had already descended and had help Oscar climb down. Alice followed me, shutting the door and latching the top of the tunnel hatch over us, surrounding us in complete darkness.

THE VAMPIRE HUNTER'S DAUGHTER
PART VI

ARCADIA FALLS

JENNIFER MALONE WRIGHT

The Vampire Hunter's Daughter
Part VI

ARCADIA FALLS

It was so dark in the tunnels I was positive I was the only one who could see anything at all. For about ten minutes, we stumbled through the tunnel, hanging onto each other's hands and bumping against one another.

"I can't do this anymore." I was at the head of the line, and I stopped so quickly it caused Alice, Drew and Oscar to bump into me and each other from behind.

Drew moved from the back to stand beside me. "Do what? We have to keep moving."

"I just can't walk in the dark like this anymore. Give me a second." I flexed my hand a couple of times and after a few deep breaths, I managed to pull up a little flame, similar to a candle flame, in my palm. "There."

In the glow of the small flame, I saw Drew grin. "Nice."

"Now we can keep moving, but we have to be quick. If we linger too long, Trevor will figure things out and catch up to us. Once we get above ground, we can figure out where to go from there."

Drew nodded but looked nervous, something I wasn't accustomed to seeing. I figured it boiled down to the fact he wasn't used to being defenseless; he usually had his guns.

"You okay?" I asked him.

He nodded again. "Yeah. Let's move." He encircled Oscar's waist to help him walk. "You doin' okay?" he asked Oscar.

"Yes," Oscar croaked out.

I turned to lead the way again, my little flame guiding the way. We had only been walking about five minutes when Alice cried out, "Oh!"

Every single one of us halted to a stop and turned.

"I totally forgot!" Alice said.

"What?" Drew and I demanded at the same time. I expected it

to be something bad, like she forgot there was no exit or something.

"This!" She reached into the pocket of her jeans and extracted a cell phone.

"Oh, my god! Alice, I love you!" If my hand hadn't been occupied by flame, I would have hugged her.

Oscar shook his head and croaked. "It probably won't get a signal down here."

Drew shrugged, "You're right, but I'm still trying."

It powered up and Drew turned it around for us to see. "He's right, no bars. Let's go."

We moved on with renewed energy. We walked for what seemed like hours, until I saw a ladder that reached to the ceiling with another hatch, like the one we came down through.

"There!" I pointed.

We rushed for the ladder.

"I'm going first," Drew told us, letting go of Oscar. He shimmied up the ladder quickly and lifted the hatch. We waited patiently while he went up and inspected.

"Drew?" I called after a few minutes.

He stuck his head down. "It's all clear. Come on."

I turned to Alice. "Let's get Oscar up first."

"I agree." She nodded. "Yeah, it will be easier for him if we help. Come on, Oscar."

I extinguished my flame and then we helped him off the floor where he'd practically collapsed after Drew had released his hold. It took both of us to push him up the ladder and Drew pulled from the opening, once he could reach him, to get Oscar out of there.

Once he was safely at the top, I called out, "Drew, see if the phone works now."

Alice and I climbed up and out.

"I already did. Our ride is coming."

Above ground, darkness surrounded us. We were in the woods. How deep in the woods, I had no idea, but the thick forest of trees blocked out any moonlight we would have seen otherwise. I shivered against the chilly fall air and wished I had a jacket.

"How will they even know where we are?"

"I just told them to follow the road to your father's and look for us on the way. You should be able to hear them, right?"

I sighed. Crap, now everyone is depending on me. That's the last thing I need.

Because the night was already upon us, vampires could come out. I was positive Trevor had either realized Alice wasn't around, found out we had escaped with her, or both. He could put two and two together pretty quickly. "We have to go, you guys. It won't be long before Trevor finds us."

If it were possible to become any more scared, I was. Any head start we'd had on Trevor was pretty much gone. I lit the flame in my hand again, and we traipsed through the woods, over fallen logs, crunching leaves, pushing through tree branches. It was a given that Trevor, or any vampire, would hear us or smell us before they saw my little light.

"Drew, what time is it?"

I turned to see him glance at his watch. "Four fifteen in the morning," he answered. "Man, I had no idea it was so late...er, early."

Thank god, at least one thing is running in our favor.

We pressed on in search of the road. Oscar looked pretty ragged. Alice and Drew both had to help him. He was so pale he seemed to glow in the darkness. He mumbled phrases like: "Never should have listened... Don't go into the water..." I was pretty sure he was hallucinating.

"Don't worry, Oscar," Alice whispered. I looked back and saw she was whispering in his ear and smoothing back his hair while they walked. She provided comfort for him, despite the fear shown in her eyes.

"The road can't be much farther. I hear cars, so it can't be that far away."

"Are you sure it's a car?" Drew asked me..

"I know what I heard, Drew."

"Just asking, Chloe." Tensions obviously were running high.

I swiped a branch out of my way, so I could pass. "I don't know. Maybe we're going the wrong way."

Suddenly, the leaves and branches stopped their crackle beneath their feet, signaling they had stopped. I looked back at them.

"It's possible." Drew turned in a circle and assessed the area. "There probably aren't many cars on the road at this time of night. We'd have been lucky to hear one at all."

Not knowing what step to take, we just stood there in silence for another moment. Only Oscar's raspy breathing made any noise.

"Let's just keep going the same way." I tried to keep the

frustration out of my voice. The last thing we needed was to be lost in the woods. I headed out in front to lead the way.

After about five minutes, I heard it more clearly. "A car!"

"I don't hear anything," Drew complained.

"But I can. Let's go!" As fast as we could with Oscar in tow, we plowed through the forest.

"I hear it!" Alice exclaimed, when we saw headlights flash their bright light through the trees. I flexed my hand and extinguished my flame, and then I bolted for the road.

"Chloe, wait!" Drew must have released Oscar because I felt his arms wrap around my waist and lift me off the ground. "It might be Trevor or one of his vampires."

Oh. That never occurred to me.

"Don't move," he ordered while the car passed. Then he whipped out the phone and dialed a number. "Yeah, it's me. Where are you?" He grunted and then clicked off.

"Where are they?" Alice asked. I sensed the urgency in her voice. She, of all of us, knew Trevor best. I didn't even want to think of the things he would do to her if we were caught.

"They aren't far, hopefully. It's hard to tell because we don't even know where we are. We're going to have to take the chance of going out into the road."

None of us wanted to go out there. The woods weren't exactly safe, but they were safer.

"Come on." Drew signaled us.

My heart pounded as we noisily crept out of the trees and onto the hard cement of the road. It felt good to be on the flat surface instead of fighting our way through the woods. If anything, it would be a lot easier to walk with Oscar.

Once again, we had to decide which way to go. Drew and I discussed which direction we thought we had come from and agreed to go left.

While we walked, Drew made another call. "Hey. We're on the road now." A pause. "Yeah, she's fine. Just hurry up." He clicked off and pocketed the phone.

"Who was that? Who's coming?"

Drew rolled his eyes. "Who do you think? The one you wanted to save you."

That wasn't true. I'd never really expected anyone to save me. I'd always figured I'd do it on my own. "That's not fair, Drew. It's not true, either."

He turned away so I couldn't see his face. "Well, all that matters is that you're safe and we're going home, right?"

I nodded. I just didn't understand why he was always so back and forth about everything. One minute we were kissing and the next he was almost shoving me at Gavin. I pushed back the tears that threatened to surface and clamped my mouth shut. I wasn't about to say anything to him in the middle of the road while we attempted to escape evil vampires.

I'd already chosen. Drew had come for me. No matter what the cost or who he had to defy to do it, he was the one who chose me over all else. I couldn't deny that. I didn't want to deny that. Yes, Gavin probably would have come, but only after he had a guarantee of safety. I wasn't mad at him or anything, but it just wasn't the same as someone risking everything, including his life, for me.

Not to mention I could practically still taste Drew's lips.

A low hum sounded in my ears, and I realized what it was: car engines. "Guys! Stop! There's a car coming." I listened harder. "No, there are two cars coming, one from each direction."

Drew looked at Alice. "Take Oscar to the trees. Now!" he ordered.

"I'm going!" she answered back. She dragged Oscar into the darkness of the trees.

We could see the headlights of the first car from the direction we had been walking toward.

"That has to be Gavin." Drew was squinting toward the headlights. "It's his Jeep."

I heard the other motor in the distance. I knew the sound of that motor.

"It's him," I told Drew. "Trevor's coming from the other way."

Drew walked to the middle of the road, in plain view of the oncoming cars. I followed him, and we stood there, weaponless, defenseless and vulnerable. I didn't have a good feeling about what was about to happen.

"He probably has guns," I told Drew quickly. "He tried to shoot me before."

Drew smiled. "Well, how else would you kill someone you couldn't touch?"

I didn't smile back. "Yeah, you laugh now, but it was my gun." That comment caused his smile to fade. He knew how much I loved my gun.

The Jeep stopped mere feet behind us after it skidded sideways in the middle of the road. I watched as the doors flew open and Gavin appeared. He had his arms full of guns while he ran toward us.

Christina popped out of the other door, and she also ran toward us. She wore jeans with heavy leather chaps over the top and a long-sleeved, tight black top. I'd never seen her decked out in hunter gear. She wore it well, unlike her hooker dress. Her hair was pulled back into a tight ponytail, and she wore a double holster. In addition, her outfit boasted several sheathed knives. I could see the dark wood of the hilts with inlaid brass that glimmered in the headlights.

"Great," I mumbled.

"Let it go, Chloe. No time for that," Drew told me.

The Mustang arrived not nearly in such a hurry as Gavin and Christina had arrived. I glanced back and saw Gavin toss Drew a gun.

"Ammo?" Drew called, checking the gun.

"It's loaded. Just check the safety. Here's extra." Gavin hurled a magazine at Drew, which he caught easily.

The doors on the Mustang popped open. In an instant, Trevor and Constance swept from the car, leaving the doors open. I held my hands in front of me and called up the fire. Two huge flames appeared in my palms. Just when the flames burned brightly, another vehicle pulled up behind Trevor's, and Vincent and my guard goon scrambled from the doors and moved behind Trevor and Constance.

I shot my flames upward in warning to the vampires.

"What the hell?" I heard Gavin's obviously shocked voice call out.

Christina flanked my right side. "Well, someone's been keeping secrets. Here's a gun too."

I did my best not to sound ungrateful. I was going to need that gun. I wished they'd had two for me. "Can you stick that in my pants?"

I wasn't looking right at her, but in my mind, I could see her raising her eyebrows and coming up with some snarky comment.

"Just do it, Christina," I said.

I felt her slide the gun into my waistband and give it a pat. "I hope it was good for you, too."

"Knock it off, and get ready to fight."

"I'm ready," she said. I heard her pull back the slide mechanism and the cartridge shifted into the chamber. "Let's kick some ass!" she yelled.

Trevor and his vampires stood in a line of four, just like us. I was right. He had my gun. It didn't look like any of the others had a gun, but there was no way to tell for sure.

It appeared as if we had ourselves a regular standoff. Both parties were simply waiting for the other to draw.

"Come with me now, Chloe," Trevor called out, "and I'll let the other hunter's depart alive."

"Don't you dare!" Drew nearly hissed the words at me.

Not that I paid much attention because at that same time I yelled, "Go to hell, you freak," and revved my fire again.

"I am not sorry for what is about to happen, Chloe," Trevor shook his head, "since you insist on having it your way."

Then he shot at me.

Time seemed suspended. I literally saw the bullet leave the barrel. I side-stepped in front of Christina and let the bullet pass. There was no time to think or try to watch every bullet, but it suddenly occurred to me that I was the only one he wanted alive, and I knew it was up to me to protect the others.

"Get behind me," I ordered them.

"Are you crazy?" Gavin exclaimed. "You'll die."

"No, he wants me alive." Yeah, so the worst that could happen was that I would be shot and not die.

Yay.

"Just do it," Christina yelled out from behind me. "She's right."

Trevor advanced and fired a shot that whizzed by Gavin's head. Quickly, Gavin fell behind me, but Drew still refused. I shook my head. I should have known he would never stand behind me.

I pushed the fire up and out. The result was probably beautiful from a distance. Droplets of fire rained down onto us like the falling tracers on the Fourth of July.

"Get back!" I screamed, meaning both Drew as well as Trevor.

"I am certain Alice escaped with you." Trevor spread his hands. "Tell me where she is."

He scanned the sides of the road and turned his attention back to us. No one answered him.

"I will allow you one last chance to come with me willingly, Chloe. It will spare your friends if you do."

"Tell him where to stick it." Christina pushed me from behind.

Before I could say anything, we were rushed by the vampires. I rushed forward too, blowing the fire out like flame throwers and screaming from a place deep down inside where I kept the rage of my mother's death. Drew and Gavin stood on either side of me. Gunshots filled the air while they shot at Constance and Vincent. Christina stayed behind me. I wasn't sure if her strategy was to stay hidden or if something else was going on, but it was okay. She was safe behind me.

That's when I felt it: the burning, ripping flesh when a bullet tore into my calf.

"Oh, my god!" I screamed in pain and fell to the ground.

My flames extinguished, and I lay there in pain. It felt like nothing I'd ever felt before. "I've been shot! He shot me!" I screamed.

Behind me, Christina shot back at him while I desperately reached for my gun. I knew I could hit him in the heart. I never missed.

"Gavin's hit!" I heard Drew yell.

"Damn it!" Christina hollered. "I'm out of ammo."

Finally, my hands wrapped around the handle of the gun in my waistband. God, my leg hurt. I aimed at Trevor, ready to take the shot, but before I could pull the trigger, a loud blast rocked the air, sounding above all the other gunshots, and Trevor crumpled to the ground.

Suddenly, the atmosphere was static. Silence interrupted the chaos, and every single person looked to see where the shot had come from. There, behind the open door of the Jeep, stood Alice with a shotgun still smoking in her hands. Her blank blue eyes were wide with shock and fear. Her face was pale beneath the dirt from the woods and Oscar's blood. We watched as her fingers released the shotgun, and it fell to the ground with an anticlimactic clank. Tears slid from her eyes.

UV shotgun shells.

Everyone's eyes were glued, unbelieving, on Trevor's body as it convulsed and a white light attempted to eat at his body, but his aged vampire blood repelled it. I'm pretty sure, had it been one of our bullets, he wouldn't even have noticed, but the shotgun shell held more UV than most ammo.

Vincent was the first to come back from the pause. In a flash, he had Drew's throat in his grasp. I shot him in the head.

Drew, covered in vampire brains and blood, kicked Vincent's falling body with his boot.

"Ugh!" he cried out. He kicked and then shot him twice in the heart. Just to be sure he was dead, Drew reached back over his shoulder and produced a wooden stake that he rammed through Vincent's chest.

White light emanated from the holes in Vincent as he eroded. The UV wove its way through his body, eating it away. He must not have been nearly as old as Trevor.

I fell back onto the cement and wondered where Gavin was shot, having completely forgotten about Constance until Christina jumped over the top of me and slammed her body into the hard surface of the female vampire. They both tumbled to the ground.

I watched, weakly trying to get a bead on Constance, but Christina kept getting in the way. Constance was much stronger than Christina, so of course, she pinned her right away. Christina growled at her like a pit bull. "Get off me, you nasty whore!"

Instead of using her hands to force Constance off of her, she reached downward toward her thigh and pulled out a large, lethal-looking knife and slammed it into Constance's side, sliding it right between her ribs. Constance screamed and released Christina to frantically swipe at the knife lodged in her. Christina rolled away from the crazy vampire, grabbing her knife on the way. I finally had a shot at Constance, and I took it, straight to the heart.

Christina was on her feet already and bolted toward the last vampire, who fought with Drew. Every time the vampire made a grab or tried to hit him, Drew deflected it. Christina took a flying leap at the vampire and landed on his back. She planted her blade into the side of his body, in almost the same spot on him where she'd stabbed Constance.

She was good with a knife.

Though my attention was focused on the scene before me, oh, my god, the pain was awful.

"Drew!" I cried out, then rolled over and tried to stand. I made it part of the way up but fell back down. I didn't even want to look at the wound. There was blood everywhere.

"Chloe, come on. We have to go." Christina stalked over to me.

"I need my gun," I said between clenched teeth. "Oscar…"

Everything was fuzzy.

"Who the hell is Oscar?"

"In the woods." I pointed. "Alice."

"Oh, there's another guy in the woods. She knelt and wiped blood off of her knife using my jeans and then sheathed it.

"Thanks a lot, you hooker," I moaned through the pain. "I need to go to the hospital."

"Gavin needs to get there more than you," she said. "Now get your ass in the Jeep."

Yeah, there was absolutely no reason why she would want to help me. Just because we killed vampires together didn't mean we had to like each other. It just meant that we hated someone else more than we hated each other. Even so, she went to Trevor's UV-scorched body to retrieve my gun for me.

I stared at Trevor for a moment as Christina ran over to him and picked up my gun from the ground near his hands. It was so quiet. His black clothes were stark against his white skin, and they were scorched where the UV had tried to burn him away.

Christina stood and held the gun in her left hand, and then drew a knife from her sheath with her right. She lifted the large knife high into the air above his heart. She drew a deep breath, but I called out before she plunged it down.

"Don't..." I don't know what I was thinking. We needed to be sure he was dead, or deader, since he was already undead.

"Damn it, Chloe!" Her eyes moved back and forth from Trevor to me, her knife still raised.

"I'm sorry..." I called back. "He was my father."

I heard her grumble while she lowered her knife and slammed it into the sheath. She stomped over to where I still lay on the ground and threw the gun down onto the pavement next to me. "You and I are going to talk about this later. We always make sure."

I nodded and reached for my gun. When I looked up at her, I couldn't look her in the eyes; they were so accusatory. I was a horrible vampire hunter, and the tears that slid down my cheeks when I stared at Trevor's body proved it.

But he was my father. It shouldn't have, but it did make a difference.

Christina rushed back to the body and grasped his feet with both hands so she could drag him out of the road while I twisted around and tried to get up. I didn't want to look at her dragging his body, but I did. It's a damned good thing I did, too.

Trevor's hand twitched.

"Christina!" I called out. It was too late. Trevor's grotesquely burnt arm flew upward so fast he had Christina's throat in his grasp before she could move an inch. I let out a blood-curdling yell while I watched her try to scream, or even to just breathe..

"Drew, help!" I screamed and fumbled for my gun. I had it engaged within seconds. I sat up and shot him in the arm. The shot was enough to force his fingers let go, and after releasing an animal growl, he curled back his lips and bared his fangs, hissing at the inconvenience the gunshot wound had caused.

Drew ran and threw himself on top of Trevor, trying to pin him with his legs.

"Get the chains out of the Jeep!" he shouted.

"What do we need chains for?" I called, forgetting the pain amidst a rush of adrenaline and jumping up to help him hold Trevor. I sat on his legs to avoid looking at his monstrous face. That was not the face I'd come to know Trevor by… it was hideous, inhuman.

"The chains are silver; they can help hold vampires."

"What? Like in True Blood! That stuff is real?"

Just then, Trevor lurched forward, tumbling us both to the ground. He stood and sped toward me, eyes bulging, fangs bared. He didn't even make it a few steps in my direction before I saw a chain whip by my face and wrap around him.

Shocked, having totally expected to be eaten by Daddy Dearest, I saw Christina behind him holding tightly onto the chain. She had swung it lasso style at him and trapped him beneath the cold silver links.

"What now?" I asked.

Trevor struggled against the chains.

"Free me at once!" he demanded.

Finally, it seemed Trevor, the refined vampire, was back, displacing the monster he had woken as.

Drew helped Christina hold the chain while I dropped to the ground and favored my leg. The pain came back, hard and fast, and I was bleeding everywhere. Drew looked to the sky. I hadn't noticed, but it was brightening on the horizon; no sun yet, though.

"We're going to tie him to a tree," Drew stated.

"What?" I asked.

It was one thing to shoot or kill someone, but it was an entirely different prospect to watch them slowly char to death.

Christina let Drew have the chain, strode up to Trevor, and got in his face. "Yeah," she said to Trevor, "we're going to make sure you burn." She drug out the last word, taunting him.

In response, Trevor snarled, "You must free me, this instant. If you manage to kill me, I swear an oath that you will find death at the hands of my avengers."

Christina flipped her ponytail off her shoulder. "I'll look forward to that. Now, let's move."

After a moment of discussion about which tree would be best to use because of the direction of the rising sun, Drew and Christina dragged Trevor to one of the trees close to the edge of the road, an exposed and solitary tree that would experience maximum sunlight when the sun finally rose.

Thank god this road was somewhat unused this time of year. That would have been all we needed for a car to come speeding along while I lay in the road bloody and shot, while my friends chained a guy to a tree. Then I'd have to explain how that guy was my father. Yeah, that would go over well.

I hadn't even noticed that the goon who had guarded me back at Trevor's house apparently had disappeared with the second car. Trevor's promise of his cohorts avenging his death was likely true. I realized more was at stake here than simply seeking revenge for my mother's death. The enormity of the situation weighed heavily on me.

Trevor struggled against them the whole way and more chains were added over the top to secure him to the tree. The UV shotgun shell, the UV bullet in his arm, and the flames that had scorched him had left him weak enough the silver chains were likely to hold him easily, if I knew anything of my vampire history, now that I knew it was all true.

For me, exhaustion and severe pain were setting in. I found myself wondering about Gavin, Alice, and Oscar, but I didn't have the energy to get up and go see how they were.

I fell back onto the cement and stared at the sky while I listened to Trevor scream at Drew and Christina. The opening in the tree line above the road was quite wide, and the sun was rising. As the rays of sunlight drew closer, I closed my eyes. I didn't want to watch Trevor tortured. I felt the sun hit me before it hit him. The warmth soothed my cold skin; it felt good. I tried to mentally prepared myself for what I knew was about to happen.

Minutes later, I heard screams from Trevor while he begged to be released. Those screams turned to painful wails, wretched, ear-piercing screams that could only have ended in death. Even though I didn't think I could bring myself to look, some part of me knew I had to.

I turned my head and opened my eyes. I saw Drew and Christina stood far from the writhing, flaming body that Trevor had become. Through the flames, I could see his dark hair had been singed off and his skin was melted like wax in some spots and black and charred in others.

Ugh. I turned my head back the other way. His suffering went on for only a few more seconds before it was finally over and the world around us was mostly silent again. My mother's death had been avenged. Trevor had finally gotten what he had wanted so badly: to see a sunrise again.

Drew moved by my side, and he spoke softly. "He's gone Chloe. It's time to go. I have to help Gavin now."

And then he was gone from my side.

"Crap!" I tried to stand again. I managed to get up and sort of zombie-walked to the Jeep, leaving a trail of bloodspots behind me.

I was coherent enough to hope Gavin was all right. Distantly, I could hear Drew tell Christina she was going to have to take Gavin to the hospital in the Mustang and then take it home. I watched them load Gavin into the car while he yelled at them to be careful, calling Drew all sorts of terrible names.

"Shut up!" Christina yelled. "We're trying to help you, dumbass."

Alice still sat behind the door of the Jeep. I bent down and grabbed her hand. "Alice, we have to go. Can you get Oscar?"

She looked up and stared me in the eyes. "Is he dead?"

She had known Trevor best. She was his housekeeper, but she had also been his lover. In a strange sort of way, she was also his partner. Of any of us, she had the right to be emotional about his death. He was all she had known for so long.

"Yes. He's dead." I glanced at the tree where his body had been. Ashes were all that was left of the once proud Trevor.

Alice cried. I had expected emotion, but she bawled uncontrollably. I didn't know what to do to comfort her, but I knew we needed to get moving. "Come on, Alice. There'll be time for this later. Right now, we have to get out of here and get to the hospital.

Gavin's hurt."

She wouldn't budge. She acted as though she hadn't even heard me.

Damn it. We really needed to go.

"Drew!" I called. I used the Jeep for support and limped around it. "Drew!"

He heaved the door shut on the Mustang and glanced at me. After we watched Christina reverse the Mustang, then slam into drive, peel out and speed away, Drew hurried over to us.

"We need to get Oscar," I said, my breath coming in short pants. Fatigue had kicked in now that the adrenaline had worn off. All I wanted was to lay down and go to sleep.

"Get in the Jeep, Chloe. I got this."

I did what he said and crawled into the backseat of the Jeep. I closed my eyes for just one second and woke up in the hospital.

Groaning, I forced my eyes to open through the fog of medication. I could feel thick bandaging all around my leg. I lifted my head a little, pulled the thin hospital blanket over, and saw my calf was, indeed, covered in a thick bandage. Oddly enough, I kind of wanted to see it. I officially had a battle wound.

I let my head fall back on the pillow and closed my eyes for a moment. When I opened them, I turned my head to the side and found Drew asleep in the chair next to my bed.

He had stayed with me.

I took that moment while he slept to examine him without him knowing I was staring at him. He sat kind of sideways in the chair, head tilted and leaned against the wall. The hood on his sweatshirt was pulled up, covering his hair. For such a tough guy, he had really long eye lashes. I was actually a little jealous of them.

He must have showered and changed, because his skin and clothes looked clean.

I watched him sleep for so long he must have felt my eyes on him. They fluttered open and settled on me.

"Hey," he whispered.

"Hey," I whispered back.

He shifted in the chair until he sat forward and leaned toward me. "Are you feeling better?"

I nodded. "Better now. I think they have me on pain meds." I lifted my wrist to show him the IV.

"I'm sorry I let you get shot."

I rolled my eyes and laughed. "Yeah, how could you?" I asked him sarcastically. "I'm not sorry. I'm just happy I'm not dead."

Finally, he smiled. "That's a good point."

I looked down at my leg. "So how bad is it?"

"Actually, it could have been way worse. The bullet hit toward the outside of the calf. It completely missed the bone. It went in and out."

"Ugh."

"You're pretty lucky it didn't hit the bone or anything." He tried to make it sound good. "You should heal pretty well."

"Well, I'm probably going to heal faster than you think," I told him

He raised his eyebrows. "The vampire thing?"

"Yeah, I should probably get out of here before the whole thing is healed up, and they think I'm some miracle child or something."

"Yeah, that's probably a good idea." He nodded.

I looked around the hospital room. "Where is everyone?"

"Alice and Gavin are down the hall in their own rooms, and Luke is around here somewhere."

"Oscar?" I really hoped he was okay. I couldn't remember anything after getting in the Jeep.

"He's being treated at home by our own medics." When I raised my eyebrows, he spread his hands out. "Well, we couldn't exactly bring him here with all those bites."

He was right. "Why is Alice here?"

Drew leaned back in the chair again. "The doctors say she is suffering from shock. Other than that, she doesn't have any injuries."

"Oh." I reached down and fiddled with the blanket. "I hope she's going to be all right... like, mentally or emotionally, or whatever."

"She'll probably be fine. They said that most of the people who go through this recover with rest and relaxation."

"Well, what did you tell them happened to us?"

He shrugged. "I told them we were walking home from the movies when some guys tried to mug us. We fought back, and they shot you guys. I suppose the cops will want to talk to you once they know you're awake, which is probably another reason to get out of here soon."

I supposed that would have been a believable story. Believable enough anyway.

Suddenly my mind took me back to the road, and I was reliving the face-off with the father I'd never known, trying to kill him. I was shot and lay helpless on the ground while the people who came to rescue me fought the vampires. I wished I could have been a better fighter and could have held my own more, or least been more help than the hindrance I felt I'd been.

I reached for the water glass beside the bed on the bedside rolling table and couldn't reach it, so Drew handed it to me.

"Thank you." I took a sip and swished it around in my mouth for a second before I swallowed.

The door opened quietly, and Luke slipped inside. "Chloe! You're awake."

"Yes." I nodded. I wanted to hug him. More than that, a feeling I didn't expect, I needed to hug him. He must have sensed this because he set his little paper coffee cup on the counter, came right over and gave me a gentle embrace.

"I missed you."

I grinned. He felt like home to me. "I missed you, too. When can I go home?"

"They said you and Alice can come home today, but Gavin has to stay longer."

I knew it was going to peeve Drew, but I asked anyway. "Can I go see him? How bad is he?"

As I expected, Drew turned away. He stood and went to the sink to fiddle with whatever was there just to avoid having to answer the question.

Luke answered, "Gavin was shot just beneath his ribs. The bullet had to be removed, so he needed surgery. Luckily, the bullet had lodged between his spleen and stomach, but missed the organs. And yes, you can see him, but they are keeping visits very short. He's asleep most of the time anyway since he got out of surgery." He paused, looked at Drew, and then back at me. "Do you want me to tell the nurses you want to go visit?"

I shook my head. "Let's wait until I'm released, that way I can wear clothes instead of a hospital gown."

"Oh, speaking of which…" he pointed at a gym bag in the corner. "I brought you some clean ones."

I squeezed his hand. "You're awesome. Thank you for thinking of that."

He returned my squeeze. "Well, that's a nice compliment, but it wasn't me. Drew called and asked me to bring them."

"Oh. Well, you're awesome, too," I called out to Drew, but the compliment felt pathetic to me.

He finally turned from the sink. "Thanks. I'm happy that you're happy. I'm going to go see if they will do the release paperwork soon." Then he hurried out the door.

Luke looked at me with a question in his eyes, and I shrugged. "In a hurry to go home, I guess."

Luke somehow managed to look even more quizzical. "I'm not blind, Chloe."

Uh-oh.

"I've known Drew his whole life. I know him better than I know you, better than almost anyone, and I've never seen him act this way."

Turning my head away, I tried to lie. "I don't know what you're talking about. Act how?"

"Don't play dumb with me, Chloe." Luke moved over to the vacated chair and sat. "I don't care what's going on between you guys. It would be natural, because you spend so much time together. I just want you to remember two things."

I widened my eyes in question.

"One, you're not quite sixteen… and you know what I mean by that. And two, you be careful with him."

I laughed. "Seriously! Aren't you supposed to be telling him that he is supposed to be careful with me? Like, when the dad says 'if you hurt my daughter, I'll kill you' and goes about cleaning his gun?"

Luke managed a weak smile. "You are resilient, Chloe. You have a quality that makes you bounce back from the bad things in your life. Drew, he dwells on the bad things and never really gets over them. If he cares about you, really cares, that is a big deal. I don't want his heart stepped on any more than it already has been."

I suddenly remembered when Drew told me about how his mother had deserted him. Oh, she had better hope she didn't cross my path anytime soon. What a loser. In a way, I felt she didn't deserve Drew.

I nodded. "Okay. I'll remember."

Drew came back in the room, followed by a nurse who carried a big clipboard with lots of papers. She gave me a wide, toothy smile.

"Hi, Chloe. We're going to check your vitals again, and if they are all good, then we can unhook the IV, and you can go home.

"Okay." I tried to catch Drew's eye, but he was busy inspecting a picture of a bird on the wall.

After my vitals came back good, they removed the IV and allowed me to get dressed. First, I was given what seemed like a million directions on how to clean the wound and re-dress it and how much medication I was allowed to take. The nurses brought me a wheelchair and gave me some crutches to use if I needed them. I doubted I would use them. I had hurt my ankle once when I was twelve, and the crutches had hurt my armpits. Drew wheeled me into the hallway and then passed me off to Luke.

"I'm going to see if Alice is ready to go now." He left me sitting in the hallway with Luke.

"Nice," I said, to no one in particular.

Luke ignored the obvious snub from Drew and pushed me down the hallway to Gavin's room. It was dark in his room, and nearly silent, except for the low hum of some machine he was hooked up to. He had an IV too, with two bags hanging from the pole.

Luke wheeled me right up to the side of Gavin's bed, where I could easily hold his hand.

"Gavin," I whispered, "are you awake?"

His eyes fluttered a bit, but didn't open.

"Gavin, I'm sorry you're hurt. I hope you can hear me, because I just want you to know how grateful I am for your help." I was grateful. Even though he didn't come with Drew, he did come through in the end. "I hope you're going to be all right."

"He's probably on heavy pain killers," Luke explained.

"I know." I nodded. "I just wanted to say thank you." I squeezed Gavin's hand. "I'll try to come visit you every day until you go home."

Suddenly, I felt his hand move in mine, and I was sure he could hear me. His body simply wouldn't let him respond. "Okay. I have to go now, but I'll be back tomorrow."

I released his hand and nodded at Luke.

"I'm ready."

He wheeled me back into the hallway, and I saw Drew waiting with Alice by the nurses' station. Alice was also in a wheelchair. She looked exhausted, but other than that, you couldn't tell anything was wrong with her.

"Hi, Alice." I waved a little.

She lifted her hand in a weak wave back at me.

"Hey," she whispered. She looked up at Luke. Apparently, they had already met and no introduction was needed. "Are you guys sure it's okay if I come home with you? I'll understand if you don't want me."

Luke waved her comment away. "Don't be ridiculous. We wouldn't put you out in the street. Where else would you go?"

Even though Luke tried to reassure her, tears formed and fell down her cheeks. She didn't sob, but silent tears continued to escape from the corners of her eyes.

"Alice, it's all right. We're going to take care of you." I tried to help. I knew it was hard for her. She had lost everything.

Drew turned her wheelchair in the direction of the elevators. "Let's go."

We wheeled out to the car in silence. I guess no one could think of anything appropriate to say. The ride home was quiet, too.

The trees had already begun to turn; red, gold and burnt orange leaves fluttered over the road as we drove.

When we reached the gates of the community, I exhaled a large sigh of relief. I was home, and I was safe again. "Does this place have a name?" I asked. "I always just call it the community."

Luke laughed. "Actually, yes, the community has a name. It's called Arcadia Falls."

"Arcadia Falls." I tasted the name. "That's pretty. I like it."

While we drove through town, I stared out the window at all the places I'd missed while I was gone: The Java Bean, the library, even the school. There were people out on the sidewalks, and every single one of them waved when we drove by. I remembered why I'd left in the first place: to protect them.

I could smell smoke from the wood stoves as it curled out of the chimneys and mingled with the crisp fall air. For the first time, I realized it was a smell that reminded me of home. It reminded me of when I'd first come the year before. Where I'd lived in the city with my mom, there were no wood stoves curling smoke out of the chimneys.

Drew's rickety old truck sat in the driveway. We pulled up next to it and parked. Quickly, before anyone could come help me, I opened the door and tried to stand. I wanted to walk by myself.

Drew eyed me, as did Luke, but neither said anything. I clung onto the car door for a moment before I took a few limping steps. Drew went around to help Alice out of car, because she didn't attempt to get out, or even move.

I knew neither of them would have helped me out. Drew was my trainer, the one who said 'If I help you, then it's not helping you in the long run.' I took a few more steps and was certain I could at least make it into the house.

"Do you want your crutches?" Luke asked. He opened the trunk and lifted out my bag.

I smiled big. "No, I can do it."

"All right, then," Luke answered, but he grabbed the crutches out of the trunk anyway.

I was exhausted by the time I reached the front door. Drew had already gone inside and helped Alice sit on the couch by the time I even made it halfway. I finally tumbled down onto the couch next to Alice, causing her to bounce.

"Hey, Alice."

"Hmmm," she mumbled.

"You're going to like it here." I took her hand. "I promise."

Later that night, after I tried to bathe myself without getting my bandage wet, I explored my room. My bow sat in the same place I had left it. I lifted it and ran my fingertips over the smooth wood and beautiful carvings. Suddenly, I wondered what purpose Sostrate'd had when she gave it to me. Sostrate was a demi-goddess, and her intentions always came with deeper meaning. So far, I hadn't used her gift for anything except to kill one random vampire.

The thought actually made me nervous that the fighting between the hunters and the vampires might not be over.

⚔ ⚔ ⚔

The next day, my leg felt worse than the previous day, for some reason. I had plenty of pills to cut through the pain. My plan to avoid the crutches wasn't exactly working either. I had to use them to get around or deal with more pain.

Alice had shared my bed with me, and it looked like that was how it was going to be for a while since we had no spare bedrooms.

After using the bathroom and brushing my hair and teeth, I fell back on the bed and tried to wake Alice.

"Hey, you." I touched her nose. "It's time to wake up."

She moaned and swatted at my hand.

"Time to get up now." Still nothing, so I shook her a bit, and her eyes popped open.

"What?"

"It's time to get up."

She sat up and rubbed her eyes, then glanced around my room.

"Why can't I just sleep for a while? I'm so tired."

I sighed. "Alice, I know you're tired, but you need to get up and move around. If you stay in bed all day, it's not good for you. It could make you depressed."

She flopped back down, rolled over and covered her head. "I'm already depressed."

"Well, you shouldn't be. You're free now. You can do whatever you want."

I tried to roll her back over.

"That's the thing... I have nothing. What am I supposed to do?"

I lay back on the pillow beside her. "I don't know. You can stay here for as long as you want while you think about it. I'm sure there is something you have always dreamed of doing. Maybe now you can work on that. "

"Now, let's get up. We need to see how Oscar is doing this morning."

She sat up. "All right, fine."

"The shower is in there." I pointed at the bathroom door. "You can wear any of my clothes you want."

"Thank you." She reluctantly pulled the covers off, got out of bed, and headed for the bathroom. I lay there, enjoying the purple comforter and staring at my mother's picture on my nightstand. Man, I missed her. If she could only see me now, all shot up and recovering from a fight with vampires.

"I did it, Mom," I told the picture. "For the last year, all I could think about was killing the man who ordered your death. But now I know that you loved him, and I don't understand how you could love him." She stared back at me from the picture, smiling. "I know you loved me more. I just wish you were here to explain it all to me, because it's more than I can handle right now."

I thought of Trevor. I wondered if I was supposed to feel any sadness for the father I'd known for less than a year.

I didn't.

The only real emotion I could muster about Trevor's death was happiness. I remembered not wanting Christina to stab him, and I wondered why I didn't just let her. It was a weak moment. I didn't want to be weak.

I knew we would still have to fight vampires. I knew that would always be an issue; we were vampire hunters, after all. With Trevor gone, we were safer, and that made me happy.

After Alice had dressed in a pair of my jeans and a sweatshirt, we tried to go downstairs.

"I could piggy back you," Alice suggested.

I shook my head. "No, I'd be afraid you'd fall. I'm bigger than you."

"How about if we just try to go down with you hanging your arm around my shoulders and using me like a crutch and the handrail for balance on the other."

"Yeah, that sounds good." I wished the vampire healing thing would hurry up and kick in. I didn't like to worry about getting around. I figured it was taking longer because the wound was so deep.

We jostled comically down the stairs and into the kitchen where we found Luke making sandwiches.

"Hello, ladies. Did you rest well?"

"Yes, except for waking up a few times because of my leg. Otherwise, I slept great."

Alice whispered, "Yes, thank you." She pulled out a chair from the kitchen table for me to sit in, and then she pulled another out for herself.

"Where's Drew?" I asked.

"He went out for his run, and then he was going to get Oscar."

"Oh good," I said. "I was wondering how Oscar was doing."

Luke put the sandwiches onto plates and cut them all in half. "He's doing well. The medics said he could leave the care center, but he's going to have to stay with us for a few days so we can monitor him. He had a lot of bites, and we just want to be certain he isn't going to have any side effects of a partial turning."

He handed us each a plate, and I asked him, "Don't you have to drink blood after you've been bitten to complete the change?"

I'd read a lot of vampire stuff while I was at Trevor's and thought that was the only way someone could become a vampire.

He nodded. "Yes, normally it would take drinking the victim's blood until their heart almost stops, then they would have to drink blood, any blood, to begin the process of the change."

Alice stared at the table, seemingly uninterested.

"But, an incident like this, with this many bites, the victim may not become a full vampire but could have side effects of vampirism, like sensitivity to sunlight and becoming exceptionally strong for no known reason."

I took a huge bite of my sandwich. "Oh, I see."

He sat down at the table with us, his own sandwich in front of him. "It's just better to be safe than sorry, so Oscar is going to stay with us for a few days."

Alice hadn't touched her sandwich. She asked, "Is it even safe for him to go home at all? Won't there be vampires who will want to want to avenge Trevor's death?"

I looked at Luke and raised my eyebrows.

"Most likely, yes. They will probably look for him, considering the circumstances, but really, that will all depend on what he wants in the long run."

Just then, we heard the door open and voices in the hallway. Drew and Oscar appeared in the kitchen.

"Hey!" I waved at them, smiling at Drew and then Oscar. "How are you feeling, Oscar?"

"A lot better than before, that's for sure." He shrugged. "But I've been better."

He did look much better, except he was still quite pale. He had a hoodie on, one of Drew's, so I couldn't see his arms where he'd been bitten. The ones on his neck were visible, however, faintly scarred dots where he'd been punctured by fangs. It seemed they should only be scabbed rather than scarred already. Maybe vampire bites healed quickly because they came from a vampire.

"What about you?" He pulled out a chair at the table and sat, running one of his hands over his hair. "Are you doing okay? I heard you were shot."

I stuck my leg out and pulled up my jeans to show him the bandage. "Yeah, it's not so bad, compared to Gavin."

Oscar glanced over at Alice. She still hadn't touched her sandwich.

"You should eat that," he told her.

"I'm not hungry." She scooted it toward him, and he scooted right back to her.

"You should eat it," he told her again. "I'm sure you need to eat something."

Without any more argument, she picked up the sandwich and took a bite of it. I ignored the fact he was using his siren stuff on Alice because it was for her good.

I turned to Luke, deliberately ignoring Drew. "Will you take me to the hospital?"

Following my lead, Drew ignored me right back by opening the refrigerator and rummaging around inside.

"Yes, I'll take you over there." Luke ate the last bite of his sandwich and stood to put the plate into the sink. "You ready?"

"Yeah." I looked at Oscar and Alice. "You guys going to be okay here while I'm gone?"

Alice stared down at the table, and Oscar nodded.

"It's okay. I'm here," Drew said, but it was more to reassure them because neither of us would have left them alone, anyway.

I nodded. "All right. Let's go then."

I grabbed my crutches, and Luke picked his keys off the hook by the door.

⚔⚔⚔

I opened the door to Gavin's room and expected to see him lying there like before. He was lying there like I'd left him, but I was surprised to see a blond-haired woman sitting in the chair beside his bed. She must have heard me hobbling through the door on my crutches, because she lifted her head and turned toward me. When she did, I saw Drew's eyes stare back at me, and I realized she must be Gavin and Drew's mother.

"Um... hi." I wasn't sure what to say. I was biased against her already, and I didn't even know her. "I just came to see how Gavin was doing today."

"You must be Chloe." She didn't smile or offer to shake hands with me.

Maybe she was mad at me. The only reason Gavin got shot was because of me, so it wasn't completely unreasonable she might be mad at me. I looked down at the sterile white floor and fiddled with my hands. I mumbled. "Uh, I'm sorry Gavin got shot."

She made a noise that sounded sort of like an 'uh huh'.

So I continued to babble. "But it was nice of him to come and help rescue me."

Gavin's mother nodded and reached for his hand. "Yes. Thankfully, he is going to be all right. He'll live to hunt another day. We take this risk on every mission." She eyeballed me and pinched her lips together. "Hopefully, next time, his head will be in the right place, and he might avoid being injured. Not to mention the fact that he never should have been on an unauthorized mission in the first place."

I wasn't sure exactly what she was talking about, but I think she blamed me, and maybe Drew, for Gavin being in the hospital.

It was time to go.

"Well, I gotta go. Will you tell him I stopped by?"

"Of course," she told me with a little bit of snoot coating her voice. She turned back to Gavin, basically dismissing me.

"Well... bye." As smoothly as I could, I backed away from her and out the door. Once I was back in the hallway, I couldn't help but mutter, "Nice meeting you, too."

Man, I really liked that woman less and less, and I barely knew her at all.

Luke was waiting for me at the nurses' station. He leaned on the counter and chatted it up with a couple of the pretty, dark-haired ones and drank coffee out of a little paper cup. I guess he'd made some friends while he was laid up in here after the attack.

"I'm ready," I told him and hobbled on by.

"What happened?" he asked, hurrying to catch up with me.

I stopped at the elevator and slammed the button for the main floor. "Nothing..."

"Doesn't look like nothing."

The elevator door opened. "His mom was there." We both stepped inside. "She just seemed... rude, I guess."

Luke didn't look surprised. I guess he probably didn't like her much either, considering how close he was with Drew. I couldn't see him defending her after knowing Drew all that time.

"Daphne Turner is...," he paused, trying to find the right words, "somewhat strange." He didn't look certain of his choice of words.

"Well, I didn't really like her much, just from what I'd heard about her... and now, her being rude to me, too, didn't help her case any."

The elevator doors swooshed open, and Luke held them while I hobbled out.

"Drew told you about Gavin?"

I nodded. "Yeah, but he wouldn't have if I hadn't made him."

"It is a big deal for him to tell you about all that."

"I know," I told him. That was the end of the conversation.

We crossed the hospital lobby and exited through the front doors. I felt bad for Drew, but maybe he was better off without a mother like her in his life. I felt horrible even thinking something like that. No one should be without a mother, but I couldn't imagine who would want one that had the ability to leave her child as a baby and then live in the same town with him without ever trying to make contact.

I felt like smacking her.

When we arrived home, Drew paced the living room again while Alice and Oscar sat on the couch and watched him. They looked cozy sitting there together. Oscar had his arm thrown over the back of the couch behind Alice. Well, I couldn't really complain. She needed comfort and attention, and Oscar was nice, and hot, too.

"What's going on?" I asked when Luke and I came through the door. "How long has he been doing that?"

I leaned my crutches against the end of the couch and flopped down next to Alice.

Drew didn't give either of them a chance to answer. "We had to drive up to the gate and meet with some guy who is apparently a courier for Trevor's lawyer."

I felt my jaw drop, and a quick glance showed Luke's hanging open, too. For a minute, I couldn't find my voice. The first of my concerns, before anything else, was the safety of everyone here. I worried we had unintentionally brought the danger to them.

"What did he want?" Luke asked.

"Don't worry." Alice shifted on the couch, effectively scooting a little bit closer to Oscar, if that was possible. "It didn't seem like he wanted any trouble." She leaned forward to pluck a paper off the top of a manila envelope and handed it to me.

I scanned the first line. "What? We have to go to a will reading? You have got to be kidding me! I don't want anything of his."

"Read on, Chloe." Drew pointed at the paper. "He didn't leave you anything."

I stared at the paper and read down the first paragraph.

"Oh."

It was Alice they wanted to meet with.

I shrugged and handed the paper back to Alice. I guess I was a little jealous I didn't get anything and she did. I had no idea why I was jealous about it. "So we have to go there and meet with this guy?"

"Yeah, there is no way we are letting them through the gates."

Luke reached for the paper and scanned it. "When is the meeting?"

Drew went back to his pacing. "In four days."

"We will be ready," I told him, and then looked at Alice. "Right?"

She nodded in agreement. "I'll be ready."

The next day, I woke a little later than I wanted. I had slept in again, and it was about nine. I rolled over and was surprised not to feel any pain in my calf. I gently pulled the blanket over and bent my leg at the knee to check and see how the wound was healing. I peeled the tape off around the square bandage, peeked at the wound and discovered that it was covered in a thick, bumpy scar tissue.

Gross!

It actually looked like a big, huge wart or something. It was nasty, but at least I could cover it with my pants. I sat up and slid my legs over the side of the bed, then slowly stood, testing the ability of my legs to hold me up. Once I was all the way up on my feet, I took a few tentative steps.

Nothing, no pain.

Yay for vampire super-healing!

At least I wouldn't need the crutches any more. It did seem a little strange that just the day before I couldn't even get down the stairs without help, but I sure as heck wasn't going to complain about it.

After a quick shower, I dressed and went in search of Luke to take me to the hospital so I could see Gavin. I needed update him on everything that had happened.

I found Luke at the kitchen table reading the newspaper.

"Morning."

He smiled and set his paper down on the table. "Feeling any better this morning?"

I nodded and headed for the fridge. "Yeah, actually, perfect. Look!"

I turned, left the fridge door hanging open, stuck my leg out toward him and wiggled it around.

"No crutches!" I declared with a smile.

He raised his eyebrows. "How is that possible? You were shot all the way through your calf."

I let my pant leg fall back down, grabbed an apple and a bottle of water out of the fridge, and closed the door.

"Vampire super-healing," I told him, then uncapped my water and took a big swig.

He shook his head in a combination of amazement and surprise. "I should have known."

"It's okay," I said, and I shrugged. "I only realized it was happening because I cut myself last year, and then I was punctured by a branch when I tried to escape from Trevor. I think it's getting stronger as I get older, because it's only been a few days, and this was more than a scratch."

Luke's paper crinkled while he folded it into a square. "It makes sense that it would get stronger as you get older."

I grinned. "You should see my fire power now."

He chuckled. "That good, huh?"

"Yup!" I polished my apple on my shirt. "Can you take me to the hospital today?"

"Absolutely. I already expected you'd ask. I'm ready when you are."

He scooted his chair out and stood up.

"Let's go now. I'm ready."

I hurried out of the kitchen and grabbed my sweatshirt off the hook by the door.

When we arrived at the hospital, I left Luke at the nurses' station to chat with his lady friends while I went in to see Gavin. I worried his mother would be in his room. I really did not want to meet up with her again.

I crept up to the door and tried to listen. I could hear voices through the door, but they sounded more like part of an action scene on television. I rapped lightly on the door before I opened it a crack.

"Gavin?" I whispered.

I couldn't see him because the curtain was drawn across his half of the room. As I had suspected, his television was on, and it was blaring male voices above the sound of revving car engines.

"Gavin?" I tried a bit louder, as I entered the room. I pushed the curtain aside and saw he was asleep.

I studied him for a moment before I woke him. He slept on his back, with his head tilted. He had an oxygen cannula in his nose, and his outturned wrist had an IV inserted. I hated to wake him, but I wanted him to know I'd come to see him. I smoothed down my hair, moved to the chair beside his bed and scooted it close to the bed.

After thinking about it for a minute, I gently took his hand in mine. He woke up then, his long eyelashes fluttered open and exposed his pretty green eyes that were so similar to Drew's.

"Hey," I whispered.

"Hi," he said, his voice weak.

"Do you want some water?" I asked. He had a pitcher and a plastic cup on the rolling table near the head of his bed.

"Sure," he nodded slightly.

I let go of his hand and poured water into the cup until it was about half full.

"How are you doing?" I asked him, handing him the water.

He adjusted his bed so he sat up more. "I'm doing better. I guess I've been better." He finally smiled. "I'm glad you came to see me."

"I came to see you yesterday, but your mom was here."

He rolled his eyes like he already knew how she'd acted. "Yeah, sorry about her. She's just overprotective."

"Yeah, I'd be the same way if I had a kid," I said.

In my head, I thought, She has two kids, not one. Maybe she should try protecting the other one every now and then.

"I'm just glad you're okay," I finished. "That's all that matters."

He nodded and closed his eyes.

"Are you tired?" I asked.

"Yeah, it's these pain killers. I sleep all the time."

Suddenly, I didn't feel comfortable at all. I had come to tell Gavin he and I couldn't continue any kind of relationship, but there never really was a relationship in the first place. It didn't seem right to say anything about that now. It all seemed petty compared to him lying there recovering from a gunshot wound and major surgery.

"What is it, Chloe?"

"Hmmm?" I had drifted away while considering my reasons for wanting to talk to him. "Oh, nothing. I was just thinking."

"About what?" Even in his drug-induced haze he managed to raise his eyebrows in question.

I smiled and hoped it looked real. "It's nothing. Just worried about you, is all."

God, I am the biggest liar in the world.

⤳ ⤳ ⤳

I left Gavin at the hospital without telling him how I felt and probably had him thinking the complete opposite of what I wanted to tell him. Sometimes it felt like I failed at everything I tried to do. I wondered when I would actually succeed at something.

I had gone up to my room after we got home and stayed there all night. I didn't want to see anyone or have to talk to anyone, especially Drew.

The next morning, I woke at five and slid out of bed quietly, trying not to wake Alice. There was something I wanted to do, and I figured I could take my run while I was at it. I dressed in black yoga pants and tank top with a pink hoodie over the top. I brushed my teeth, brushed my hair and pulled it into a ponytail. Finally, I grabbed my MP3 player and earbuds off the dresser on my way out the door.

I tiptoed down the stairs, trying to be as quiet as I could, and turned the corner to go into the kitchen. At five in the morning, I should have expected others might be up, but when I slammed into Drew coming around the corner, I yelped in surprise and punched him in the face out of reflex.

"Ow!" Caught totally off guard, he covered his nose with his hand. "What the hell, Chloe?"

"Oh, my god. I'm so sorry!"

I moved forward instinctively to try to look at his nose.

"I didn't mean to hit you… you surprised me."

He grunted and held his hand up in the 'just give me a minute to recover' signal. After a couple of deep breaths, he removed his hand from his nose, examining it to see if there was blood. Finding no blood, he whispered, "Why don't you be more careful?"

I tried to sidestep away from him because he was in my path. "You scared me. I didn't know you were down here."

He sidestepped also so I couldn't pass. "I'm always up this early."

"I know, but I haven't been here for a while, okay?" I sidestepped back the other way. "Let me get by!" I hissed at him, trying to keep my voice down.

He surprised me by grabbing my upper arms and pulling me toward him.

"No," he said simply and lifted his hand. I felt one finger run gently down my jawline. I tried to pull away from him. I didn't want to play his kiss-me-one-minute-ignore-me-the-next games that morning. I had plans for the day. My efforts were useless, however. He cupped my face with both hands and kissed me.

Oh, man.

I kissed him back. I let him pull me close and wrapped my arms around his shoulders as his moved to my waist.

When it was over, which was far too soon in my opinion, I pulled away and ran for the door. I didn't want him to say anything like before about how he shouldn't have done it or how we wouldn't be doing it again. I didn't want him to ruin it.

The only thing I heard before I jammed my earbuds in was him calling out for me to wait.

While I ran, I chose ear-blasting, blood-pumping music that wouldn't make me cry.

What the heck am I going to do about this?

I just didn't think I could take any more. It was time to make some kind of decision, on both ends. I still had Gavin to deal with. He would probably be upset if he knew I was going to choose Drew over him. Oh, for crying out loud. I never thought in a million years this would happen.

I ran the trails through the woods, over the tops of the dirt and crunchy autumn leaves, with music blaring in my ears and sweat running down my face. When I emerged from the woods on the edge of town, I ran down the side streets all the way to the other side of town, toward the cemetery... toward my mother.

I didn't even slow when I passed through the tall iron gates that surrounded the small cemetery in the woods. I ran between, and probably over, some of the graves, trying to remember where my mother's plot was located.

Finally, as the sun began to rise, I arrived at the spot under the huge maple trees, which now had golden leaves, and I dropped to my knees before her headstone. With a yank, I ripped the earbuds out and let them fall to the ground. My fingers dug into the grass surrounding her plot.

I had been holding back tears since I'd left the house, but as soon as I looked up and my eyes met her name on the headstone, the dam broke.

"Why are you gone?" I screamed at her. "You should be here to help me!"

I fell back onto my butt, wrapped my arms around my knees and rocked back and forth until the tears diminished.

"I need you," I whispered to her, hoarsely. "I need you."

No one spoke back to me. Her ghost did not appear. The sounds of nature were all that could be heard around me. My mother's headstone, where Sostrate had first appeared, remained the same. No demi-goddess appearances for me today, I guess. It was just me, talking to my dead mother.

I'd half expected… no, I had hoped and wanted Drew to come after me. But he hadn't. So I sat there until the need to pee drove me back home.

Back at the house, I entered quietly. Finding no one, I removed my shoes and headed back up the stairs to my room.

Alice was in bed, awake, staring up at the ceiling. She turned her head toward me when she heard the door open. The moment she saw me, her eyes widened. "What happened to you?"

"Nothing, I just went for a run." I waved her off and headed for the bathroom to pee. When I came back out, I fell down onto the bed beside her.

"It looks like you've been crying." She turned onto her side to face me.

For a moment, I didn't say anything.

Finally, I decided to go ahead and let it out. I told her all of it… Drew, Gavin, my mother…all of it.

When I'd finally exhausted the whole story to her, she lay there for a moment, taking it all in, and then she said, "Well, except for the part about your mom not being here, none of that really sounds so bad."

I sighed. "Really? Because it feels crappy to me."

"I'm sorry it does, but what can I say? I would love to have two guys after me."

"But that's the problem. Drew acts like he likes me one minute, and the next he ignores me."

She shrugged like it was nothing. "Confront him, then. Tell him it's either one way or the other."

"He told me that he doesn't ever want to be second to anyone," I said.

She raised her eyebrows. "So he has already told you. See, what's happening here is that he is telling you to make the choice. You have to tell him now."

I rolled back over to stare at the ceiling again. "I'm waiting until Gavin is better so I can tell him first. I need to make it clear to

Gavin that I have feelings for Drew."

"Oh, I see."

We both lay there in silence, staring at the ceiling. I decided to change the subject. "Alice?"

"Hmm?"

"When we found Oscar, he had all those bite marks."

"Yeah."

"How come I have never seen you with any bite marks? I know you gave Trevor your blood."

She released a long sigh and closed her eyes as if she were blocking out a memory.

"Because they aren't where you can see them."

I must have given her a confused expression, because she suddenly flung back the purple comforter, and her eyes filled with sadness. She gently pulled up her shorts just enough to show me that her inner thighs were thick with the scars of vampire bites.

"Oh, Alice," I breathed.

She let her shorts fall back down and covered up with the comforter again.

I decided that since I'd shared, Alice needed to share something, too. "Did you love my father?" I asked her.

She nodded. "I did. I don't know what kind of love, but he was all I knew."

I could understand that; I had all along. "How could you love someone who was so cruel?"

She shrugged. "I don't really know. I think…" she thought a moment, "I think that it's easy to love someone when they take care of you, give you everything you need, and give you such a grand home." She smiled, and I saw her eyes sparkle. "Chloe, he was never horrible. Not to me."

I just couldn't believe that. I wanted to believe that he was horrible to her on a daily basis, but I knew that wasn't true because, somehow, this psycho freak had made my mother love him enough to live with him and create a child with him.

"How could you have betrayed me like that, Alice? I understand you would do whatever Trevor asked of you, but he was going to kill me."

"You think I never thought of that?" Her voice took on an edge. "Do you really think I had the power to defy him? I wouldn't dare, not over something like what he had been planning for you. This plan of his had been in place since before you were born. I wasn't about to go there. I never told him no. Why would I? He saved me."

I guess I could understand that, but her betrayal was hard for me to swallow. I just couldn't trust her.

After a pause, she finished by saying, "And I didn't betray you; I betrayed Trevor. I realized what he was doing to you was wrong, and I was going to help you. I knew it would be the end of my life if he caught me, but I didn't care."

I pondered that for a moment. It was true.

We both lay back down to stare at the ceiling and feel sorry for ourselves.

Several days passed quickly. Oscar was situated with Drew in his room and the house had quickly become very crowded. It wasn't a big house, by any means. It was more on the quaint and small side, so it was hard to get used to two extra people living with us. For me, especially, since I had just come from having a whole suite all to myself for almost a year.

We were sort of a silent and brooding bunch, keeping to ourselves. I still went to see Gavin twice more and hoped each time his mother wouldn't be there. The whole situation sucked, because I didn't want to give Gavin the wrong idea about why I was coming to visit; I didn't want him to think I didn't care about him at all, either. I mean, he was shot trying to save Drew and me.

He finally came home the day before we were supposed to go to the meeting with the lawyer about Trevor's will. I knew I wouldn't see him until after he was up and around. That was probably a good thing. I really felt like Drew and I needed some more alone time.

But before the alone time, we had to go see the lawyer.

The day of the meeting, Luke sat us down to explain the situation.

Our living room was suddenly bursting with vampire hunters. Oscar was excluded because there was no reason for him to be involved in the plans. Alice was allowed, since she was the reason we were going in the first place, and we needed to protect her.

"The mission, this time," Luke stood in front of the television, speaking to the group, "is to keep the peace..." He paused. "We have no targets, even though the destination is the Talon business building, downtown on First Street."

A round of moans and mumbles made its way through the

group.

I looked from Luke to Drew and around the group. No one looked happy.

"Why no targets, Luke?" Joe called out.

I was confused. "I don't understand why you all look so upset?"

Luke leaned on the wall beside the television. "The Talon business building is a vampire-run establishment. Any particular business you can think of that a vampire would need is run from that building."

"What? Are you serious?" I threw my hands in the air. "How come this hasn't been taken care of yet?"

Drew put a hand on my shoulder in a pathetic attempt to calm me. "Hunting vampires is not always as simple as it may sound. We cannot simply stroll in there and annihilate the whole building." He removed his hand. "We need to stay anonymous to some degree, and taking out an entire building that is smack in the middle of town is not discreet."

"I just don't understand. Why can't we do that? Then it would be over, and we would have a few hundred less vampires to hunt than we do now."

Joe stepped into the conversation. "If we take out the whole building, we would literally have a vampire versus hunter war on our hands. And I know it may look like there are a lot of us, but there aren't nearly enough to fight a war with the undead. Besides, there is legal stuff to think about. If we blew the building up, it would be investigated. Part of what we do is to stay invisible. There are cops who are vampires, not to mention agents for the government, and crime investigators. We cannot risk the community."

Drew nodded. "Which is why we take them a few at a time."

I understood that part. No one wanted to risk the community. This was our home, children and babies were here, and no one would risk losing their children to the authorities. I could only imagine what would happen if the authorities were to come here and find the arsenals that were stored in the homes.

I nodded. "All right. But now we have to go in there. With all those vampires?"

I shuddered with thought of being so vulnerable.

"Yes, we have to go in," Luke said. "Alice has to be at the will reading, and this is actually the perfect excuse for us to get a look inside that building."

I sighed. It was going to be a long day.

>)>)>)

We arrived at the Talon Building with an entire entourage of hunters surrounding Alice as if she were the President of the United States. The building stood tallest among the other buildings on the street. Unlike Trevor's windowless house, this building was made purely of tinted glass, which reflected the lights of the busy city.

Our group, prepared for anything, entered through the large double doors of the building. From the outside, we looked like an ordinary group of people, but we wore weapons strapped onto every available spot on our bodies underneath our clothes. We were trained killers… well, most of us.

Of course Gavin wasn't with us because he was still at home, but oddly enough, Christina came. It was probably because her father was on this mission. Other than that, the rest of the group were seasoned hunters. Drew, Luke, Sara Jane—who was the second grade teacher at school—Joe, and a couple others I didn't know well made up our group.

As we strode across the grey marble floors of the lobby, toward the elevators, I felt like we should have had a soundtrack. It was right out of the movies. No one even looked our way. It was nighttime, but the lobby was bursting with activity like it was midday lunch hour at the mall.

We stopped in front of a bank of elevators, and Luke stepped up to the directory list beside the buttons and ran his finger down it.

"Here it is, Maxwell and Associates." He pushed the up button for the elevator.

The rest of the names on the list made me want to laugh. Luke was right when he said every business a vampire would need was in this building. Aside from lawyers, there was also a psychiatrist's office, a bank, a real estate agency called Everlasting Realty, and a dental office called Deadly Smiles.

While we waited for the elevator, I turned to check out the people in the lobby. Most were dressed in business suits. Few wore any kind of casual wear like we did. Nearly every one of them had the pale white skin of vampires.

Oh, my god. Suddenly, the gravity of where we were—of the situation— hit me like a ton of bricks.

I glanced around to see how the rest of the group was dealing with this. Most of them had their backs to the elevator doors so that they could see the lobby.

I nudged Drew. "I still don't understand how this is possible."

He shook his head. "How do you think vampires have lived among us for so long? It's because they look like people, but are far more powerful."

The elevator doors whooshed open, and Drew shoved me forward so we could all smash into the small space. That was insane. I just couldn't stomach the feeling. I couldn't wrap my mind around how could we just waltz in there and feel safe doing it. Alice had better be feeling damned lucky she had us.

I felt bad after thinking that last bit. We were making her come here. She had said before that she didn't want anything from Trevor.

I elbowed her and asked, "You okay?"

She met my eyes and nodded, but I could tell she was scared. She had lived around vampires for a long time, but she was protected because she was in Trevor's home. This was definitely a different experience for her.

The elevator doors opened, and we all moved into a busy office with a cubicle farm taking up the floor space.

A pale, dark-haired woman sat behind a tall counter to our left. She smiled, her crimson red lips turning up at the corners.

"Hello, how may I help you this evening?" she asked while she cradled her telephone.

Luke stepped forward. "We have a meeting with Abraham Maxwell."

"Oh, perfect. He is expecting you. Please follow me." She stepped down from the platform and led us down a long hallway alongside the cubicles until we arrived at an office with glass walls sectioning it off from the rest of the space. She rapped on the door and peeked through the window.

I could see a man who looked about twenty-five sitting behind a large mahogany desk on the other side of the glass. He turned away from a computer screen, saw our large group outside his windows, and beckoned us in with a smile.

Miss Crimson Lips opened the door and held it for us.

Abraham Maxwell stood and gestured to the couches while we filed into his office. "Please, have a seat."

I glared at him as I passed, but Luke smiled and nodded, extending his hand. "Thank you for having all of us."

I really hoped this was going to be over soon. I didn't feel comfortable being in an entire building full of vampires. With not much room to sit, I managed to squeeze onto a couch beside Alice and Sarah Jane. Drew remained standing beside the door.

Maxwell lowered himself back into his chair. "Won't you sit?" Drew shook his head. "I prefer to stand, if you don't mind."

"Not at all." Maxwell turned his attention back to Luke. "All right, I have summoned you here to commence the reading of Trevor Krasimir's last will and testament. I have asked you here a bit early because I wish to explain to you that everyone who is listed in the will must be present for the reading." He raised his eyebrows. "Therefore, we will be joined by others shortly."

Oh, great. I could tell by the look on this guy's face that I wasn't going to like this at all. I peeked over at Drew. Boy, he looked mighty irritated at the whole situation.

The lawyer sat back in his chair and eyed Drew as well. "Being as you are here on vampire business matters, nothing more, I trust there will not be any problems from your hunters."

The whole group stiffened and shifted simultaneously. These people had a gene in their blood that made them want to kill vampires; they couldn't help it. I could see already how hard it was for them to sit here in an office across a desk from one and not put a bullet in his heart.

Luke said, "No problem from us as long as a truce remains with yours."

Maxwell stood and stuck out his hand. "It's a deal."

Luke took the vampire's cold hand. I could almost feel him cringe inside. "Deal."

Deal, my ass! Ugh!

Just then, Miss Crimson Lips rapped on the window again.

"Come," Maxwell called out.

The door opened and the one person I could have gone the rest of my life without seeing again entered.

"Vanessa," I mumbled.

She wore a floor-length, white fur coat, and her chocolate hair was piled up on top of her head in a huge mass of curls. I couldn't see the expression in her eyes, because they were hidden behind a pair of large, black sunglasses that contrasted with her pale skin, making it seem even whiter than it was.

Freakin' wonderful.

Maxwell stood up to greet her. "Nice to see you, Vanessa.

Would you like a seat?"

I chuckled to myself while I watched Vanessa scan the room. We were taking up all the couches and chairs, so there was nowhere else to sit.

Ha! Take that, freaky psycho vamp.

My victory was short-lived. Miss Crimson Lips produced a chair from the other room and sat it off to the side of Maxwell's desk, as far from us as she possibly could.

"There you are." She offered the chair to Vanessa.

I was surprised Christina had kept her mouth shut the entire time. It probably had something to do with her father being there. Funny how people were totally different around their parents.

Maxwell shuffled a few papers on his desk. "We await one more, and then we can begin."

One more… who else was coming?

Vanessa removed her sunglasses and peered at me with a smug look. "It's so nice to see you, Chloe. May I inquire as to why you are here?"

Oh, the nerve. "Trevor was my father," I responded. "Why wouldn't I be here?"

She waved her perfectly manicured fingers through the air. "Oh, I don't know, Trevor not really giving a damn about you wouldn't have anything to do with it, now, would it?"

"Enough!" Maxwell snapped at Vanessa. "We are here to discuss the last will and testament, and that is all. Any other issues can be addressed elsewhere."

Yay, Maxwell.

Once again, there was a rap on the door. After it opened, I was surprised to see Dahlia there. She was as beautiful as ever, her porcelain skin and pale hair making her look like a goddess of some kind. Only today, instead of interest, I saw anger when she laid eyes on me.

She quickly capped it and removed black leather gloves from her hands.

"Hello, Abraham. It is so nice to see you."

It occurred to me this was the first time I had ever heard her speak. Her voice was delicate and beautiful, like the rest of her.

He took her hand and kissed the back of it, then led her to another chair that had been set beside Vanessa's. "And it is even more so to have you here, Dahlia."

She glanced at where Alice and I sat smashed together and gave us a nod.

I wanted this to be over. At least we were able to get on with the reading.

"Very well. Now that we are all here, we can commence the reading." Maxwell sat in his chair and pushed a button on his phone. "Margaret, would you please bring the television?"

"Right away, Mr. Maxwell," she piped back through the intercom.

Not a minute later, there she was, rolling in a flat screen on a cart. She parked it off to the side where everyone would be able to see it.

"Trevor left us a video will. In support of the video, there is paperwork to accompany it."

He stood and inserted a DVD into the disc drive underneath the television, then took his chair while Margaret dimmed the lights.

Suddenly, a face I never wanted to see again appeared before us. I shifted uncomfortably and gave Alice's leg a squeeze before I stood. I couldn't handle sitting and staring at his face, especially with Vanessa and Dahlia in the room.

While Trevor spoke, I moved to stand beside Drew. He silently moved behind me and wrapped his arms around me. I knew it was hard for him to make himself vulnerable by not having quick access to his guns.

I snuck a glance at Christina and saw her staring at us. Our eyes met, but she quickly looked away. I could see jealousy there, still. Somehow, I didn't think she and I were ever going be friends.

"If you are watching this, then I no longer exist," Trevor stated. His dark hair and eyes focused on the camera. "If you are sitting in this room, it means you were important to me in one way or another, and I have given you something of importance that I possessed during my existence."

His face, his voice, everything about him made me shake. I hated him. Even though he was gone, I still hated him.

"Let's begin with my estates. All of my homes, including the one in Greece, and everything in them, I bestow to Alice Matthews. Alice, you may do whatever you wish with the homes. I know I haven't said in clear enough words what you meant to me. So maybe the wealth and importance of such a gift will show you just how much you meant to me. If I could have come close to loving anyone else but Felicia again, it would have been you."

Alice burst into tears. I had thought we were past this, but I could understand how being able to see his face would be hard on her. Christina, of all people, got up from her space on the other couch and grabbed the box of tissues from Maxwell's desk. She handed them to Alice with a slight nod and then went back to her spot.

I was proud of Christina then.

"Next, the three clubs I own will cede to Vanessa Darling." Trevor smiled into the camera. "Vanessa, I expect these clubs to be run in the same fashion I have managed them in the past. If you have any problems with the clubs on your own, contact Abraham Maxwell to see about finding a prospective buyer."

Vanessa sniffled, as though she were actually upset he was gone and she had three of his clubs.

"Now, I have several items in a safe. They are very old, and I would like them to return from whence they came. Dahlia, the jewels inside my safe are those that were stolen from your crown several hundred years ago. I have no more use for them. I apologize for our past conflict. I took the jewels to make your people hate you. It was that or kill you... and I couldn't bring myself to kill you... not you... I regret our troubles in the past, but I am honored to have known you.

"Finally, there is a matter of my bank accounts. I have an account for each of the clubs that will be turned over to Vanessa, but my personal accounts shall be payable to Alice Matthews. This shall be an easy transition to Alice and... Alice, you will never go back to where I found you. Make something great of yourself."

Oh, holy hell! He pretty much gave her everything. I looked over at her and saw her clutching her hands together. Sarah Jane had her arms around her, trying to provide some sort of comfort.

Trevor had one last message for us.

"I have no regrets for the life I lived, for the things I did during my existence, and I hope that every single one of you treat your lives in the same way.

"One last note: Chloe, if you have survived me and are in attendance to see this, remember that you are my daughter, my blood flows through you. If you have survived, then I am still immortal, in a sense... make yourself extraordinary."

What a load of crap! Ugh.

Trevor faded away and the lights came back on. There was silence in the room except for Alice's sobs.

Reluctantly, I pulled out of Drew's arms and looked up at him. "Thank you," I whispered.

He nodded and went back into door guard mode.

"Well," Maxwell said, drawing the word out. He shuffled some paperwork. "There is a lot of paperwork that needs to be filled out. Alice, we need identification and signatures from you for the bank and title transfers. There are three homes in the United States and one in Greece."

"I don't want anything."

I had sat down next to her again and put my hand on her leg.

"Alice, you have earned this. You gave him your heart and soul; you earned it with your blood. Don't make that into nothing."

"At least keep the house in Greece," Sarah Jane suggested, "and the money."

Vanessa made a choking sound. "How crass to be discussing this here. Some of us are distraught."

I'd had it with that hag. "Shut up, Vanessa!" I flexed my hands and prepped to blow her away.

"Chloe!" Luke scolded me. "Not here."

"Luke, you told me this would stay under control." Maxwell stood, quick on the defense.

Vanessa also stood. "Our game is not yet over, young one."

Dahlia stood. "Perhaps it would be beneficial to everyone if the hunters leave and the papers are signed another day."

"No," Alice said. She stood on shaky legs. "I'll sign them now."

She moved from the couch to the desk where Maxwell had the papers. "Mr. Maxwell, would you be so kind as to help me find buyers for all the homes except the home in Greece? I don't care to live in any of his homes here."

Maxwell smiled kindly at her. "I would be happy to do that for you, Ms. Matthews. Please, just sign each of these papers here, here, here, and here." He marked an X everywhere she needed to sign. I felt uncomfortable with us not reading anything she signed, but we were all more than ready to leave.

Alice signed while Vanessa and I glared at each other. She knew absolutely that I would burn her beautiful brown hair right off her head if she made the slightest move toward me, or any of us, for that matter.

"There, all done." Alice clicked the pen and set it down in front of Maxwell.

"Thank you, Ms. Matthews. I will send your information by courier and call you to let you know when the transactions are completed."

Alice sniffled. "Thank you so much, Mr. Maxwell."

As soon as the words were out of her mouth, the entire group stood and made for the door. We didn't run or anything, but it was evident that none of the parties involved were happy about being there.

On the way out, Luke shook hands with Maxwell again. "Thank you for your time."

And then we exited the office and quickly walked to the elevators.

✗✗✗

Back at home, Oscar sat at the kitchen table anxiously awaiting our arrival.

"What happened? How did it go?" He stood. "Alice, why are you crying?"

Luke patted Alice on the back. "Honey, why don't you go on up and get some rest. We can explain everything to Oscar."

She sniffled, nodded, and then headed up the stairs.

I pulled out a chair and sat down, while Drew made his way to the fridge.

Oscar looked back and forth amongst all of us and threw his hands up. "Well?"

Luke opened a bag of carrots and started to chop them up. "Well, nothing. It was procedure. Alice got pretty much everything he owned except the night clubs and some jewels."

"What was with that anyway?" I asked. "Was Dahlia some kind of royalty?"

Luke had his back to us and continued to chop. "I'm assuming that was the case."

I leaned on my elbows on the table. "I'm just glad that's over."

"Me too." Drew set a glass of water next to me on the table and sat beside me. "I didn't trust any of those vampires at all. I was on edge the whole time."

I yawned. I was super tired, and it was late. I wasn't used to staying up late because I had woken so early in the morning.

"I think I'm going to go to bed," I announced. "Are you running with me in the morning?" I directed my question at Drew.

He took a swig of his water. "Yup. Just remember I'm up when you come down here in the morning."

"Very funny," I told him, pushing out my chair.

"What's funny about that?" Oscar asked.

"Chloe punched me in the nose the other day when she came downstairs and ran into me." He touched his nose. "Pretty good hit, too."

"Ugh, you didn't have to tell everyone," I complained.

He laughed. "It doesn't matter. We know to avoid you in the mornings."

"Ha ha, you're so funny," I muttered and left the room. "Good night everyone," I called out.

I left the guys laughing in the kitchen and went to my room where I changed into my nightclothes and fell into bed beside Alice.

⤛⤛⤛

It was my birthday.

Not that there were going to be any huge celebrations, but it felt good that the day I turned sixteen had finally come. With Trevor dead, I didn't have to worry so much about being an ingredient in a vampire day-walker recipe. In less than twenty-four hours, I wouldn't have to worry at all. It felt almost like I had been freed from some sort of prison.

I peeled back my purple comforter and tried to get out of bed as quietly as I could. I didn't want to wake Alice, although, I was about ready to make her start running with me. It would be good for her. I knew exercise produced endorphins, and endorphins made people happy. She could use that.

Pretty soon, I was going to have to get back to my regular training. I was keeping up with the exercise and stuff, but not the butt-kicking part. I threw on my black yoga pants and a shirt with matching black hoodie. I twisted my hair into two braids and put a stocking cap on. It hadn't snowed yet, but it was getting chilly outside.

Slowly and quietly I tiptoed out of the room and down the stairs. Thank god I didn't run smack into Drew. He sat on the living room floor doing stretches.

"Good morning," I greeted him and joined him on the floor to do my own stretching.

"Morning," he answered.

We stretched our muscles while the news played on low volume in the background. Neither of us said anything until we were outside. It was still dark, but you could see that daylight was coming.

"You ready?" he asked.

"Yeah, let's go." I started off before he had a chance to get ahead of me and headed toward the trails. The leaves crunched underneath my running shoes with every step. He caught up to me, and we kept pace together, running for about twenty minutes on the trails, then down into town. We stayed on the sidewalks until Drew veered off onto another trail I'd never been up.

"Where are we going?" I called out.

He stopped and waited for me, because I'd lagged behind a little bit.

"It's a surprise. I want to show you something."

I shrugged. "Okay. Should we keep running, or should we walk?"

He took his hood off his head. "We could walk, if you want. It does eventually end up being kind of a hike."

After a while, I noticed the trail sloped uphill.

"How come you won't tell me where we're going?" I complained.

"Quit asking. We'll be there soon."

"Fine." I huffed back at him. I just wanted to know where we were going. It was a nice walk. The trees and bushes hadn't completely died yet, and the air was crisp but not freezing. The trail continued to slope upward, but it was rockier than the lower trails. We had to make sure our footing was just right or we'd fall. It wasn't much longer, maybe about ten minutes of rocky trails, and I heard the sound of a river.

"I hear water. I didn't know there was a river out here. How come you never told me?"

He stopped in front of me and turned around.

"Just stop asking questions and go with it, all right?"

He took his pack off and extracted a water bottle, took a big swig and handed it to me.

I took a long drink, too. I don't know why I hadn't brought my own water. Then again, I didn't know we would hike all this way. We moved on, and about twenty minutes later, Drew pushed through a particularly rough trail with tree branches that blocked the pathway. We emerged in front the most beautiful waterfall I'd ever seen. It was so tall I couldn't even guess how high it stood. The water came over the side of the cliff and pummeled into the pool below where it churned and sprayed droplets of water everywhere.

It was utterly amazing.

Drew stood beside me, taking in the beauty of this sacred place. "This is where the community got its name. Arcadia Falls."

He took my hand and led me to a large rock beside the water's edge.

"It's amazing." I sat on the rock and pulled my knees up in front of me. "Does Arcadia mean anything?"

Drew nodded and climbed up onto the rock beside me. "Of course it does. It means a place of simple pleasure and quiet."

"Well, this is definitely that." I nodded in agreement.

"Also, in history, Arcadia was a part of Ancient Greece, in the Peloponnesus. This region of Greece was known for its isolation and mountainous beauty."

I laughed and slapped at him. "Sometimes I think you know everything."

He smiled and looked away. "Yeah, right. Believe me, it's far from everything. There are a few things I wouldn't mind knowing right now."

I stared out at the waterfall. "Like what?"

My question was met with silence.

"Come on, like what? Maybe I can help." I adjusted my hat on my head. "I know a few things."

"Then tell me what you and I are going to do."

That was a question I hadn't expected. I felt blood rush into my cheeks and my whole body heated up a little bit. "Um…"

Because of my slight hesitation, he shook his head. "You don't have to answer."

"But…" I swallowed and decided to just go for it. Nervously, I reached out and touched his shoulder. "But I do have to answer. I've been waiting to talk to Gavin."

He scoffed at the mention of Gavin.

"No wait," I told him. "Hear me out. I've been waiting until Gavin got better to talk to him, because… well, I wanted to tell him that he and I should continue to be friends only. That's it."

There was more silence. Oh, man, I should have never said a word. I shifted, wanting to get up and run away. Drew must have sensed the fight or flight in me and put a hand on my leg.

"Don't."

My cheeks burned even more, and then I blurted out, "And just for the record, we never really had a relationship or anything. We just went out twice."

"I know," he whispered.

"And you said that you wouldn't be second to anyone, so I didn't want you to be second to anyone. The moment I saw you running toward me after I fell, I knew it was you. That was when my decision was made. It was even before you kissed me, not that that wasn't a deal breaker or anything."

Oh, my god, I was babbling like a crazy woman.

"Stop. You don't need to explain."

"But I do need to explain. I need you to understand that you are the one who came to rescue me. You knew what my heart wanted, not what my lips said. I need you to understand that I chose you. That I do choose you, and you are not and never will be my second choice... ever."

Good gracious, it was time to find out what had I done.

Drew took his hand off my leg and got up off the rock. I watched in horror as he walked away from me and stood with his hands on his hips. The tears were threatening to break free. I don't know what I'd expected, but it wasn't for him to just walk away.

"Drew?"

I crawled carefully off the rock and crept toward him.

"Drew?"

Suddenly, he spun around to face me. "You waited all this time to tell me that?"

Shocked, I threw my hands out to the side. "I didn't know you wanted to know. I thought you would have wanted me to talk to Gavin first."

Again, he didn't say anything. I met his eyes, though, and I saw the answer I wanted to see.

"So... are we okay?"

He moved forward a couple of steps, closing the gap between us. "I think we are more than just okay."

He reached out and took my freezing cold hands in his and pulled me close. I closed my eyes, hoping he would kiss me again.

I was not disappointed. I felt his lips touch mine, and my body literally sizzled. My hands were no longer cold, and my cheeks were warmed by my own fire, not by embarrassment. The waterfall coursed and crashed behind us while we kissed longer than ever before.

Happy birthday to me!

Drew was the first to pull out of the kiss. He still hugged me to him.

"Do you like it here?"

I leaned my head on his chest.

"Of course, I like it here. And now, this place has a special meaning for me, too."

"Oh, yeah, and what would that be?"

"The place you and I ended up together for real?" It was a question, directed at him. I needed confirmation we were on the same page.

"It will be that for me too, from now on," he told me softly.

I knew I shouldn't say anything. I didn't want to ruin the moment, but I had to ask. "So, did you still want me to talk to Gavin?"

He shook his head. "Not right away. He is still recovering. Eventually, he will figure it out and you can talk to him, or we can. Whatever you want."

"Thank you," I whispered.

He laughed and pulled away. "Why in the world are you thanking me?"

"Because, you saved me, you train me, you want me for... um, your girlfriend? I just wouldn't be who I am without you. I can thank you for that if I want to."

He puffed up his chest and gave my hand a squeeze.

"Well, you're welcome, then." He looked at his watch. "We had better go. Luke will be wondering why we're so late."

"Yeah, you're right, but I'd rather stay here."

"We can come back soon. That is another thing... Luke is going to bust his top when he finds out about this."

I stopped in my tracks. "You mean, he didn't tell you?"

Drew knitted his eyebrows together. "What do you mean? Didn't tell me what?"

I laughed. "Oh, he already knows. And he gave me some long lecture about how I was supposed to be careful with you. You know, like a dad warning the boyfriend. Only way different than that."

Drew burst out laughing. "He did not!"

"Oh, yes, he did. It was when I was still in the hospital."

"Well, I'll be damned. I don't know what I would do without that guy."

I took his hand again, and we walked away from the beautiful waterfall, toward the trail.

"I feel the same way."

⤙⤙⤙

Back at home, we found Luke, Oscar and Alice sitting at the kitchen table eating bowls of cereal and talking about what the future held for them.

"You are both welcome to stay here as long as you need to," Luke offered as Drew and I entered the kitchen and made for the fridge and cold water bottles.

We both cracked one open and guzzled half our water down.

"Hard work out?" Alice asked, raising her eyebrows.

I raised mine back at her but didn't answer her sarcastic question. She directed her attention back at Luke.

"Well, I'd like to stay longer, if you'll have me. Of course, now I can help pay rent or something. I just need to figure out exactly what I want to do."

Luke swallowed a bite of his cereal. "Of course, that sort of decision takes time. And there is no need to help with anything but groceries."

Oscar nodded. "I hate to admit this, because it's not very manly, but I'm actually afraid to go home. I'm afraid there might be vampires waiting there to kill me." He rolled his eyes. "God, that sounds so pathetic."

"Perfectly understandable," I said. "I would feel the same way. I'm okay with you both staying here."

Luke looked up at Drew with a question in his eyes. "What about you?"

Drew shrugged his shoulders. "I'm okay with it, I guess." He looked around. "It's kind of crowded, but temporarily... it's not so bad."

"All right, then," Luke addressed Oscar and Alice, "you can both stay until you find other accommodations. If you stay long enough in the community, perhaps become a part of it somehow, the board will discuss you getting your own homes in the community."

Alice and Oscar agreed. So it looked like we were going to be a full house for a while.

Luke scooted his chair out and got up to deposit his cereal bowl into the sink. "Looks like we have a birthday to celebrate today."

I waved it off. "Nah, I have everything I want. We don't need to celebrate."

Drew refilled his water bottle from the faucet.

"Well, maybe we want to celebrate."

He took swig off the water and capped it, then walked out of the room.

"Where are you going?" I called after him.

Alice, Oscar and Luke followed Drew out of the room, so I had no choice but to follow. In the living room, I had totally missed the huge stack of presents that sat on the coffee table.

"Oh, you guys! You didn't have to do this."

Although I was sixteen now, the child in me rushed forward to rip into all my gifts. Alice gave me a pair of boots that would be nice for school. Yeah, I had to go back to school. Oscar gave me a leather-covered journal with a carved bow and arrow on the front. Luke gave me a new gun, this one a pink and black Glock, and it rocked! I was totally excited about having my second gun, but nothing would ever compare to my first baby Drew had given me.

My last present on the table was from Drew. It was a tiny box. I opened the box and found a bullet dangling from a silver chain.

"Drew," I breathed. Normally, a girl would be excited about a diamond or any other kind of necklace, but this was, for sure, my kind of gift.

He cleared his throat when I handed it to him and moved my hair aside so that he could help me put it on. "I wanted to get the bullet that you were shot with, but that wouldn't look good on a necklace. So this is supposed to be symbolic of your battle wound."

"I love it!" I told him as he let my hair fall back down. "It's perfect."

"I hoped you would like it." He backed away.

Suddenly, the room became very warm. "Is it hot in here?" I asked.

Before anyone could answer, I got my final birthday gift. A mist filtered into the living room and Sostrate appeared in her jungle hunter outfit, only this time she held a long wooden spear in her hand.

"Greetings, my children."

Drew and I had seen her before, but Luke, Alice and Oscar

looked like they were going to pass out.

"I come today because Chloe has reached her sixteenth year." She eyed me with a loving look. "Soon, she will reach the full potential of her gifts and must hone them to perfection."

Drew smirked. "I think she is doing a fine job of that, so far."

Sostrate shook her head and chastised Drew with her eyes.

"Andrew, Chloe will need your help." She lifted her free hand and gestured to Alice, Oscar and Luke. "She will need all of your help. Your paths have not crossed with this young hunter's for no reason. You all bear special gifts that will help her to win the coming war."

"What?" I slammed my fist on the table, causing even Sostrate to jump. "Are you kidding me? A war? I thought this was over!"

"Chloe!" Luke hissed. Apparently, I was not supposed to sass the demi-goddess.

"No! Damn it! I just escaped from evil vampires. I don't want to fight a war with them."

Sostrate moved closer to me.

"My child, you are a hunter. The war will never be over until the vampires are eradicated. The war is brewing already, and you must all train." She ran her eyes up and down Oscar and Alice. "Yes, even you two. You are not hunters, but you are descended from those who bear great power."

To everyone's surprise, Alice spoke up. "I beg your pardon, goddess, but I am no one special. I have no power."

With a slow and delicate movement, Sostrate crouched down before Alice.

"My child, you do not know your power, because you did not know your family. You are a child of the earth. Some call them witches, but the earth is in you, and you bear the power to call upon it."

Alice didn't appear to believe her. "I don't understand."

"You will, child; you will."

Oscar and Luke sat spellbound and stared at the beautiful demi-goddess.

"I need your word that you will all work hard to train, plan, and support each other in preparing for and fighting this war."

"No!" I called out. "I don't want a war."

"Child, there will be war regardless of whether you want it or not. Whether you win or not depends on you."

"You have my word," Luke and Drew said in unison.

"And mine," Oscar whispered.

"And mine," Alice finished.

I sighed and lowered my head in defeat. I couldn't say no when everyone else was committed. "You will thank me later, child. I know this is hard for you. With these powerful people and their weapons to help you, hunters will be victorious." She backed away from us slowly, and the mist closed around her. "Goodbye, my children, until we meet again."

Oh, great. Impending war, just what I wanted.

The one thing that stuck in my head through all of that was that this war would never be over until the vampires were eradicated. She was right, and I would never really have avenged my mother until they were all gone.

So, now… Chloe Kallistrate, vampire hunter, was going to hunt the world for vampires and kill every single one.

Well, perhaps I was getting ahead of myself. I wasn't going anywhere, yet… not until after the birthday cake.

LOOK FOR MORE CHLOE IN THE SERIES:

THE ARCADIA FALLS CHRONICLES

about the author

Jennifer Malone Wright resides in the beautiful mountains of northern Idaho with her husband and five children. Between the craziness of taking care of her children, whose ages range from fourteen all the way down to six months, and being a homemaker, Jennifer has little time left for herself. The time she does have left, usually leading far into the night, is spent working on freelance work or her beloved fiction.

When she grew up, Jennifer always had her nose in a book. She has been writing stories and poems since grade school. This love of the written word and her strong interest in the paranormal is what has led to her first novel *The Birth of Jaiden*.

In addition to being a mother and homemaker, Jennifer is also a very proud military wife. Moving around the country for the last ten years has made her a bit of a nomad and she finds it difficult to be in one place for too long.

Jennifer is also the author of *The Birth of Jaiden*, a paranormal novel filled with action, suspense, and even a love story.

Find out more at www.jenniferwrightauthor.com

Made in the USA
Lexington, KY
19 October 2012